When Phoebe looked back from the nets to the shore, Alice was nowhere to be seen. Damn and double-damn, she'd lost her again! Her heart thumped so hard that it was hard to breathe. She'd lost Alice before—almost really lost her and had almost died trying to get her back. After all that they'd been through before, how could she have done this again? Becca would kill her.

"Alice!" she called, fighting down panic, and rushed down the shore. Things squished under feet. Something splashed over her toes. She broke into a run.

"Alice!" How had she disappeared so fast?

Ahead fishermen loosening fish from their turquoise mesh nets looked up as she ran up to them. "Alice? Have you seen my niece?"

Their blank stares said that she'd found people who spoke only Malayalam, the local Keralan language. Great.

The nets. Alice had to have gone for the nets. Of course, now there were more people around, out for their morning stroll.

She shoved past them, apologizing, her gaze on the nets. Alice had been excited about the nets being raised and lowered. The one net still seemed to be still. A shout came and through the trees bordering the beach, slow as the sun rising over the horizon, the huge net began to swing upward.

The trees blocked her view as she rushed toward the net.

That was when the screaming started—shrill and frightened. The kind of free-form scream a thirteen-year-old might scream.

She'd heard the same kind of screams in her school as her students lay dying.

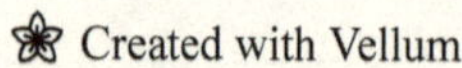 Created with Vellum

ALSO BY K. L. ABRAHAMSON

MYSTERY (WRITING AS **K.L.** ABRAHAMSON)

Phoebe Clay Mysteries

Through Dark Water

Beneath Malabar Nets

The Detektiv Kazakov Mysteries

After Yekaterina

Mareson's Arrow

The Tsarina's Mask

Ivan's Wolf

FANTASY MYSTERY (WRITING KAREN **L.** ABRAHAMSON)

The Aung and Yamin Mystery Series

Death By Effigy

A Death in Passing

Death in Umber

BENEATH MALABAR NETS

A PHOEBE CLAY MYSTERY

K. L. ABRAHAMSON

1

The diesel-stained Goa-Ernakulum train slowed, its wheels squealing on the iron rails as the metal behemoth slowly ground into Ernakulum Junction Station. The sun had barely finished rising, but the air was already hot and humid. So sultry, even with the train's wind, the fans couldn't dispel the heat. But then, it was hot and humid all along India's southwestern Malabar coast.

The wheels' rumble and grind gradually diminished, replaced by the clamor of voices—those from the train's hallway preparing to disembark and those from the surging crowds on the siding waiting to board.

Letting the grimy curtain fall back over the dust-blurred window, Phoebe Clay settled back on the straight-backed, bench seat next to her sister and closed her eyes, trying to find the strength for the effort to come. Another night of feigned sleep in an optimistically named First Class sleeper stateroom didn't leave much energy to spare.

The cabin's two fans beat the tepid air into what might pass for cool here, but wouldn't in any temperate country. Well-flattened, red vinyl seats had folded down into equally well-flattened sleeper bunks —four of them. The two-foot-wide stretch of stained linoleum floor between the lower bunks was filled with belongings and three sets of sandaled feet belonging to Phoebe, her sister, Becca, and her niece, Alice. The postage-sized tray-table was permanently sticky—probably from some of India's overly sweet orange soft drinks. At least she hoped it was soft drink. There were other sticky things that she could think of, but she didn't want to go there.

This was one of those moments when she really wondered what she'd been thinking, bringing Becca and Alice on this trip. The train thumped, bumped, swayed, and juddered under her just as it had all night. She felt tired and gray—as gray as Alice's white t-shirt.

Seated across from Phoebe on the other lower bunk, Alice shouldered her backpack and stood to look down at them. Becca slumped beside Phoebe. Judging by the gray pallor around her eyes, she hadn't slept any better than Phoebe.

"So? Aren't we going? This is our stop, right?" At thirteen going on thirty, Alice was all long arms and legs and body swiftly shifting from girl-child to a young woman with a penchant to roll her sea-blue eyes. The last vestige of her girlhood seemed to be the braids in which she'd plaited her long blonde hair, inherited from her mother. For modesty, more acceptable to the country, she wore loose cotton trousers (under protest in the humid heat) and a baggy t-shirt that had been pristine white when she left home.

"It is, and we will stand up when the brakes on this locomotive don't threaten to knock us down again," Phoebe said. "We aren't all as young and athletic as you. Besides, who needs to carry these packs any longer than we have to?" She patted the top of the pack that she had begun to think of as 'Stoney-the-Pack' for the millstone it was becoming. The darn thing seemed to weigh more every time she hauled it on although she had bought virtually nothing on this holiday.

"Alice, maybe it's better to stick together. Why don't you wait? We'll be ready to go in a minute," Becca said, her usually intense blue gaze filmy with fatigue. "It'll be a crush out there and neither Simon nor Zamir have come by to tell us to disembark." Becca's voice was a little sharper than usual. While she might almost trust Simon, their guide, she definitely didn't trust Zamir, their good-looking thirty-something guide-in-training. With puberty, Alice's hormones were raging and she'd made goo-goo eyes at Zamir when she met him. Unfortunately, he continued to be all too charming.

"Mom!" Alice used her eye roll as if her mother's concerns were nothing. "I'll be safe. I'll just step outside the door, okay?"

Becca hesitated and then gave a defeated nod. "But stay where I can see you."

"You bet!" Alice slid the stateroom door open and stepped out before Becca could change her mind. The open door admitted the gently wafting scent of latrine from the again optimistically named washrooms at the end of the passenger car. She wrestled her pack out into the narrow corridor and the door slid shut behind her with a rattle.

Becca closed her eyes and leaned her head back. Her honey-blonde hair was longer than Phoebe's. It was pulled back into a ponytail but flyaway strands stuck to the sweat on her cheeks. In her early forties she was still model-thin compared to Phoebe's solid build, but worry lines had formed around her eyes and shadowed the corners of her mouth, aging her slightly beyond her years. Phoebe had caused some of those lines.

"What was I thinking, bringing a thirteen-year-old to India?" Becca said.

"Uh… you were worried about your fifty-something older sister running off to Myanmar and thought that an organized tour of India with her was safer and would keep said older sister out of trouble," Phoebe offered.

Becca's eyes opened wearily. "There is that. I know you can take care of yourself, but you've got to admit that travel in third world countries is harder than you realized."

"The third world category is political, not economic," Phoebe said, dropping into school-teacher mode because she didn't want to admit that Becca was right. Phoebe had dreamed of solo travel around the world. Taking this tour was the first step, but it wasn't going exactly as planned. "During the cold war, third world was the term applied to countries that were neither NATO involved—the first world—nor in the communist block—the second world."

"Whatever." Becca rolled her eyes so like her daughter that they both broke out laughing just as the train did its final judder and stopped.

"If it matters, I *am* really glad we're doing this together. How often do I get to adventure with my favorite sister?" Phoebe said.

"Only sister."

Phoebe shrugged 'get over it' as the cabin door rolled open.

"We're here. Come. Come. Chop. Chop. We need to keep moving." Their guide, Simon Roy, stood in the doorway. He was a diminutive man, shorter than Phoebe's five-foot-six, with graying hair he wore swept off his brow, a pointy goatee, and a particular penchant for aftershave that even this morning came off him in waves. As usual, he was dressed in buff-colored safari shorts and shirt that showed off his pasty legs and arms. A tilly hat perched on his head, and a silly pink pocket poof with rainbow embroidery stuck out of one hip pocket. He clutched a briefcase in one hand and in the other dragged a roller suitcase that was, at best, a wine color. Alice claimed that it was embarrassingly close to hot pink.

Phoebe nodded and stood. "We'll be right out."

A curt nod and he let the door slide shut again. No offer to help with their bags. No offer to get them a porter. From the hallway, Alice motioned at them to hurry up.

Phoebe met Becca's gaze. Standing, they were of a height. "Tell me again how you found him and this tour."

Becca shuddered and sighed. "He was recommended by the friend of a friend because he's Canadian?"

"Recommended for what?"

"Well… the tour was recommended. We *have* seen a lot."

"And have the bedhead to prove it." Phoebe ran her fingers through the matted gray-blonde hair at the back of her head. Her stomach growled. Simon apparently thought that moving from place to place was more important than a good night's sleep—this was the third time they'd had an overnight train. But then, he apparently thought a lot of things that Phoebe didn't agree with—like they didn't really need meals when they were on a train, whether daytime or night. And it was okay to smoke pot or make sexual comments in Alice's presence.

She wrestled Stoney up off the floor and onto her back, then helped Becca on with her pack and together they stumbled out the narrow door to follow the disappearing form of Alice down the corridor toward cacophony and—heat.

Simon and Zamir were just stepping down from the train. Jeannie and Trevor, the other two people who had joined the small tour, were standing on the concrete amid the press of people. When Phoebe had first met Trevor and Jeannie, she'd thought they were a couple, but had soon been disabused of that idea. They'd apparently known each other a long time and shared an interest in photography. They were traveling together on the tour before taking off on their own in Northern India.

Alice had already disappeared into the crowded platform.

Becca swung down with an "oomph" while Phoebe paused in the train car doorway. Based on the Indian train stations she'd already seen —and according to Becca it was too many—Ernakulum Junction Station was typical. Dusty concrete platform. Dust-colored paint on the concrete walls and too many people pushing and shoving with the attendant noise that involved. Jewel-tone sari-clad women sat with their children on the concrete floor amidst the flotsam of their luggage. Men in dark trousers and white shirts were everywhere, like refugees from office towers. A few men wore white pajama things that looked cool in the humid heat. A few bright turbans in gold or red or cobalt blue. That was the thing about India—too many colors, too much noise, and the stench of diesel that seemed permanently imprinted at the back of her tongue so that she felt like she'd spent the tour so far on sensory overload. She craned to see and spotted a blonde head near a kiosk that, by the steam and hot oil smoke, looked to be selling Indian breakfasts of chai and, perhaps, vada.

Phoebe's stomach growled again as she swung down from the train and felt the lurch of Stoney settle once more on her spine.

Becca was craning around for her daughter.

"She's looking for breakfast," Phoebe said. "There's a breakfast kiosk that way." She nodded to their left.

"Breakfast should wait until we reach our hotel," Simon said crisply as if the matter was closed.

She caught Trevor's roll of the eyes and turned to Simon, who had begun to roll his suitcase in the direction away from Alice. The silly rainbow scarf bobbing in his hip pocket made his stride a distinct sashay.

Trevor was in his thirties with a shaved head and darkly tanned skin that gleamed in the morning sunlight and was probably great in the heat. He had piercing blue eyes and a way of looking at her that made Phoebe think he really *saw* her—inside and out. She put it down to him being a photographer. Jeannie, also a photographer, had long red hair that had frizzed in the humidity and made a halo around her face, even though she tried to contain her hair in a bun. Freckles and cat-green tilted eyes made her the stereotypical redhead, but oddly her pale skin had accepted a lovely golden tan. She'd been friendly on the trip and had taken Alice somewhat under her wing when the girl had shown an interest in photography.

"Hold on a minute, Simon. How long will it be until we reach the hotel?" People jostled Phoebe's shoulders, but she stood her ground.

Simon kept going.

In exasperation she caught up to him and grabbed the pink poof out of his pocket.

He spun around, fist half raised so for a moment she thought he might hit her. Then he stuck out his palm. "Give it back. Now."

She did. "It's just a stupid pocket poof. Geez. I think you need a new one. That one's all worn."

He gave an exasperated shake of the head. "What is it, now?"

"I asked how long it would be until we reach our hotel. Alice is clearly hungry and I am, too. We haven't had a meal since noon yesterday."

Simon shrugged. "It's not far. Just across the bridge."

Just beyond Simon, Zamir shook his head. "At this time of day, it could take an hour at least, possibly two."

Simon's lips flattened into a line. "How would you know? You've never been here."

Phoebe checked her watch. "It's ten now. That would put us at the hotel closer to lunchtime than breakfast."

"Fine then. What do you suggest?" Simon asked, a vein pulsing along his jaw.

"Well…" She'd like to suggest that he do his job and find them breakfast at a reasonable hour, but that wasn't a fight she wanted to get into now. She turned back toward the kiosk. "Alice has clearly found us something to eat." Which was more than Simon had managed to do on any of their train rides. "Who's up for chai and vada?"

Jeannie mouthed a 'thank you' at Phoebe as they all wrestled their bags in Alice's direction.

"Good job," Becca said to her daughter when they reached her. "But please, please, please, stick closer to us."

"Mo-om!" The eternal cry of the put-upon teenager.

"I'm only saying this because I love you. You're beautiful and blonde and you don't know anything about this country. Anything could happen to you."

"I'm not doing anything! I'm wearing the long pants and t-shirts like you wanted. Next you're going to want me in a burka!"

Becca gave a mother's weary sigh. "Now who's being overly dramatic. I just worry that something could happen and we won't be around to help."

Zamir appeared at Phoebe's side. He was broad-shouldered, with a wide mouth that liked to smile and a warm brown gaze. He brought with him a small glass of spiced chai that smelled deliciously of cardamom, cinnamon, and pepper, and a square of newspaper with two, three-inch, crispy discs of deep-fried chickpea flour—vada. He deposited them with Phoebe and returned again with the same for Becca. Both women thanked him. Alice used the opportunity to escape her mother and went to the counter to claim her own.

"You know, she's pretty capable, right?" Phoebe asked around a mouthful of the crisp nutty-flavored breakfast bread. She sighed with pleasure at her first sip of chai, hot and sweet, and figured she might survive the morning.

"Thank you," Trevor came up to her, licking his fingers. With his permanently black five o'clock shadow and his sun-darkened skin, she figured he had Mediterranean heritage. "I could eat a dozen of those things, but I've held myself to three. Doesn't he get it that people need food?"

"Trevor, be nice. He's trying," Jeannie said, coming up beside him. She nibbled at her vada with small white teeth that matched her fox-like features. The pert nose and slightly tilted green eyes went with the wild head of red curls, but there was something about her that made Phoebe a tad cautious of the woman. As if Jeannie was hiding something. And she was constantly watching everything and everyone, but that might simply be a result of her interest in photography.

"Trying is right," Trevor said with a shake of his head. He glanced over at Simon, who was standing apart from everyone checking his watch impatiently as he drank his chai. "The guy is weird. What the heck is he doing leading tours when he doesn't even seem to like people?"

"He likes some people," Jeannie said. "He has to like people to provide a house and so on for Zamir and his wife and kids. That's a pretty neat thing to do—help out someone less fortunate."

"At what cost?" Trevor leaned into them and lowered his voice. "I swear the guy tried to come onto me once he realized Jeannie and I weren't a couple and wanted separate rooms."

"What the heck are you implying?" Jeannie's sharp gaze flashed as she finished the last of the vada and crumpled the newspaper wrapping.

"I'm not just implying," Trevor said. "Those two," he lifted his chin at Simon and Zamir. "They room together. They're always together. For God's sake, Simon met Zamir when he was weightlifting at Chennai beach. Can you get more gay than that?"

"I don't care about people's sex lives. I prefer to live and let live," Phoebe murmured. "Besides, sexual orientation has nothing to do with how well you lead tours."

"Well, he's not done too well with it, has he?" Trevor asked. "I'd fire him, but he's already got all our money and I refuse to give him the satisfaction of simply walking away."

"I'm going to reserve judgement," Phoebe said. Even though she had to admit she didn't much care for Simon and thought he was a lousy guide. Still, you never knew what was going on in the other person's life. She still suffered from episodes of PTSD after the shooting death of three of her students, and that impacted how she dealt with others. There could be something going on with Simon. You just never knew.

Alice had drifted over to Zamir's side and he said something that made her laugh. Phoebe drank down the last of her chai and adjusted Stoney on her shoulders. "Time to go, I think. Simon's almost frothing at the mouth."

It took exactly an hour and a half for the minibus Simon hired to travel the fifteen and a half kilometers from Ernakulam to their hotel in the old city of Kochi. It was a drive that started through the usual cacophony of Indian traffic in modern Ernakulam with the modern business buildings plastered with signs advertising gilded red wedding saris, far-too-ornate Indian jewelry, and designer sunglasses. Eventually they left the too-busy canyon streets behind and soared up over a bridge before being deposited amid walled Indian military complexes that Simon said made up Willingdon Island and crossing a second, smaller bridge to the old city of Kochi.

Here, like Goa and wealthy parts of Chennai, tall, spreading trees shaded the roads that passed between what looked like English country homes. They passed cricket fields and soccer pitches.

"Stop here," Simon said and the driver turned into a driveway under sweeping, broad trees that led to a stone fence and a long, low, open-sided building that faced the road. Beyond the building, more low structures stood, and to either side, open fields were filled with ramshackle rows of wooden frames and something fluttering white.

"Is this where we're staying?" Alice asked, clearly alarmed. "I thought you said there was a pool?" There was nothing that looked like any kind of hotel room or pool and the kid liked her comforts.

"I have some—business—to conduct. It will not take long. You can wait or you might wish to take a look. Your choice. It's not on the itinerary, but this is a laundry—the dhobi khana—that the British started about 1920. Tourists are always welcome."

Arms crossed, Alice slumped back in her seat, clearly not planning on budging for any kind of laundry. Becca shrugged and sat back. Trevor and Jeannie looked at each other and hauled their cameras out.

"I'll take a look and stretch my legs," Phoebe said, clambering out the side door. Zamir stayed with Becca and Alice, and Trevor and Jeannie set out, cameras at the ready.

The air smelled of strong soap and water and something else she couldn't place. Phoebe paused at a plaque on the wall that described how the laundry had been established during the British colonial period when British officers decided that people from the Indian state of Tamil Nadu made the best launderers and they imported an entire community to Kochi. Generations later they were still here.

The first roofed building was open-sided above a shoulder-height wall on both long sides. It held long concrete shelfs along the long walls. In a space that could have held twenty people or more, five men and women were busily ironing. The cloth steamed under their flashing, coal-heated irons as they thumped down on damp cloth or clattered as they were replaced on their stands. A heap of glowing white sheets sat on the floor, bundled on another white cloth, awaiting pressing. White towels and shirts hung from the log building rafters. Piles of ironed sheets were neatly folded and tied in bundles awaiting pickup in piles at one end of the building.

Interesting. Phoebe followed Simon, Trevor, and Jeannie through the ironing shed and found herself facing another long building, this one with small rooms with open front walls. All of them held large plastic tubs, but only two of the twenty or so were in use—men pulled white cloth from vats where they must have been soaking and then soaped the cloth again in smaller tubs before beating it on well-worn washing stones set in the floor of the room's opening. Then they rinsed the cloth and wrung it out. The wrung cloth was stacked to one side, presumably awaiting hanging. One man gathered up the clean cloths and carried them past Phoebe, so she followed him down the open space between the two buildings to the rickety looking wood frames planted in the open fields. The man swiftly tucked the edges of the cloth under ropes strung along the wood frame and the white cloth unfurled, revealing itself as monogrammed sheets—probably belonging to some hotel.

"It must be a problem when the wind comes up. All those nice clean sheets blown into the dust," Phoebe said.

The man glanced in her direction. He had to be at least sixty, though it was hard to tell with the Indian people. Their lives were so much harder than the lives of people in Canada. He had a cap of steel-gray hair, high cheekbones, and skeins of lines that framed his surprisingly hazel eyes. He wore a neat white shirt, rolled up at the sleeves, and a blue sarong that was folded up over his knees.

"That is never a problem. The ropes hold everything in place." He finished hanging his sheets. "I am Kalki. You have not seen our laundry before?"

"True. I'm Phoebe. The place is amazing. I don't think I've ever seen such white sheets." And she wasn't just blowing smoke, either. These sheets positively gleamed.

"It is tradition. We have washed this way for ten generations." He picked up a folded shirt that was on top of a stack waiting to be taken inside. "We wash in good clean water and beat stained cloth on stone. Sometimes we use a little chlorine to make sure things are white. We are very good at starching just the right amount whether for sheets or a professional man's shirt." He held it out to her. The shirt was board stiff, and yet the cotton was soft and pliable.

"That's amazing!"

He smiled. "The secret is in the rice water. We know how long to soak the cloth to get the right texture."

She stroked the soft cloth, but a movement out of the corner of her eye swung her around. Simon was striding away from the row of low sheds behind the wash building. He didn't look happy, but then he rarely did. Pleased perhaps and even smug, but happy? Not that she'd seen.

Behind him, a younger man came around the corner of the building and watched Simon leave. She turned back to Kalki and caught him watching as well. He jerked back to her as if his attention was still elsewhere.

"Has your family always done this?" she asked.

He did one of those charming head-waggles she'd noticed that Indian people use. "Always. I am not an educated man. This is what I know. My children, though. They are very smart. My daughter has a degree in business from the local university. My son will soon be graduating from Harvard University with a medical degree. I am very lucky to have such children."

"I'd say your children are lucky to have you. You must have washed a lot of sheets and ironed a lot of shirts to put them through school."

He gave his little head-waggle again, neither yes, nor no, but his gaze kept getting pulled back toward the corner of the building where the young man had now disappeared. "I am only an uneducated old man."

"Phoebe! If you want lunch, we need to get going!" Simon called from the ironing building. "Jeannie and Trevor are already back at the van."

"I'm being paged!" she said brightly and turned to go. "I think I've disturbed your work long enough. Thank you so much for your time and conversation."

Kalki's gaze snapped from Simon to her. "You are with him?"

"He's our tour guide."

He seemed to hesitate and then he smiled at her. "I wish you well, Phoebe. May the gods smile upon you and keep you safe."

He gathered up the shirts and pushed past her, striding away back to the ironing shed and leaving her to hurry after Simon. She met him at the van.

"What brings you here?" she asked him, nodding back at the laundry.

"What do you think?" He snapped, but then seemed to soften. "I like to get my clothes laundered here when I'm in town. I just wanted to check that they could fit me in."

She blinked as she climbed into the van. There hadn't been a lot of activity in the laundry so fitting him in shouldn't have been a problem. When they left, they wound into an old town of tightly packed buildings and narrow roads. Phoebe told Becca and Alice what she'd seen, while Jeannie and Trevor reviewed their photos together. Whitewashed, street-side shops displayed incense, rainbow-colored tika powders used for bindi and holy markings, ornate brass bells, and hand-dyed clothing. Displays spilled into the street and doorways. Then the road swung into a broader avenue along the shore and Kochi Harbor—one of the best in the world—and the Arabian Sea stretched out before them in shimmering shades of turquoise.

"Oh!" Alice said and craned around as the road struck inland again. "I want to go there."

"You'll have time later. First, we get lunch and then you have your tour," Simon said. It was the first thing he'd said since leaving the laundry and he still didn't look happy.

"What about unpacking and taking a shower?" Becca asked, shoving back the tangled hair around her face.

"You'll need to be quick," Simon said. "Good. This is it. I haven't booked here in a while, but for the money it's good."

The minivan pulled up in front of a building like something out a northern European fairy tale. The place was two stories of white-painted plastered wood with dark green shutters beside each window. A small white picket fence surrounded a narrow garden of bright lilies and jasmine that perfumed the heavily humid air as they climbed out of the van into sunshine. A broad, black-painted wooden door stood open at the top of three stairs. Phoebe hefted Stoney up from the back of the van because Zamir and Simon sure weren't going to help anyone and then suddenly a young man in a tan uniform was beside her and claimed Stoney from her. He grinned and waved her ahead of him toward the open door. Another young man had relieved Becca of her pack and Jeannie and Trevor were getting similar treatment. Only Alice managed to sneak past to the doorway with her pack on her back. She disappeared into the darkened doorway ahead of Phoebe.

Pausing at the top of the stairs, Phoebe was struck by the quiet. A few vehicles. Voices of school children. A distant thunder that might be ocean waves. Bird song. She inhaled the perfumed air deep into her lungs, closed her eyes, and turned her face to the sun. This was more like it. She could get used to this.

She turned and entered the building.

Shadows. Open arches across the lobby that gave out onto the glare of a small garden pool and restaurant. It took a moment for her eyes to adjust. Comfortable looking wicker chairs with plush lime-green cushions filled the cool tile floor in groupings that would encourage conversation, though at the moment they were only filled by the collapsed figures of her travel companions. A heap of luggage lay on the floor beside them. A long, mahogany registration desk filled one wall with an efficient-looking young woman waiting on Simon. She was a striking woman of perhaps thirty, dressed in a turquoise sari, with her dark hair coiled at the back of her head. A small, ruby-tone bindi sat between her brows, marking the third eye and her married status.

Phoebe found a chair and groaned at the comfort. "Why couldn't they have seats like this on the train?"

"Because people wouldn't get off again?" Alice offered. "Did you see? There's a pool! A nice one!"

Phoebe grinned at her niece. So far on their adventure they'd seen very few pools. After their first few days in Chennai, their hotels had been less than stellar, either with no pool or pools with water that was a suspicious-looking green that none of them wanted to swim in.

"It looks like a nice place." And a part of her wondered what had changed that suddenly they were booked into such a nice place, when so far everything about this tour had screamed budget. But then, that was what you got on Phoebe's and Becca's limited budget.

"I'm telling you: that rate is not what I was quoted." Raised voices from the front desk turned Phoebe around. Simon was arguing—again —with the front desk staff.

"And I am telling you that the rate for a room in this establishment has never been and will never be as low as you are suggesting. Now I must ask: do you still want the rooms?"

"Of course," he snapped and signed the registration ledger.

The woman somehow managed to look apologetic as she gave one of those charming, ubiquitous, Indian head nods and handed over a number of keys. Simon turned and saw Phoebe watching. He looked down at what he held.

"Phoebe. This is Becca, Alice, and your key. You're on the first floor." He nodded at a door just to the right of the registration desk. "Jeannie, Trevor, you're on the second floor as are Zamir and I." He tossed Phoebe a key and turned for the stairs that made a graceful arc up one corner of the lobby. "Be ready in thirty minutes." He called down as he climbed the stairs.

Thankfully, the kind young porter grabbed Becca's and Phoebe's bags and wrestled them into the large room that gave directly onto the lobby. For a moment, Phoebe hesitated at being so close to the center of things. It could be noisy. But changing rooms would involve Simon and undoubtedly more raised voices because that was all Simon seemed able to use when he was dealing with the locals. He spoke to them as if he thought the barrier of language made them deaf—and there wasn't even a real barrier of language given English was a lingua franca in a country that had hundreds of languages and dialects.

The room was actually lovely. Two queen-sized beds filled one wall with a twin comfortably fitting on the wall across from them, with a door that gave onto a clean private washroom. Clean tiles underfoot and clean cream walls with louvered and screened windows that gave onto the front garden. The hint of jasmine and lily wafted through the air.

Becca settled on one of the queen beds and lay back with a sigh.

"Dibs on the first shower," Alice called and dragged her pack into the washroom with her.

"Remember there are three people who want a shower before lunch," Becca said.

"I'll be quick. I just want to rinse the dust off." Alice pulled bathroom door closed.

As if any teenaged girl was ever quick in the shower.

A knock came at the still-open door and Phoebe swung around. The front desk clerk was there.

"I hope everything is to your satisfaction?" she asked.

From beyond the bathroom door came the sound of running water and Alice's cry. "The water's gloriously warm!" Then she broke into some modern pop song that Phoebe didn't know.

Phoebe grinned. "I think that's the final verdict. I'm Phoebe. This is Becca. The songstress is Alice." She nodded at the bathroom.

"I am Avni, your hostess. Welcome to the Scandinavian Guesthouse. If there is anything you need, please don't hesitate to ask."

"Thank you, Avni. We appreciate the welcome and we'll try not to be too much trouble. We may need extra towels, if that's not too much of a problem." There had been a single towel laid out on each bed.

The song continued in the bathroom.

"Unlike other people who shall remain nameless," Becca said glancing up to the second floor as she swung off the bed and began unpacking. She hauled out clean capris and a blouse and her toiletries.

Phoebe turned back to Avni. "Sorry about Simon. He can be a bit—much. He seems to have difficulty dealing with everyone."

"Mr. Roy is well known here…"

The bathroom serenade stopped.

"I thought—"

Miraculously, the bathroom door pulled open interrupting Phoebe's thought. Alice stepped out wrapped in a sarong, toweling the long damp strands of her hair.

"I thought I should dress out here so you guys could shower." She stopped when she saw Avni. "Oh. Company. Hi! I'm Alice." She grinned and stepped up to shake Avni's hand, surprising Phoebe and apparently Avni, who hesitated at this bold young thing.

Then Avni shook her hand. "I am pleased to meet you, Alice. I am Avni, your hostess. I believe my daughter may be your age. You are fourteen? Fifteen?"

Alice's smile broadened. Nothing pleased a thirteen-year-old more than being told they looked older. Oh, for those days again.

"You are here for five days. Perhaps there will be time for you and Aimi to meet each other."

"That would be great, don't you think, Aunt Bee?"

"It would be wonderful. Thank you, Avni."

Their hostess withdrew in a rustle of silken fabric. While Becca showered, Alice quickly dressed in clean cotton trousers with an ornate elephant print around the waist and cuff, and a loose cotton short-sleeved top of bright orange that she'd bought in Goa. She settled on the edge of her bed as she combed out her tangle of hair. "So where are we going on the tour this afternoon?"

Phoebe shook her head. "After that train ride, everything feels loose in my brain; but I seem to recall something about the old town, a synagogue, and fishing nets."

Alice frowned. "Doesn't sound too interesting. But it *did* look like interesting shopping. Hint, hint."

Through the bathroom wall came the sound of water and a loud sigh of delight.

Phoebe rolled her eyes. "You are going to run out of money if you keep spending like you are."

"I'm not looking for anything big…"

Loud male voices through the window stopped Alice's protest. She went to the louvred window to listen. "Great. It's them. Again."

Them, meaning none other than Simon and Zamir. Phoebe joined Alice at the window and looked out at the sun-filled street. There was only a lone male walking about half a block down the street and no one else in sight, but the voices were loud and clear from upstairs. They sounded angry, but she couldn't hear what they were saying.

"It's really none of our business," she said and eased Alice away. There'd been sporadic arguments throughout the trip. Simon was officious and demanding of everyone around him who wasn't a paying customer, just as he'd been to Avni. Zamir seemed to take the brunt of it. And take it and take it some more, but every so often he'd stand up for himself and there'd be what Simon euphemistically called a disagreement. It didn't really impact the tour except that whenever the fireworks came out, Phoebe and the others had learned to vacate the area.

When Becca exited the washroom looking squeaky clean in white trousers and flowing caftan shirt, which were about the least practical thing Phoebe could think of in a country as dusty as India, Phoebe quickly sluiced herself off in a lovely warm shower and then turned the water gradually colder to cool down from the Kochi heat.

Kochi sat on the Malabar Coast of India—a place that held mythic status to travelers—like Zanzibar or Timbuktu. Kochi's famous deep-sea harbor was, according to the guidebooks, one of the best in the world and had led to visits from ancient mariners from as far away as China, and to the Portuguese takeover, the British takeover from the Portuguese, and the eventual handover of the area to the Indian government.

When she stepped out of the shower and pulled on clean clothes—dark grey capris and a maroon, Indian cotton short-sleeved shirt, she felt like a new woman. She fluffed her short-cropped blonde hair that she had had frosted on the tips to hopefully hide the gray and went out to the others.

Both Becca and Alice had their day packs on their shoulders.

"Let me guess. Simon's waiting."

"He says we're to come to the restaurant. He has lunch waiting," Alice said.

"I thought we were going out for lunch…"

"Apparently not," Becca said. "The hotel brochure says that lunch or dinner are included in the price. I can't see Simon paying for a restaurant meal with that kind of offer available."

Sighing, Phoebe grabbed her day pack and cross-body purse and locked the door behind them.

The guesthouse restaurant was a scattering of glass-topped wicker tables in the shade of jasmine and bougainvillea vines that had been trained over a trellis to one side of the pool. A large tree grew up through the pavers around the pool and dappled the turquoise water with shade from the omnipresent sun. Phoebe was already sweating by the time she settled at a long table where the others were waiting.

"Nice place, huh?" Trevor said.

Phoebe nodded.

"Nice shower," Becca said.

"Mmm. I could have stood in that water for hours." Jeannie closed her eyes in apparent rapture.

A waiter appeared and set down two large platters heaped with saffron-colored rice dotted with flecks of vegetables and larger pieces of chicken. The table went silent except for Simon, who helped himself to a heaping plateful, being careful to select a healthy portion of the meat.

"I took the liberty of ordering for us so that we could get on the road quickly," he said. "Dig in." He used his fingers to eat in traditional Indian style. "It's good."

Phoebe eyed the yellow rice and glanced at Becca and Alice.

Biryani.

Chicken biryani.

Again.

As if that was the only Indian food available in Southern India.

Alice looked close to tears. Before the trip, Phoebe, Alice, and Becca had gone for Indian food a number of times and Alice had always waxed on about loving this chicken and rice dish. Then they'd arrived in India and the chicken was often boney and they'd eaten the darn stuff practically every second day—when they weren't on a train, of course. There'd been none of the lovely curries that they'd enjoyed at home.

"At least have a little," Phoebe said softly as she spooned a small amount onto her plate. "You'll be hungry if you don't."

"We need to buy some fruit," Becca said. "And I want vegetables again in this lifetime."

They ate in silence, with Simon and Zamir polishing off the major share of the food. When they were done, Simon pushed back his chair and stood.

"So, this afternoon Zamir is going to be your guide. I have a few other things to take care of. Have fun." He graced them with a smile and left the table as the rest of them shuffled to their feet.

"I thought you hadn't been here before," Phoebe said to Zamir.

Zamir gave an embarrassed little head bobble. "Don't worry. We'll be fine. I am Indian."

As if that could fix all the things that had been wrong with this tour. She glanced back at Simon as he climbed the stairs to his room. Trevor and Jeannie watched him go, and Trevor shook his head. There'd been times Zamir had shepherded them before and he'd always done a great job, but they were paying Simon to be their guide… What did Zamir, a Tamil who had never been to Kochi before, possibly know about the old city?

If they hadn't spent so much on this tour, she really would have considered walking away from it long before now. She hadn't, however, discussed that possibility with Becca given it was Becca who had chosen the tour.

"You know," Jeannie said, "I don't know if it was the chicken, but something's not sitting well with me. I think I'm going to give the tour a pass and spend the afternoon in my room." She rose and, with a nod to Trevor, carried her camera bag back upstairs.

"Shall we go?" Zamir said. He pulled a ball cap down on his head and headed for the guesthouse door. Like a gaggle of baby ducklings, they trooped after him.

Phoebe waved to Avni as she followed the others out the door.

2

The tour didn't go well. A dusty old palace with too little to see and too many sweaty tourists. An ancient synagogue—currently closed to the public for renovations. A spice market that was unconscionably devoid of spices—except for high-priced packets for sale to tourists, and traffic that trapped the minivan in the street for so long that everyone had voted to return to the hotel—only to find that the pool was only open another hour and then closed for the dinner seating. The only good thing was that Jeannie was feeling better.

The day had left Alice irritable, Becca once more apologetic for selecting this tour though no one blamed her, and Phoebe exhausted for trying to smooth everyone's ruffled feathers before she fell into bed at half past ten regretting that she'd agreed to go with Alice, Trevor, and Jeannie for an early morning walk to the Chinese fishing nets that were the tourist symbol of Kochi.

She fell asleep knowing she definitely did not want to repeat a day like today again.

. . .

Phoebe rolled over in the oh-so-comfortable bed. The room was velvet dark. The delicious scent of something baking suggested that a good breakfast would be waiting when she got up. She snuggled into the covers, the room's air conditioning almost too efficient.

"Come on, Aunt Bee. It's time to get up."

A soft glow through her eyelids said Alice had the washroom light on with the door half closed.

She squeezed her eyes shut tighter.

"I could tickle your feet like you did to me…"

Phoebe hauled her feet into the center of the bed against the encroachment of thirteen-year-old fingers, then sighed and threw the covers off.

She rolled up to sitting and groaned. This age thing was really no fun. Between having to get up to go to the toilet in the middle of the night and the aches and pains that came with getting older… "You're going to owe me big-time for this."

Alice did one of her eye rolls again. "And you and Mom say *I'm* moody."

Phoebe blinked against the half-light that silhouetted Alice standing fully clothed with one hand on her hip, the other clutching her camera bag. "What time is it?"

"Time for you both to be quiet and let me sleep," came Becca's groggy reply as she pulled her sheets up over her head.

"Six twenty-five," Alice whispered.

And they were supposed to be meeting Jeannie and Trevor at six thirty.

"Crap. Go on out to the lobby and tell them I'll just be a minute." She grabbed clothes she'd laid out the night before and ran for the washroom, did her teeth and threw water at her face, pulled a brush through her hair and hauled her clothes on, then ran out of the room to the shadowed lobby. Alice, Trevor, and Jeannie stood alone amongst the empty lounge chairs. There was no one at reception, but a light beyond the pool said someone was at work in the kitchens. So did the potent scent of something sweet and bready baking. Phoebe's mouth watered.

Trevor checked his watch and stifled a yawn. "Not bad. I thought you'd keep us waiting." He lugged a large camera backpack and collapsible tripod over his shoulder, but bags under his eyes said he might feel closer to how Phoebe felt. Jeannie, with a pack that was only slightly smaller, looked the same. They must have stayed up for a while after Phoebe'd fallen into bed so she had no sympathy for them. Getting up this early was their crazy idea.

"I'm just hoping that we'll be back in time for breakfast," Phoebe said. She glanced at the still-dark dining area beside the underwater lit pool. A cup of chai was calling her name. Actually, at this moment, a coffee would be even better.

"It's possible. It'll depend on the light." Jeannie said with a sigh. This morning she had her cloud of red hair semi-contained in a disheveled pony tail that suggested she'd barely rousted herself from bed. She wore a shin-length Indian cotton skirt in purple and a fuchsia t-shirt. "We want to capture sunrise over the Chinese fishing nets." She checked her watch—vintage Mickey Mouse that Alice had oohed and aahed over. "And for that we should get going."

They shoved the main door open and headed out into the dim gray light of dawn. Trevor referenced a hand-drawn map that Avni had made for him last evening, turned right in the street and led them on. The street was quiet, though the sound of vehicles wafted through the trees. Doves coo-cooed softly in the branches. A whiff of jasmine floated on a salty breeze. They passed an ATM located in what looked like an apartment building surrounded by trees. A small discreet sign advertised a bank name that Phoebe didn't know. It was a far cry from the security-conscious structures in her native Vancouver.

They rounded a corner and in barely five minutes found themselves at a parking lot by the water. Small vendor kiosks of sun-faded red, blue, and yellow had their shutters pulled down and their wares stored away elsewhere, but the colors still gave a deserted carnival feel. Beyond the kiosks, a lone weightlifter did reps in an open-air, muscle-beach area where barbells littered the concrete.

Jeannie and Trevor led the way up to the walkway that sided the water and stopped.

"Now that's what I'm talking about," Trevor said as Phoebe caught up to them.

"Wow," Alice said.

They stood overlooking a small bay as the sun came up behind them. Where the light struck, the water was purest turquoise, affixed with glaring white breakers. Farther out, the water was azure and stretched across the channel to what could be an oil refinery judging by the huge tanks, though there was no smoke to be seen. A massive freighter was approaching the channel, the rumble of its diesel engines cutting through the roar of the waves.

Their small bay curved around to a rocky headland to their left and became just another part of a sandy coastline to their right. At the base of the headland, a man in red stood juxtaposed against the dark stone. He waded chest deep into the water carrying something and then threw it. The something whirred away from him, spreading out into a circular, turquoise net that splashed into the water. The fisherman pulled his net back to him and returned to shore to begin picking his catch out of the webbing.

Alice brought her camera up and started snapping photos and with the striking red against the azure, Phoebe could understand why.

Trevor nodded and then swung off his pack for his camera. He took a few shots. Jeannie didn't bother. She touched Trevor's arm. "The nets, remember."

He lowered his camera. "Right. Let's get going. The nets should be down here a ways. We just need to follow the water."

They headed down the paved walkway along the shore, passing more of the fishermen throwing nets into the waves and small boats heading out into the deeper water. Phoebe had to almost drag Alice away from the amazing scene of the whirring nets gleaming in the sun, but Trevor and Jeannie kept going and Phoebe didn't want to get separated from them. A few hardy souls—both foreigners and locals— jogged the seawall past them. There would probably be families as it got later, but 6:30 a.m. was at least cooler than the temperature they'd experienced the day before.

The freighter cruised past them, churning its way farther into Kochi's deep-water harbor as the seawall curved around a slight headland. Ahead, huge kite-shaped net structures made of elongated timbers perched on stork leg pilings along the shore. Some of the kite-shapes were bowed low, the nets dipped into the water. Others silhouetted dripping, four-sided nets above the water against the streaming, early morning light. Below them, along a debris-strewn beach, small fishing boats launched into the water, and above the beach, a line of trees bordered the seawall. The stench of sea wrack filled the air, but there were none of the gulls Phoebe had grown so used to during her Pacific Northwest kayaking forays. Instead, the air around the boats and the fishing nets was filled with black crows.

"Wow, again," Alice said, bringing her camera to her eye to snap a view of the scene. The camera had been a Christmas gift from Phoebe after Alice had moaned that she had nothing to remind her of the beauty they had seen amid the wild adventure of their kayaking trip to Johnstone Strait off British Columbia's scenic west coast.

Jeannie and Trevor set up tripods to capture the scene. Their discussion had taken a foreign-sounding turn with terms like neutral density, long exposure, and other more esoteric things like aperture and ISO. It was Jeannie doing most of the talking and Alice listened with interest, but the photographers' discussion seemed even beyond her. Given Trevor already had his camera up and was taking pictures, Phoebe had to wonder who exactly Jeannie was talking to. But then some people had to talk themselves through their processes.

"How about we go closer to the nets, given you don't have all the lenses they do?" Phoebe suggested.

Alice nodded and the two of them set off along the shore, Alice hurrying ahead like an eager puppy, held up only by the frustratingly slower speed of Phoebe's older legs.

"Look! They're going to raise one of the nets!" Alice said and snapped a photo as she rushed ahead and then stopped to wait for Phoebe.

"Go on. I'll catch up. Just don't go too far, okay?" Phoebe waved her on.

Alice nodded and was off like a shot, scooting along the seawall until she found a set of stairs that took her down through a line of trees onto the sand. Phoebe followed to the stairs and sighed. The only good thing was that Alice was hard to miss as the only blonde amid the darker heads of the locals. She'd be hard to lose sight of.

The beach, however, was filthy. Plastic water bottles, old clothing, lost nets, drink containers, Styrofoam boxes, etc., clotted around a dead sea turtle. Driftwood caught shoals of half-decomposed fish and broken plastic that crows and mangy dogs dug through. Phoebe picked her way through the mess, trying to keep her sandaled feet clear of the worst of the debris while keeping Alice in her sights. Beyond Alice, the huge old fishing nets rose and dipped.

The nets were ancient technology brought by the Chinese when they visited India before Columbus ever found America. The Chinese were more or less gone except for their modern-day investments, but the nets had stayed behind and, from what Phoebe had read, the technology had spread all up and down the Malabar coast. They worked on a cantilevered weight system with huge rocks tied to ropes to offset the weight of the net. Men walking along the narrow wooden net supports provided the additional weight that would raise the net or send it dipping into the water.

All but one. One net, in the line of eight or nine that edged the channel, was in the water, but apparently refused to be raised. Perhaps it was a large haul of fish or—given what was on the shore—more likely garbage that held the net in the water, but the fishermen were laboring, hauling on the rock-weighted lines to slowly, slowly, raise the net.

When Phoebe looked back from the nets to the shore, Alice was nowhere to be seen. Damn and double-damn, she'd lost her again! Her heart thumped so hard that it was hard to breathe. She'd lost Alice before—almost really lost her and had almost died trying to get her back. After all that they'd been through before, how could she have done this again? Becca would kill her.

"Alice!" she called, fighting down panic, and rushed down the shore. Things squished under feet. Something splashed over her toes. She broke into a run.

"Alice!" How had she disappeared so fast?

Ahead fishermen loosening fish from their turquoise mesh nets looked up as she ran up to them. "Alice? Have you seen my niece?"

Their blank stares said that she'd found people who spoke only Malayalam, the local Keralan language. Great. More boats pulled to shore blocking her path to the line of huge Chinese nets. Alice must have gone around them.

Another set of stairs ran up to the seawall.

Phoebe stumbled over driftwood piles and clots of plastic bottles and ran up the stairs. Back the way they had come, Trevor and Jeannie were still taking photos. No Alice with them. Which meant that she had to have gone on.

Phoebe turned down the seawall toward the nets. The wind rustled the spreading trees that would provide shade in the sunshine, but now were a nuisance for blocking her view. The nets. Alice had to have gone for the nets. Of course, now there were more people around, out for their morning stroll.

She shoved past them, apologizing, her gaze on the nets. Alice had been excited about the nets being raised and lowered. The one net still seemed to be still. A shout came and through the trees bordering the beach, slow as the sun rising over the horizon, the huge net began to swing upward.

The trees blocked her view as she rushed toward the net.

That was when the screaming started—shrill and frightened. The kind of free-form scream a thirteen-year-old might scream.

She'd heard the same kind of screams in her school as her students lay dying.

3

The scream pierced the morning and froze Phoebe in her tracks. The world stilled around her. Nobody moved. The ocean breeze stopped and turned from warm to frigid. The ship anchored in its wake. The harbor water iced over. The crows stopped their swirl in the air above her and the sun no longer rose. All she could smell was rot and death—of fish caught by fishermen, of the dead sea turtle, and something else like perforated gut from a bullet wound. Or perhaps that was her memories. She wanted to run. She wanted to take cover and protect herself.

Instead she shuddered and suddenly the world moved around her. Crows rose and fell. People turned in their tracks and the ship rumbled on toward its berth as if nothing had happened.

Phoebe stumbled and almost fell.

Alice. Where *was* she?

The piercing scream died away somewhere near the water and Phoebe leapt down a second set of stairs and plunged down to the beach under the huge Chinese fishing nets. Fishermen flooded around her. So did joggers and other people from the seawall.

The wind off the water was full in her face, blowing sea salt air and the stench of fish. People jostled and shoved her, hampering her progress and yet pushing her along. The clamor of voices was too loud in her ears. Too reminiscent of shoving students along. Herding them into a classroom to hide.

Ahead, where the fishing net strained out of the water, a beam of sunlight through the trees found a familiar blonde head.

Alice.

Relief flooded through Phoebe as she arrived. Alice stood rigid, her face gone white, her blue eyes wide. Two sari-clad women fussed over her and tried to turn her around. She shook her head and shook her head again, and yet seemed unable to look away from the net beyond.

They stood at the edge of the great net that had struggled to bring its catch up from the water. The fishermen operating it still struggled, but the sagging curve of net was out of the water as the great timbers groaned.

Phoebe followed Alice's immobile gaze and finally understood the fishermen's challenge. At the bottom of the net a figure sprawled, dark water sluicing off the body and the seaweed and debris caught with it. Alice turned into Phoebe's arms and buried her face in Phoebe's shoulder.

Phoebe stroked her soft hair. "It's okay. It's okay. People die, Alice. You're okay." Which was more important than anything. With Alice safe in her arms, Phoebe could almost breathe again, could almost slow her racing heart.

The timbers groaned as the net rose and steadied at its highest level. Fishermen tied it off and crowded the wooden scaffolding around the net, staring down at their unlikely catch.

Alice lifted her pale, tear-stained face and glanced once more at the grim sight. She swallowed. "Don't you see who it is?"

Phoebe frowned and forced herself to take a second look.

"Look. The skin's light—white. He's wearing shorts." Alice pointed.

The crumpled figure lolled loose-boned amid the seaweed in the morning sun. It was hard to tell, because the body was backlit, but gradually she could make out four white limbs tangled with weeds and garbage. A torso in khaki, stained dark by the water. The sunlight caught on steel-colored hair and then she saw it—the face peering blindly down at them. Narrow. Gray goatee.

She swayed, clutched Alice's shoulder for balance, and desperately needed a place to sit. She turned Alice around so the girl could no longer see Simon Roy's body dripping above them. Not that she'd ever forget the sight. Phoebe's first sight of a body was etched indelibly on her brain.

She caught Alice by the shoulders, nodded her thanks to the women who had helped her, and guided Alice toward the seawall. It wasn't easy. It seemed as if the entire population of Kochi arrived at exactly that moment to see the dead man caught in their famous nets. A siren's blare through the cacophonous crowd said someone had called the police.

Up on the seawall, they both collapsed on a bench that looked out over the water. It didn't help. Alice sagged beside her. Phoebe pulled her into her side. Her insides jittered and jerked like water dropped on a hotplate. If she could just find the strength, she'd be up and running. Back to the guesthouse. Back on the train. Back on the plane to Canada and safety locked in her apartment.

But she couldn't.

She had Alice to care for, just as she'd had the students before.

"How—how could that be Simon? How could he be there? Dead? I don't understand," Alice said, her voice sounding too loud in a dead space between the breeze and the waves.

"Neither do I," Phoebe said. She felt numb and unable to move. To prove she wasn't, she kissed Alice's forehead. "It's an awful thing." The end of a man, a life—even if he wasn't a particularly likeable man.

She shook her head and Alice looked up at her. "What is it?"

Phoebe sighed. "I was wondering how he died." And how his death was going to affect the tour. Not to mention what Becca might say given it seemed like Phoebe's holidays with Alice were doomed to have something awful happen. Thankfully it was Becca who'd made the arrangements this time.

Through the press of people on the walkway, Trevor and Jeannie arrived.

"What's happened?" Jeannie asked. "We heard a scream."

Phoebe looked up at them. "It seems our illustrious leader has died."

"He's in one of the nets," Alice added. "Or at least his body is." The tremble in her voice said she was still shaken.

Phoebe squeezed her into her side and caught Trevor and Jeannie exchanging glances. "He must have fallen in the water somehow and the net caught him."

Trevor shook his head slightly. "I'll bet the police have a tough time with this one. Simon might be Canadian, but he must have visited here a number of times. I get the feeling he hadn't made many friends."

Alice pulled away and straightened. "You mean like Avni, that nice lady at the hotel?"

Phoebe sent a warning look Trevor's way. The last thing she needed was Alice getting upset, but her mind was already whirring away. "Simon's death was likely an accident. And his discussion with Avni was just a little disagreement, I think."

"Simon was arguing with Zamir, remember?" Jeannie said.

Phoebe glared a warning at Jeannie, too. Would these two not get the message that they had a thirteen-year-old in their midst?

Across from them, people began to surge up the stairs from the debris-covered beach, the two sari-clad ladies from the beach at their head. Just behind them came a police officer in a khaki uniform. He had thick black hair and a moustache that set off the dark eyes half-hidden by the peak of his uniform hat. Around his waist he wore a tan equipment belt loaded with a gun, a radio, and a truncheon.

"This is the girl and the woman," said one of the women. "They seemed to know the man." She stepped back to let the officer approach.

He glanced back at the crowd as if to check that they were watching, straightened his shoulders, and stepped up to the bench. Phoebe stood to face him, keeping Alice behind her. Trevor and Jeannie stayed back.

"Identification, please," the officer asked.

Phoebe glanced at Trevor and Jeannie. No help there. She fished in her cross-body purse and brought out her passport. "My name is Phoebe Clay. This is my niece, Alice."

The officer flipped through her woefully empty passport pages, pulled out his notebook, and took down her name. He glanced down at Alice. "Her identification?"

"Alice?" Phoebe asked.

Alice shook her head. "Sorry, Auntie Bee. I left it in the room. I thought it would be safer."

She looked scared and still shell-shocked by what she'd just seen.

Phoebe turned back to the officer. "I'm afraid she doesn't have her identification on her. It's in our hotel room."

"Where do you stay?"

"At the Scandinavian Guesthouse."

"We're on a tour," Trevor added, coming to her rescue.

"And you are?" the police officer asked.

"Trevor Smith and Jeannie Gerard." He lifted his chin at the water. "Is it really true? Simon's dead?"

"A body has been found. It has not been officially identified," the officer said, but Phoebe nodded.

"Shit. This's bad." Trevor said, rubbing his face. Jeannie looked lost deep in thought.

The officer asked for passports and took down their names.

"You." He turned back to Phoebe. "Who is this Simon?"

"Simon Roy. He's—he's our tour guide. We're on a tour. Five of us were. Through southern India. We started in Chennai."

He waved that information away. "What were you doing by the fishing nets this morning? That is not a place for tourists."

"It's not? I thought they were the iconic photograph of Kochi," Jeannie said, then shut her mouth at a sharp look from Trevor.

The officer glanced at Jeannie. "You and your friends may go." He turned to Phoebe. "You will come with me."

"But I've done nothing wrong."

The officer caught Phoebe by the arm. "This way, please. There are others to talk to."

He dragged her a step or two, but he wasn't asking Alice to come too. That was good, wasn't it? She'd heard about police in other countries not exactly conforming to policing standards back home. There were plenty of horror stories about tourists ending up in foreign prisons...

Phoebe craned around. Alice still stood by the bench. "Alice, go back to the hotel with Jeannie and Trevor. Stay with your mom. I'll see you there."

To ensure the officer didn't change his mind about Alice, Phoebe almost pulled him along with her into the crowd.

He guided her back down the stairs to the beach and toward the water and the nets. Her feet sank in the damp sand. It was hard to walk and to pick her way through the debris with his firm grip pulling her off balance.

The crowd still encroached on the scene, but now uniformed men stood among the fishermen on the wooden walkway around the fishing net stanchion. It looked like they were arguing. Finally, one of the fishermen slid down the net surface with a rope. He tied the rope around the body's chest and then had another rope tossed down to him that hauled him back up to the fishermen's platform. Two officers heaved on the rope that held Simon's body and it slid loose of the debris and then slowly, slowly dragged up the side of the net like some strange sea beast. Around her, people snapped photos with their phone cameras.

The body reached the edge of the net and officers grabbed his arms and flopped him onto the platform. Phoebe's stomach twisted at the thud and the boneless way his body moved. For all Simon was an officious little man, he didn't deserve to be treated like a piece of human flotsam. He would have hated this. His prissy nature would have rebelled against absolutely all of this.

"You come," Phoebe's officer said and dragged her toward the net.

"Where are you taking me?" she asked and held back as he urged her up onto the narrow rickety planks that formed the raised walkway to the net.

"Someone must identify the body." He guided her up and on to the swaying wooden planks that seemed to bow almost to breaking at every step. Her knees felt weak and every part of her screamed "No, no, no!"

She'd seen enough dead bodies. She didn't want to see more. This was supposed to be a family vacation. A chance to see the world. She was not supposed to get caught in another situation that brought her face-to-face with a body.

As they advanced onto the narrow planks, the wind off the water turned cold and threatened to buffet her right off. She slowed, planting each foot with purpose and fighting the police officer's insistent tug until finally she reached the slightly wider platform next to the net. There were too many people there. Five fishermen and three officers on a platform meant to hold the cantilevering rocks that operated the net—not all of the men plus a sprawled body.

And not her. Was the wood strong enough to hold her?

At the officer's insistence, she edged around the fishermen and police to the body. The stink of death rose off of him. At least it smelled like it. Decay, salt water, and mud had overcome Simon's overly sweet aftershave.

He lay in his sodden khaki shorts and shirt with his arms and legs splayed wide, his head turned slightly sideways, water trickling from his mouth. There was something misshapen about the back of his skull and his eyes and eyelids were gone, revealing permanently open eye sockets.

Her stomach churned. She swallowed back bile and looked away from the gruesome face. Arms and legs looked whole. No sign of injury to his body. Hands overly white and clawed in death—maybe rigor mortis was settling in? She tried to keep her study clinical. Clinical would stop her from being sick. Clinical would keep her from screaming. Clinical would hopefully keep all the other memories massing at the edge of her brain from seeping in and overwhelming her.

"Simon Roy," she said, but it came out as a whisper. "His name is Simon Roy." This time her voice had steadied. She turned away from the body. "He is—was—Canadian. He was our tour guide. He lived half the year in Chennai."

And that was virtually all she knew of the man. That and that he was gay and proud of it.

"Very good," said another voice, strong, warm, with a cultured English accent almost like a schoolteacher assessing a student.

She swung around, almost losing her balance, but a strong hand caught her elbow. Another man had joined them on the platform, this one with the same ubiquitous black hair and moustache of the police officers, but his skin was a shade of caramel instead of the darker shade of some of the Keralan officers. Instead of a uniform, he wore a neat gray suit and blue tie and a pristine white shirt that could have come from the laundry the tour had visited their first day in Kochi. His hair was a little shaggy on top, and he had a little swagger as if he thought himself a cut above other people. His cool hazel-green gaze said he was sure of it.

"And you are?" She managed to keep her voice steady.

"Detective Parmar Mathias." He inclined his head in her direction, halfway courtly, the other fifty percent clearly condescension as if he expected hysteria from a foreign woman.

She might be foreign but she sure as heck wasn't going to show hysteria.

"You've saved us the challenge of having to identify him, though his consulate will need to confirm it. That is very good." He stepped up beside her and the weathered plank underfoot groaned a warning as he peered down at Simon.

Phoebe waited for the sound of splintering wood and readied herself to jump. Thankfully, it didn't come.

"And your name, Madam?" he asked her.

"Phoebe Clay. And before you ask, I'm Canadian, too. There are five of us on a tour."

He gave a curt nod as if he already knew.

"What do we have? What do we know?" he asked no one in particular as he knelt down beside the body. He studied Simon's head and then examined his white, water-wrinkled hands. "Hmm." He held up a hand. "What does this suggest?"

She peered down. Simon's usually neat fingernails were torn and ragged. There were scrapes and bruises on the knuckles.

She met Mathias's dark gaze and saw his half smile. The man was playing with her.

"A fight, perhaps? But I'm not a police officer." She straightened.

He stood beside her and looked down at the body. "Pens in his right pocket. His left shirt pocket is buttoned, but this pocket here is unbuttoned and torn." He indicated the left-side pocket of Simon's Bermuda shorts. "What did he keep there? A notebook perhaps? A wallet? Do you happen to recall?"

It was a good observation and she was surprised she hadn't noticed. "A scarf or poof—do you know what I mean? A small cloth. It was an odd piece of cloth—a rose color with rainbows embroidered on it. I touched it once and it was very soft, like it was old and worn. He always wore it." Rainbows. She wondered whether he knew the significance of rainbows as a symbol of the acceptance of the many forms of sexuality, whether lesbian, gay, bisexual, transsexual, queer, or… There seemed to be letters being added to the LGBTQ movement all the time.

He nodded. "The water could have taken it away." But the way he eyed the torn pocket, she didn't think he believed it.

"Or it could be down there." She nodded to the bottom of the net and the clot of debris.

"True."

He said something in Malayalam to one of the uniformed officers. The uniformed man didn't look happy, but he clambered over the side of the net, and with the help of a rope held by the fishermen, slid down the sloping side of the net to the dripping mess at the bottom. There, he balanced precariously and gingerly dug through the smelly mess. By his face, it was disgusting and probably something he would harbor against Detective Mathias for the rest of his career.

When he'd been down there ten minutes and had fished through the seaweed, bottles, and mud, he stood and shook his head.

"Interesting," Mathias said. "The water probably took it."

"Or he could have lost it in the struggle," Phoebe offered.

He glanced at her sharply. "Struggle?"

His gaze pinned her like a fly and she found herself defensive. "You said—you said his hands indicated a fight."

"No. It was you who suggested a fight when I asked what could have caused the injuries to his hands." He cocked a brow at her. "There are other things than a struggle that could have led to such injuries and the one to his head. He could have fallen and the scrapes were from attempts to help himself before he hit his head. I will await the pathologist's report before coming to conclusions."

It was true and it felt like all the blood had drained from her head and her legs were unsteady. Or maybe it was the boards under her feet that now felt like quicksand. Had she just incriminated herself? Those horror stories she'd heard included tourists being imprisoned on trumped-up evidence. She snapped her mouth closed and said nothing more, instead watching the slow climb of the officer up the side of the net as his now-filthy shoes kept slipping out from under him. It would have been humorous except for the situation.

When the officer reached the platform, he tried to brush himself off and succeeded only in smearing the mud and seaweed on his clothes. Mathias waved him off and turned back to Phoebe.

"Ms. Clay. You will accompany me to the police station to answer my questions."

He said it politely, but it wasn't a question—more a statement of fact. The jittering feeling that had been shaking her insides since she'd heard Alice scream ramped another notch. She swallowed and nodded. "I need to call my sister and niece and let them know. They'll be worried about me." She pulled her mobile out of her purse.

He waved the phone away as if it made no matter. "You can call from the station."

She was going to call Becca anyway, but didn't want to risk him doing something like confiscating her phone. She slipped the phone back into her bag.

He half bowed her toward the narrow planks that led to the shore.

With a sigh and her stomach flip-flopping with concern, she edged onto the planks that led back to the shore, but kept one eye on Mathias. She didn't trust him, didn't trust him at all.

She shuffled her way down the swaying plank, uncomfortable with the fact that it was Mathias who caught her elbow and steadied her wobbles. At the far end, she stepped down onto the sand and sighed in relief.

Mathias smiled down at her. In other circumstances he might be considered handsome and charming, but at the moment it felt as if he was gloating at having a foreign tourist in his power—a female one. Everyone knew women were considered second class in India.

Lips pressed together to keep from speaking her mind, she pulled back her hand and marched up to the seawall to wait for him. Unfortunately, his longer legs had kept up with her. So much for making a statement. She wondered whether she should demand to call the Canadian consulate.

"My car is there." He lifted his chin toward a parking lot beyond the crowd along the seawall and a second line of spreading trees.

"Aren't you going to move him?" she asked. Back at the fishing net, the uniformed officers still stood over Simon's body.

Mathias shrugged. "Someone else will see to that. I have come. I have surveyed the scene. Now forensics will take over and I may speak with you to gather further information about our dead man."

As if he was reading off the instructions for an investigation. Had he even investigated a death before? She hoped tourists didn't die suspiciously in Kochi every day. Well, the sooner she could get him to realize that she had played no part in Simon's death, the better it would be for the investigation. She set off for the parking lot and climbed into the small Tata sedan he led her to.

The police station was a short, but far-too-long, silent drive from the shore down tree-lined streets to a junction near an old walled church with numerous shops up narrow side streets. She checked her watch. Only eight thirty, which explained the uniformed children in the streets. The kids were going to school while she could be going to jail. The juxtaposition made her head hurt and the jitters evolved to tremors in her hands. She hadn't had those since immediately after the incident at her school. Had she survived the school shooting only to find herself accused of killing their darned-fool guide?

Not that he was a fool, exactly. Just—unpleasant and odd.

Mathias pulled up in front of a two-story stone building with a small, black-painted cannon to the left of an open door. She climbed out of the Tata sedan and waited for Mathias as he hauled his taller frame out of the small car. "You will follow me, please."

He led through the doorway and Phoebe followed, pausing to look back to the street. Then she stepped inside wondering whether she'd see the church steeple, shopkeeper windows, and artist murals again.

4

———————

Detective Mathias waited for her just inside the police station door in a dim, cool space that was clearly a public waiting area. It had a worn tile floor. A chest-high counter blocked one end of the room. Humidity-stained cream walls bore two framed images, one a likeness of the Keralan emblem of two elephants rampant, the other a faded sepia photograph of Gandhi. Low wooden benches filled the center of the room and were occupied by a motley mix of Indian humanity, with a dreadlocked tourist and apparently his girlfriend huddled in one corner. Feet shuffled on the floor at their entrance and eyes locked on her.

"My office is this way," he said and crossed the room to lift a portion of the counter barrier out of the way.

Phoebe stayed by the door. "Uh-uh. You said if I came to the station, I could call my sister and niece. I want to do that first, please." She prayed he didn't smell her fear.

His eyes widened slightly as if surprised at her bravado, but then, with that mocking smile of his, he nodded. "I did say that, yes. You may phone."

She hauled it out and hurriedly punched in Becca's number in case he changed his mind. Barely a ring had time to sound before the line connected.

"Phoebe! Are you all right? Where are you? What's happening? Alice can barely speak she's so upset and Jeannie and Trevor only said Simon's dead and that you went with the police."

"That's about the size of it," Phoebe said, eyeing Mathias as he checked his watch. The place smelled of sour cloves and body odor. "I'm at the police station."

"Oh, my God! Are you arrested?"

"No, I'm not arrested as far as I know." But Mathias's expression left her uncertain. "I'm here, now, so I guess I'll find out. The detective —a Detective Mathias—has some questions. Maybe write down his name. I'm at Fort Kochi Police Station according to the sign. Maybe— maybe get in touch with the Canadian Consulate and let them know what's happened. They'll need to know about Simon at least. Okay? And I'm fine. A little shaken, but fine. I think they just want to know more about Simon." She could hear by the tremor in Becca's voice that she needed that reassurance. Phoebe just wished someone would reassure *her*. "I'll call you again once I know what's going on. Okay?"

She heard Becca's calming gulp. "Okay. But if I don't hear from you in an hour, I'm coming to get you."

Phoebe hung up, stuck her phone in her pocket so that Mathias would have to work a little harder if he wanted to confiscate it, and turned to him. "Thank you. My sister was very upset. She doesn't handle this kind of thing well."

A dark brow tilted at her. "And you do, by comparison?"

"In comparison, yes," she said firmly. If she could get through the school shooting and the kayak adventure she and Alice had been on, then surely to goodness she could face this officer's questioning, too. She met his gaze and held there, then decided to change the tenor of their relationship. "How can I help your investigation? What is it that you want to know?"

"We will see," he said and ushered her ahead of him through the counter.

His 'office' was actually a cramped, yellow-walled interview room with only a scarred wooden table and two chairs. The door shut behind them and the cloying warmth of the stifling air felt like plastic wrap over her skin. She turned to face him and felt sweat trickle down her back into the crack of her bum.

"Please. Sit." He pointed to the chair across the table.

She edged around the table and sat, but Mathias didn't. Instead he towered over her as if to indelibly impress her with the difference in their positions. Phoebe simply met his gaze. She was *not* about to let this man intimidate her. She waited, because she had a feeling whoever spoke first would be the loser in this meeting. The person who spoke first was usually nervous at the silence and guilty people were usually nervous. She had done nothing to be nervous about.

Finally, he nodded and seated himself. "So, Phoebe Clay, what brings you to Kochi?"

"That's your question? You had to bring me to the police station to ask it?" She drew in a breath to quell her slowly rising anger. What the heck did this detective want? "As I told your uniformed officer, and you, five of us are on a tour of southern India. Simon Roy was our guide." She sat back in her chair and looked at him.

Finally, he smiled and nodded. "That was mentioned. Can you tell me more? How long were you traveling? Where have you been? What have you done? I am seeking context of how you came to be here."

And Simon. It would give him context about Simon.

"All right," she nodded. "We—Becca, my sister; Alice, her daughter; and I—arrived in Chennai two weeks ago. We joined two other people on the tour along with Simon Roy and his assistant tour-leader-in-training, Zamir. We spent five days at the beach and then we went to Ooty by train to see the hill station and tea plantations but we were only there overnight. We left the next morning for Mysore—sorry, Mysuru." She self-corrected to the non-British pronunciation. "We spent three days in Mysuru—saw the grand palace, visited a bird sanctuary and some of the markets and temples. We spent a lot of time just driving through the countryside, too, for the photographers on the trip—that would be Trevor and Jeannie—and my niece, Alice. From there we went north to the old city of Hampi for two days, then down to Goa for three days and then here. Do you want me to tell you where we go next? I could get you a copy of our itinerary…" She smiled sweetly at him. At the same time her fists clenched in her lap.

He'd been taking notes in a plain black police notebook, but glanced up at her smile. This time there was no taunt to his expression. "It sounds like you moved a great deal. No time to truly know any of our great cities or our people. Too bad. Now, tell me about Simon Roy during this time."

She thought about where to begin. Shook her head. "I'm sorry. I'm trying to put my thoughts in order. From what I saw, Simon Roy wasn't an easy man to be around. He didn't seem to like people a lot. At least not people like Becca and Alice and me. Actually, he didn't seem to like Jeannie and Trevor that much either. Or Indian people in general." She thought some more. "Perhaps it would be better if I described him for you and then told you how I got those impressions. Would that be satisfactory?"

He nodded.

Well here goes nothing. He could either appreciate her honesty or arrest her.

"Simon Roy wasn't a very likeable man. He made it difficult to like him. He was officious—always expecting people to do things his way and when he wanted—the 'I'll tell you when to jump and you ask how high,' sort of man. And if he didn't get what he wanted, there was either an explosion or he would simply do what he wanted and sabotage the other person. Early on in the tour, Trevor and Jeannie wanted to get out early for the best lighting for their photography. Alice, too, for that matter. But every morning Simon would take his time finishing an extra cup of coffee or reading the newspaper, he'd leave paying bills until the last minute and then have his credit cards not be accepted—that sort of thing. Trevor and Jeannie were actually thinking of leaving the tour. They didn't, but they were frustrated until Zamir, the assistant guide, started being available for their early mornings. In fact, through a lot of the trip, Zamir did more of the guiding."

"And what did Simon Roy do if he wasn't guiding?"

"I'm not really sure. He read a lot of newspapers and did crossword puzzles when he'd go with us to a location. He'd sit and read or something and send us on our own. At a few places he said it was too expensive for him to pay entry fees for him or Zamir, so they'd send us into the place alone. Sometimes he'd visit people he knew, I think. There were a few times he told us he'd been shopping, and I know a few times he bought things like fudge and fruit and so on, but he never shared it—just took it back to his room."

Mathias nodded as he wrote. He looked up at her when she'd finished. "These friends of his—tell me about them."

She shrugged. "I don't know much. He was friends with Zamir, of course. Or sort of friends." She thought about it a moment. "Actually, I'm not sure what their relationship is. Zamir told me and the others that he and Simon met on a beach when Zamir was a young man. They apparently became friends and Simon bought a piece of land and built a house for himself and one for Zamir and his wife and children. I suppose that could suggest they had a good relationship. Or it could suggest indebtedness. I don't want to hazard a guess, but a good relationship isn't what I've seen."

Mathias glanced up at her, encouraging her to go on.

"They argue sometimes—a lot, actually. Simon was generally rude to every Indian person we ever met on the trip. He liked to order people around and talk loudly, as if they couldn't hear or were too stupid to understand. There were times I thought he was very unreasonable. For example, in one place our driver had driven all day. He took us back to the hotel and everyone agreed that he could have the night off and spend it with his family who lived an hour away. An hour later Simon got it into his head that we needed to go out to a restaurant for dinner. So, he called the driver and ordered him back to take us." She shook her head. "It wasn't necessary, but what Simon wanted came first." She sighed. "He said that he paid the man for a day and a day was twenty-four hours."

"You were talking about Simon's friends," Mathias prompted.

"Was I?" She shook her head. "It didn't feel like it. I feel guilty talking ill of the dead, but…"

"You didn't like Simon Roy?"

"I already said that. I would never recommend a tour with him. With another guide, definitely." She sighed. "He did have friends. One of his friends joined us briefly in Ooty, but left again in Mysuru. Otherwise I didn't see him with anyone other than Zamir—I just got the impression that he was meeting people. His friends. Maybe they weren't and one of them killed him."

And it was odd that she did have that impression Simon had been meeting people when she hadn't actually seen him do so. There were definitely times when she'd been sure Simon had simply stayed in his room or by the pool all day, but there were other times when she'd got a different sense about him. What was it that made her feel that way? She looked up and found Mathias looking at her, his pen poised for anything more she had to say.

"I think I'm sounding like a judgemental old busybody. I don't like sounding that way."

He leaned back in his seat, as if accepting that she didn't want to discuss Simon anymore. He tapped his pen on the tabletop and studied her. Then he nodded.

"Let us change directions for the time being. Tell me about your time in Kochi."

She spread her hands on the rough wood table and shook her head. "What's there to say? We've hardly arrived." She swallowed and looked up at the ceiling. The lone, fly-speckled light bulb seemed to radiate heat and sweat was flowing freely between her shoulder blades and yet Mathias sat there looking cool and collected. The worst of it was that the stifling air now felt old and stale and unoxygenated—as if their conversation had sucked all life right out of the room.

She fanned herself, feeling the walls close in. They dipped and swayed and she closed her eyes to steady them or herself. She wasn't sure which.

"Ms. Clay? Are you all right?"

She didn't want to show weakness, but... "It's the heat. I think... I think I feel faint." And furious. And sad and guilty that she'd brought Alice into something like this again.

She opened her eyes and read real concern in his gaze. He pushed up from his chair and went to the door. "Water," he ordered someone in the hallway.

When he turned back, he held a plastic bottle of water. He cracked the lid open and offered it to her.

She took it and drank, not caring whether her suddenly desperate need was apparent. She finished the bottle and wiped her lips. The walls receded and she took a breath.

"Thank you. I'm sure that wasn't pretty, but Kochi is very hot." And the office more so, but she wasn't going to point out that he'd weakened her. She also wasn't sure why that was important.

He came back to the table but left the door open. A faint breeze that smelled of ocean and too many people entered the room. It didn't cool things down, but at least the walls stopped closing in.

"I'm sorry," Mathias said. "I forget that foreigners have difficulties in our temperatures."

She'd bet good money that he knew perfectly well. This room was a pressure tester. The trouble was, she couldn't tell whether she'd passed or failed.

"Are you able to continue?" he asked, and surprisingly, she thought he meant it. His sometimes-mocking gaze had turned serious. "Would you like more water?"

"Actually, I would." She nodded and he went to the door again, speaking to someone in Malayalam and returning with two bottles this time. He sat and handed her a bottle and cracked the second and drank deep.

"It *is* warm in here," he allowed.

She opened her bottle and sipped the cool liquid. At least she didn't feel like she was going to faint. The hint of breeze actually cooled her down enough so that she could focus on other things—like how uncomfortable the hard, wooden chair was.

The tromp of booted feet came from the hallway and a uniformed officer stepped inside with a folded package of newspaper that Mathias directed him to place on the table in front of her. She wondered what horror this could be until she inhaled the heavenly odor of vada. Was the detective toying with her, knowing she hadn't eaten?

"Please. Eat. I thought perhaps you had missed your morning meal, contributing to your dizziness." He pushed the greasy newspaper toward her and she tentatively opened the package, releasing fragrant steam. Under Mathias's scrutiny, she pulled out a vada and nibbled at the edge.

"Good. You have food and water." Mathias nodded. "I had asked you about your time in Kochi. What had happened, and you had told me that you'd barely arrived. Can you expand on that?"

She nodded around a mouthful of vada. "We arrived yesterday on the overnight train from Goa. We ate a quick meal at the station and Simon wasn't happy about the delay getting to the hotel. We arrived at the Scandinavian Guesthouse just before noon and registered. Simon got into an argument with the woman at the counter about the room rates. This wasn't unusual. He got into arguments everywhere and I frankly wasn't paying attention because I was tired and just wanted my room and a shower." Like she did now. She adjusted her position in the increasingly uncomfortable chair.

"After we checked in, Becca, Alice, and I shared a room. The whole group had lunch where Simon announced that he wasn't coming with us on our tour that afternoon. Not that it was much of a tour. Things weren't open and we were tired and, frankly, a tad grouchy, so we went back to the hotel by around four and laid around the pool until dinner. Simon joined us late—I don't know where he'd been—and then Alice, Becca, and I excused ourselves and went to bed. We left Simon and the others there." And she had died once her head hit the pillow. She shook her head.

"I didn't hear a thing all night until my niece got me up at six thirty because I'd foolishly said that I would go with her and Jeannie and Trevor when they went out to take photos of the fishing nets. We walked down to the seawall. Trevor and Jeannie stopped to set up their tripods and cameras but Alice wanted to get closer to the Chinese fishing nets. I went with her down onto the beach, but we got separated because she's faster. I lost sight of her for a moment and was looking for her when I heard her scream. I guess she'd been attracted to the fishermen working to raise the net and had seen Simon in the net when they brought it up. When I caught up to her, I just wanted to get her away to some place less traumatic so I took her back up onto the seawall and got her a seat. That's where the police found us and they forced me to return to the net where Simon was." She shrugged and met Detective Mathias's gaze. "Then you arrived."

He nodded and looked down at his notes. He had elegant hands with long fingers and well-groomed, short nails.

"You said Simon announced that he wasn't going on your tour. Did he say why?"

Thinking back, Phoebe shook her head. "I don't remember anything. No one asked him, probably because he'd done it so many times—not gone with us I mean. Maybe Avni, the hotel desk clerk, knows. I seem to recall something in their initial conversation when he was registering us. I think he might have said he was meeting someone."

"No idea who?"

She shook her head.

He scanned his notebook again and flipped back through the pages. The breeze from the hallway died and she could hear footfall and the scrape of waiting feet on the linoleum.

"You mentioned that on occasion Simon Roy had challenges paying hotel bills with his credit cards. Did you get the sense that he had money problems?"

"Nooo..." She thought about it. "Well, maybe there was some suggestion of it. I'm not sure. We paid a lot for the tour—over four thousand Canadian dollars apiece—and yet he booked trains that meant we couldn't get meals that were supposed to be included. I already told you that, at some places we visited, he and Zamir stayed outside because he said tickets were expensive. The restaurants we went to were usually very basic, too. If I never have another dosa or chicken biryani again, I'll die a happier woman." She shrugged "Sorry" at him.

"So there may have been money problems?" he asked, pen poised above the notebook.

She shrugged. "I really can't say for sure. It would all be speculation."

"Perhaps." He paused, studying her. "From what you've seen of Simon, who would want to kill him?"

Phoebe sat back in her chair, momentarily shocked by the question even though she'd thought of the possibility. "Kill him? But you said his injuries were consistent with a fall. An accident."

But all his earlier questions took on a new meaning. He wasn't just gathering context. He was in the early stages of what might be a murder investigation. The vada suddenly felt like lead in her stomach and the scent of the greasy remains in the newspaper about made her gag.

Mathias simply waited, just as he likely waited for a pathologist's report.

She inhaled. "I-I'm not sure. Fire him, yes. That would be everyone on the tour, I think. But kill him? None of us knew him well enough except Zamir, and I just can't see him killing his benefactor." She shook her head desperately wishing she could leave this room, this man, this city—heck, all of India—behind and return to real life. "I'm sorry I can't help you."

He snapped his notebook closed and slid it into the breast pocket of his gray suit. Then he stood. "Thank you for your information, Ms. Clay. I should have the pathologist's report by tomorrow morning and that will clarify whether or not his death was accidental. I will have an officer return you to your hotel. You will please tell your travel companions that I may wish to interview them as well. They are to be prepared to come here at ten o'clock tomorrow morning. I will call to confirm."

She stood up to face him. "I don't mean to tell you your business, but perhaps you could come to the hotel instead. This room is very uncomfortable and the hotel is not. Besides, depending on the pathologist's findings, you may want to interview the hotel staff as well."

His gaze narrowed and suddenly she didn't want to be on the receiving end of this man's interrogation. "Why would you say that?"

"Because it's what I would do if this was more than an accidental death. I've—been involved in a couple of police investigations before…" And barely survived both occasions.

He arched a brow at her. "And these would be?"

She couldn't help it. She had to look away, because the question unlocked a door she tried her best to keep carefully locked in her mind. "A few years ago there was a shooting in the school where I taught. I was a key witness in the subsequent investigation." She swallowed back the bile at the back of her throat and went to edge past the table.

"You mentioned a couple of investigations." He was right beside her, looking down. This was an investigator who would keep digging and suddenly she was confident he thought Simon's death was more than an accident. She fought to stop the shaking that threatened her calm.

"Last summer I took my niece out on a kayaking trip. There was a body found…"

He must have read something in her face for he suddenly bowed his head to her. "It sounds like you have had too much to do with unnatural death, Phoebe Clay. And now there is Simon Roy to deal with." He stepped back to allow her past him to the doorway.

"Ms. Clay?"

She turned to look at him.

"I am sure it goes without saying that you and your friends are to remain in Kochi at least until we are certain what we are dealing with."

She breathed in a sigh of cooler ocean air and nodded.

"Good." He patted his notebook in his pocket and went to follow her from the room. "You will tell your friends that I will be at the hotel at ten o'clock tomorrow morning to provide an update. I may wish to interview them then."

Surprised, she looked up at him and caught his infinitesimal nod. Something had changed between them. She just couldn't say what it was.

5

The exterior of the Scandinavian Guesthouse had never looked brighter or better as she crawled out of the marked police car, waved at the driver, and headed through the white picket fence for the door. The sun gleamed on the building's white paint and dark green shutters. The brilliant red and yellow lilies swayed in the garden. The jasmine was a white perfumed cloud around the doorway. She closed her eyes and inhaled to clear her head of the scent of grease and vada.

Then she stepped into the welcoming cool interior. Huge wicker fans turned the air over her heated skin. She stopped to let her eyes adjust to the dim lighting and was suddenly enveloped in strong, young arms.

"Auntie Bee, you're all right!" Alice squeezed her as if she would never let go. Then Becca appeared over Alice's shoulder.

"Thank God. I was about to call the consulate to meet me at the police station." The past few hours seemed to have etched worry lines around Becca's eyes and mouth.

Phoebe put her arms around Alice's and Becca's shoulders. "I'm okay. Everything's okay. I've been through far worse."

She hoped it wouldn't be that bad again.

"The detective wanted to ask questions about our trip and Simon.

They're not sure whether his death was an accident or not. I think he was trying to get a better sense of who Simon was." She shook her head. "I felt bad. I don't think I painted a very positive picture of our fearless leader."

"Leader, my ass," Becca murmured, then caught Phoebe's glance at Alice. "Sorry, but it's not any worse than she's heard before. If your detective had asked me, I'd have given him an earful."

"Actually, you might get your chance. He said he'll be here at ten o'clock tomorrow morning. He'll be able to confirm what happened to Simon one way or another. I hope the pathologist rules it an accident, but if he needs to, he'll interview all of us."

Becca frowned, then collapsed into one of the lobby's cushioned wicker chairs. "He thinks one of us did it."

"I have no idea what he thinks, but when we spoke, he hadn't ruled out accidental death." It might be a white lie, but by the expression on Becca's face it was what she needed to hear. "I think he wants to talk to all of us to get a sense of Simon. If the pathologist's report suggests it wasn't an accident, well, then he'll be interviewing the hotel staff, too."

Becca's fingers worked the hem of her shirt, her knuckles as white as the fabric.

Phoebe crouched down beside her, Alice stepping behind her mother to massage her shoulders.

"Becca, what is it? What's got you so spooked?"

Becca rubbed her face and suddenly shook her head. "It's nothing. I'm sure it's all as you said. It's just—this wasn't supposed to happen, was it? This was supposed to be a fun family holiday." She stood and gave Phoebe a strange look. "I'm going to go lie down. This heat is exhausting." She left Alice and Phoebe and crossed to their room. The door closed solidly behind her.

"She's been acting like a crazy woman ever since Jeannie and Trevor brought me home and we told her Simon was dead," Alice said. "Was it bad? Did they lock you in a cell and everything?"

"Yes. They shone a light in my eyes and beat me with a telephone book so I wouldn't show any bruises." She looked through the tops of her eyes at her wide-eyed niece. The girl was growing up so fast, but there was a level of innocence that believed everything she read in her mystery novels.

Then Alice grinned. "Auntie Bee! Tell the truth!"

"All right. It was fine. No lights in my eyes and no phone book. We talked in an interview room, but it was very hot. Thankfully the detective agreed that he should interview everyone here. That bodes well for everyone, I think. You included."

"They'll want to interview me?" Alice said, her voice catching in a squeak.

"Of course. You spotted the body. And you've dealt with him as long as we have."

Alice sat down on a wicker loveseat and looked up at her with a panic that didn't fit with their genteel surroundings. "What will I tell them?"

Phoebe sat down beside her and caught her hand. From beyond the pool came the sound of lunchtime diners and footfall down the stairs.

"Well. I'd start with the truth. The truth is always a good thing."

Alice swallowed, but nodded. "Even if you know things that might hurt someone important?"

Phoebe frowned and glanced at the closed door of their room. Was there something she didn't know? Something about Becca? But there was no way on this earth that Becca could have killed Simon. Not just because Simon was probably stronger than Becca, but it simply wasn't in Becca's nature.

She pulled Alice into another hug. "Alice, the truth is always best. That way you don't have to keep straight all the lies that you've told. At my age, my memory isn't that great."

Alice pulled back. "You're not *that* old. Only old enough to be my mother."

"And then some," Phoebe said dryly, but the concern in Alice's gaze said that the girl really did know something—or think she did. "What is it, Alice?"

"Aah, you are back." Zamir came up to them, his handsome face pained. The reddening of his eyes suggested that he'd been crying. "They did not arrest you for Simon's murder."

"Murder? What makes you say that? All the police know for sure is that he died." Phoebe stood, pulling Alice up with her. "Even if someone killed Simon, why would they think I did it?

"They don't know how Simon died yet, Zamir. They just had questions about him. I provided some information, but they will be here tomorrow morning at ten o'clock to interview everyone. The detective said that we are not to leave Kochi until the cause of death is known."

"Not to leave?" Zamir ran his fingers through his thick hair and glanced at the currently unattended reception desk. "But we only have reservations here until day after tomorrow and we have reservations in Varkala and onward in Kanya Kumari, Madurai, and Trichy."

"If the tour's to continue, I suppose you'll have to extend our stay and change the reservations," Phoebe said.

"I don't have credit cards like Simon! Everything is in his name. How can I change things? How will we pay?" He spun toward the registration desk, the grief overlaid with sudden panic at all the things he now had to deal with.

From what Phoebe had seen of Zamir so far, the young man might be a charming tour guide, but he had only a limited sense of business or reality. So far he had regaled them with his plans to be a Tamil movie star and to run a gem sales business. He might be a husband and father, but his panic said this was his first taste of real responsibility.

So much for Simon training him for the business.

"Zamir, slow down. I know this is awful, but as long as we're required to be here, we're in this together. Maybe we can work on it together at lunch. You know, make a list of all the things that probably need to be done. That will make it easier to work through them. How does that sound?"

He nodded, but his gaze darted around the room, up the stairs, toward the dining room, and held the longest on the door to the street as if running away might be his preferred action.

She caught his hand. "Listen to me. We'll help you. We will."

She'd said almost the same thing to her student, Rick, but in that case no one had helped. Not even her. And three people had died for it. She wouldn't let that happen again. She thought a moment. Given the relationship between Simon and Zamir, if Simon had been murdered, was Zamir in danger?

She held on to his hand and gradually his panicked gaze settled. He nodded. "Then I will get paper and a pen." As if even that was an accomplishment. He looked at his watch—a Seiko and probably a gift from Simon. "Please call the others for lunch."

He hurried off up the stairs.

"Alice, honey. Would you go get Jeannie and Trevor? I'll get your mom." Phoebe watched Alice head for the stairs. She was a good kid, but she still wasn't much more than a child.

Phoebe sighed. At the moment she felt like the only adult in the room, but that could be because she was the only one who was so familiar with death.

It wasn't a good feeling.

The lunchtime meal was in a shady spot by the pool, and they'd managed to snag the one spot with some privacy created by a burgeoning screen of pink and orange bougainvillea. Zamir sat on one side of the table flanked by Jeannie and Trevor. Phoebe sat across from Zamir, with Alice and Becca to either side. Both Jeannie and Trevor looked fresh from showers, but there was a tension around them Phoebe hadn't noticed before. Trevor seemed withdrawn, as if lost in thought, and Jeannie had seemingly developed creases between her brows since this morning. Had they, too, leapt to the conclusion that Simon's death was a murder? If so, why? Murder wasn't something that happened in most people's experience. It shouldn't be the first thing people thought of. Unless they were somehow involved.

Reflected turquoise light from the pool created shifting kaleidoscope masks of color and light across everyone's faces. All of them had assumed the worst when they'd heard of Simon's death.

Becca hadn't wanted to come to lunch, claiming she wasn't hungry.

At the moment she clung to Phoebe's right hand and wouldn't look at anyone around the table. Alice was also subdued though she looked at the menu with the interest of a growing girl.

Zamir had experienced the added insult of the police telling him that he was to move his things from the shared room to another, single room. All Simon's belongings were to remain untouched in their now off-limits room.

At the head of the table was an empty place setting that no one could bring themselves to look at. Simon might be dead, but he was here in spirit. His overbearing presence kept everyone relatively silent. She nodded at Zamir to start the conversation, but a waiter bustled up to take their orders.

It was a round of omelettes and coffee except for Phoebe, who asked for the lovely spiced chai. Becca didn't seem to be interested in food at all. She kept looking at her hands, flexing her fingers.

A chill ran through Phoebe, but the coffee and chai were brought and everyone looked at her. She held up her hands. "This isn't my meeting, other than to remind you that we've had a horrible shock and this isn't over yet, but I will say that the police don't know what caused Simon's death. It could be an accident, so please don't think the worst. The police will be by tomorrow at ten to tell us. Until then they've said we mustn't leave Kochi. That's all I have to say." She nodded at Zamir.

Trevor shoved his chair back from the table and swore. "You can say it wasn't murder all you want, but the police don't tell you not to leave town unless they suspect something. Jeannie and I should have left this idiot tour when we could. This is garbage being held hostage by the Indian police."

"Trevor, stop! You're just frustrated. Stop before you say something you shouldn't!" Jeannie said.

Trevor glared at her. Then he took a deep breath. His jaw worked, but he nodded and pulled his chair back into the table. "So what do we do now?"

Phoebe wasn't sure whether he was asking her or Jeannie.

Zamir pulled a pen and a folded piece of paper from his breast pocket. Fumbling, he unfolded the paper and set it on the table in front of him. Nothing was written.

He looked up expectantly as if everyone would simply know to feed him the information they needed to consider and he would write it down. When no one spoke, he licked his lips and looked remarkably nervous, given Simon had intended to pass the guiding to this man. Time to see what he was made of. From out on the street came the sound of a car passing by.

Finally, he nodded at Phoebe. "She has suggested that there are things we must do given what has happened. If the police force us to stay in Kochi, this will require changes to our itinerary that we will need to discuss. If we stay here longer, we need to decide what to take off our tour later."

Trevor shook his head. "Why would we even want to continue the tour? It's been a disaster from the get-go."

Zamir frowned. "You have paid for a tour. Surely it should happen. Simon always said there are no refunds."

"It isn't the money, Zamir," Phoebe said, sitting forward. "Well, the money is important, but it's more about people feeling safe, and right now I don't think Becca, Alice, and I feel safe traveling in India anymore."

Jeannie frowned and looked at Trevor and then Phoebe. "Isn't the tour the least of our worries? Isn't there a chance the police will accuse us of Simon's death?"

A ripple of fear seemed to circumnavigate the table until it reached Phoebe. She pressed her palms on the glass-topped table. "I don't think so. Detective Mathias had me concerned to begin with, but I think he is careful and does not jump to conclusions. The challenge is that as far as we know, we're the only people Simon knew except for his mention of meeting someone, and that could have been made up strictly because he didn't want to come on yesterday's tour of Kochi." She glanced at Zamir. "Perhaps we should think about the things we can control—like the things Zamir mentioned… Regardless of what the police do, there are things we need to do. After all, we don't know how long we'll be in Kochi."

Zamir nodded and looked around the table. "There are issues, you see. All of the credit cards were in Simon's name and that is what he used to pay for things like this hotel, for instance. I am not sure how to proceed—or how we can pay for things—like our bill."

"What?" Trevor half-rose again before Jeannie pulled him back down.

"Calm down. We need to discuss things calmly and strategically. Think about it," Jeannie said and patted his arm.

He pulled his arm away. "A lot of money was paid for this tour. You better not be telling us the money is gone."

Zamir gave a head waggle. "Of course not. It is simply unavailable."

"Well, you better make it available," Trevor said, leaning on the table. "I think everyone around this table will agree that this tour has not been great and now you're saying we might have to end it here and not get our money back?" He turned to Jeannie. "This whole thing has been a farce right from the start."

Zamir licked his lips as if uncertain what to say under the force of Trevor's threatening glower. Jeannie looked like she'd eaten something sour, and the last thing they needed was for a fight to break out between the photographers. Sighing, Phoebe decided to intervene, even though her head was aching.

She shoved her chair slightly back, the scrape of the metal on concrete hopefully jarring the table occupants out of their resentments. "Perhaps that's one of the things you need to write down, Zamir. You'll need to contact Simon's family and his banks. Maybe he has a business account that holds our money? And there's the travel agency that we booked through. They might know what we can do. And did Simon have a lawyer? If so, the lawyer might help."

Zamir wrote furiously, then looked up at her like a deer in the headlights. He clearly was out of his depth. She turned to Becca. "You work in a bank. What do you think?"

Becca shook her head, but finally sighed and seemed to rouse. She glanced at Zamir and then away. "Did Simon let you sign for anything on those cards?"

"Sometimes he told me to, so I did."

"So maybe Zamir had authority to use the card. Usually they just issue another card in the second person's name, but perhaps here they don't." She shrugged and seemed to sink back into whatever lethargy she was in.

"I would say contacting the credit card companies and then the tour company are the first things to do. In fact, we should all contact the tour company. I'm sure they have responsibilities given their relationship with Simon, but they have a responsibility to us, too, as their clients." She looked back at Zamir. "If we're going to stay in Kochi, don't we need to do something to extend our reservations?"

"Yes. Yes." Zamir set his pen down. "That is another thing. Our reservations here are only until tomorrow night. We need to make arrangements."

"Oh, my God," Trevor grumbled. "Can this get any better?"

Zamir looked at Phoebe for help.

"I suppose the first question is whether there is space in the Guesthouse. If not, then we need to find another place to stay. Zamir, you need to check with Avni to see if we can extend our reservations. If not, you need to find us an alternate hotel."

"One with a nice pool, please," Alice piped up and grinned at Phoebe.

"A pool is the least of our worries. A pool is a luxury," Phoebe said, catching Alice's hand. "So, stop being demanding," she said with mock sternness.

"There is the matter of paying," Zamir said as the waiter brought their food.

Luscious, fluffy omelettes loaded with peppers and onion and cheese were placed before them. The delicious scent sent Phoebe's mouth watering. She'd forgotten she was hungry with everything that had happened. Only her growling stomach reminded her.

Trevor used his fork to cut through the omelette and brought a piece to his mouth. "I thought you were going to take care of the credit cards," he said around chewing.

Zamir head-waggled again. "There is the matter of the cost of this place. It is far more expensive than most places we stay. It was only budgeted for three days. If we are to stay longer, who will pay?"

Trevor's face flushed, but Jeannie grabbed his arm. She looked across at Phoebe. "Maybe—maybe we can make an arrangement. Zamir pays a base rate and we pay the balance or something."

"If we all have travel insurance, wouldn't that help?" Alice said.

Out of the mouths of babes. Why hadn't Phoebe thought of it?

"Alice is right." Phoebe scanned their faces. Trevor angry. Jeannie calculating. Zamir like a puppy. Becca still withdrawn, and Alice bright as a pin. All of them dealing in their own way. The challenge was managing it. Classroom management suggested giving each of them something constructive to do. "We have a challenge. We are required to stay and Zamir is doing all that he can. Let's work together and not get angry. Getting angry helps no one."

A round of unenthusiastic head nods went around the table, stuttering out with Becca. Her omelette sat untouched, while Alice, who should be most affected, wolfed hers down. There was something so clearly wrong with Becca that Phoebe almost dragged her sister back to their room right then and there.

"Eat," she said, nudging Becca with her elbow. "You have to eat something."

"I'm not really hungry," Becca said. She turned pleading blue eyes to Phoebe.

Phoebe shook her head. "Come on, Becca. This is the best food we've had on this tour. You need something to keep up your strength. I'm betting you didn't eat breakfast, either."

"I slept through breakfast. But I had a coffee."

"Coffee is not a meal." Phoebe shook her head. "Either eat something or I'll be forced to turn all preachy teacher on you. Do you want that?" She tilted a brow at her sister.

The wind rustled in the bougainvillea. The water lapped gently against the pool edges.

"Say no, Mom." Alice leaned around Phoebe to grin at her mom. "I really advise you to say no and eat. She can be unbearable when she goes into teacher mode!"

"Hey!" Phoebe elbowed her niece. "Is that nice? I've always been nice to you. I even say nice things to your face!"

With a sigh, Becca picked up her fork, cut the omelette, and forked a piece into her mouth. She chewed and swallowed but, from her expression, it might as well have been sawdust. When she'd eaten half the omelette, she turned a weary gaze to Phoebe.

"Enough?"

Phoebe nodded.

"Good." Becca pushed to standing. "I'll leave the rest of you to your discussions." She headed back to their room, her shoulders rounded as she wound through the lobby chairs. She moved like an old woman—all she needed were the gray hair and wrinkles—but she was ten years Phoebe's junior. What the heck was going on?

Phoebe knew that she should take care of Becca, but first there was the matter of agreeing on who was going to do what before the tour completely fell apart. She turned to Alice. "Maybe go make sure your mom's all right."

Alice nodded, did a final scrape of the debris on her plate, and left the table, looking far more mature than her thirteen years. But then kids grew up fast these days. Especially the only daughter of a single mom.

Sighing, Phoebe turned back to Zamir. "Let's see your list. We need to decide who's doing what."

She scanned the list. "It seems to me that Zamir's priority has to be dealing with the credit card companies, but also the banks. You need to tell them what happened, but you also need to ask them for help in this because Simon had our money. It must be in his accounts. You need to see whether they can free up enough to cover our stay in Kochi and the rest of the tour in the event we decide to continue."

Two male Indian hotel patrons in bright swim trunks splashed in the pool, their sari-clad girlfriends or wives watching from a sun-drenched table. Their calls and happy laughter felt incongruous with the somber discussion of Phoebe's group. But it couldn't be helped. The tour that had been set up so that she, Alice, and Becca could have an adventure together had just turned into something less savory.

"Do you think you can do that, Zamir?"

He looked at her with his lovely liquid eyes and gave his equivocating little head-waggle. "I will try."

"Not try. You'll do this and it needs to be done today. Understand?" She felt like a schoolteacher talking to him this way, but one thing she had learned on this trip: It was that the head waggle was a wonderful way to hide a 'maybe' that was seriously leaning toward 'no'.

She looked at Trevor and Jeannie. "I'll talk to Avni about the rooms, and I can even call the tour company we booked through, but you might want to do it given you have some pretty strong feelings." She tilted a brow at Trevor.

The two photographers looked at each other and then Jeannie nodded. "We can take that on. We'll keep you and Becca posted."

"Good. We'll hold off on looking for alternative hotel arrangements until I've checked with Avni. Once I've spoken to her, I'll let the rest of you know what she's said, but there is the matter of paying. If Zamir can't get the banks and credit card companies to help us, we may have to figure out how to take care of our bills and then seek reimbursement through our travel insurance." She held up a hand to stop Trevor's response. "I agree with you—we paid our money and so we should have our costs covered, but these are unusual circumstances. It's not like Simon ran out on us, and we all know banks and credit card companies can be pretty rigid. They may just freeze everything. I don't know about you, but I'm going to dig out my travel insurance and contact them, too."

"I know where our papers are," Jeannie said to Trevor.

"Everyone know their tasks?" Phoebe asked.

When they nodded, she stood. "Then I'm going to leave you and check on my sister. This whole thing has clearly upset her."

Across the sunlit courtyard, she entered the cool dimness of the lobby. The fans spun lazily overhead, but her thoughts spun wildly through all the things to be done. The comfortable lobby chairs were empty, but Avni stood behind the registry desk. Today she wore a deep blue sari with golden embroidery on the edge. She looked graceful and lovely—more like something you'd see in a Raja's palace mural than a working woman.

"Hi," Phoebe approached the desk.

Avni looked up from stapling receipts. Her face lit in a smile that was swiftly replaced by sympathy. "Ms. Phoebe! I am so sorry at this most horrible situation. Mr. Simon—he will be—missed."

Phoebe tilted a brow at her because the 'missing' part had been less than convincing. "It's a difficult situation. I need to speak with you about it. As for Simon, he's left us in a bit of a pickle."

Her smooth, caramel-colored brow furrowed. "A pickle?"

"He left us in difficulty. We were supposed to leave Kochi day after tomorrow, but the police have told us that we must stay. We would like to stay here, if possible. Can you tell me whether you have space?"

Avni seemed to hesitate, but then nodded. "Let me check our reservations." She turned to the computer monitor behind the counter and typed in a few commands with elegant manicured hands. "For how many days, please?"

Phoebe considered what she knew of police investigations and came up with nothing in terms of how long they might have to stay. "Let's say three or four more days as a start. Would that be possible? And can you tell me the room rates, too. We may have to pay individually given all of Simon's affairs are up in the air."

Avni straightened. "Are you saying that Mr. Simon's payment may be in jeopardy?"

Taking a deep breath, Phoebe worked her neck. Tell her the difficulty she suspected was coming or allow it to come and let the hotel be caught in the middle just like everyone else?

"If I were you, I would immediately process payment for our rooms for the time already booked. That will stop some of the problems. Ensure that you include the meals that we've already had."

Avni met her gaze. "This death is bad."

"It is."

"Mr. Simon. He was a difficult man when alive." She plucked at an imaginary loose thread on her sari.

"And not much better when he's dead, apparently." Phoebe

considered Avni and knew what she was about to do could get her in hot water. Detective Mathias would tell her to keep her nose out of police business but, darn it, she was already involved. Her whole family was and she'd got them into it. "Were you here yesterday evening, Avni?"

The woman's face smoothed into reserve. "I was here until eleven."

Phoebe nodded. "That is a very long shift, given you were here at noon when we checked in."

"I—I had taken a second shift when the evening clerk was sick." Her fingers pick-pick-picked at the edge of her sari shawl.

Phoebe considered. "Did anyone come to the hotel to see Simon while you were on shift? Hadn't he said he was meeting someone?"

Avni did a definitive shake of her head. "There was no one, Madam. No one at all. It was very quiet here. It is the low season, after all."

"Low season. Right." Phoebe rubbed her face and looked around the room. Shadows and more shadows and nothing clear at all. No one was here and Avni didn't seem too busy. At least that might mean there were rooms available. "Did you see Simon leave the hotel last night?"

"Last night?" As if Avni hadn't heard. It was what a student might have said if they didn't want to answer a question Phoebe asked in class.

"Did you see Simon leave?" From outside came birdsong and the sound of student voices as they headed back to school from lunch. From down the road came the sound of vehicles and underlying it all came the distant rumble of what might be thunder, but was the ocean waves on the shore.

And there came the little head waggle. It wasn't even a conscious thing, but it spoke volumes.

"Mr. Simon was here most of the evening. He read his newspaper in the lobby and then he went out. He said for dinner, though he had already eaten in the restaurant. I have his bill here." She patted the stack of receipts she was working through.

"What time was that?" Phoebe asked. Maybe she could get a

picture of when Simon had gone and where and it could help solve this case so that they could continue their tour.

"Maybe 10:30 or so." Again that little head waggle, so Phoebe wasn't sure whether to believe her.

"So he left at 10:30 alone."

Avni's gaze slipped away around the lobby. "Yes. He was alone when he went out." But there was no head waggle. Did that mean it was the absolute truth or that she was hiding something?

"Do you have any idea what restaurant he might have been going to?"

Shuffling her papers, Avni looked up at her. "Ms. Phoebe, surely these questions are the job of the police. Perhaps you should turn your attention to your family and allow me to perform my job?" She held up the papers she was sorting as if in proof that she was working.

Was Avni hiding something?

Phoebe caught herself. She was being paranoid. "You're right, of course." She sighed. And Becca needed her more than she needed the information. "Thank you for your time, Avni. And like I said, process that bill now, before the credit card companies decide to freeze the account. And please let me know if rooms are available."

With a guarded expression, Avni looked back at Phoebe. "This is highly irregular, but I'll take your advice." Then her gaze softened and she turned back to her computer. "It appears that we should be able to accommodate your additional dates. I will ask you later how you intend to be paying."

"And the rates?"

Avni frowned and touched the keys again. "One hundred and seventy-five for each room. That is the best I can do."

Seven hundred dollars for the extra days. Thank God for credit cards.

"Thank you." Well, that was something at least. Phoebe turned from the front desk to her hotel room. Now there was dealing with Becca.

6

———

hoebe opened the door of the room she shared with Becca and Alice. Even compared to the shadowy lobby with its wicker furniture and ceiling fans, the room was gloomy. The louvers over the windows had been pulled tightly shut, leaving only the thinnest lines of the day's bright sunshine to sneak through. The ceiling fan whirred overhead stirring the air, but it was still close, the humidity of coastal Kochi sneaking in. Phoebe reached to turn on the air conditioner and turn off the fan, but movement across the room stopped her.

Knees drawn up to her chin, her arms wrapped around them, Alice sat on her bed with her back to the wall. She shook her head "no".

Her eyes now adjusted to the lack of light, Phoebe's gaze fell on Becca, curled on her bed with her back to the door. Phoebe crossed to Alice. "What's going on?"

Alice just shrugged, but her eyes were filled with glassy tears and worry. "I tried to turn on the lights and air con…" She eyed her mother.

"She told you not to?"

Alice nodded. "She yelled," she whispered.

Well, she'd see about that, because she was not going to be cowed by her younger sister. "Why don't you go have a swim. It's lovely and warm in the sun."

Alice hesitated, but finally found her swimsuit in the heap of her clothing by the head of her bed. Throwing concerned glances at her mother, she disappeared into the bathroom to change. Phoebe waited until she was done and had slipped out the door to the pool. She heard her greet Avni and Avni's muted reply. Then Phoebe flipped the lights on.

"Don't!" Becca bolted upright, her blue eyes wide, her blonde hair wild about her face. "Don't do that!" Her white t-shirt was wrinkled and so was her cheek from the pillow. The puffiness of her eyes said she'd been crying.

"Why?" Phoebe crossed her arms where she stood by the door. "What's going on, Becca? You've been acting strange ever since I got home and now you've gone and scared your daughter. You think that's the best thing to do?"

Sniffing, Becca shook her head. "No. I'm upset is all. This whole thing is upsetting and—and it's all my fault for suggesting this tour instead of letting you go and visit Myanmar alone like you wanted."

Phoebe leaned back against the wall, considering. What Becca said was true in terms of the suggestion for the tour, but something didn't ring quite true. "That's a huge leap, don't you think? You didn't kill Simon and we've had a good time together—regardless of Simon and his death. We're going to have an adventure getting through this and isn't that what this trip was all about? Building memories of how we overcame adversity together. Now we have to do the work. There's a lot of things to do and this isn't helping." She waved around the room and went to the first louvred window and opened the slats. Light spilled into the gloom.

Becca shuddered and hugged herself. "I—I just can't stop thinking about that poor man. And Alice. How she must have felt when she saw him. Oh, God! And I just yelled at her!" She scrubbed at her face, and if anything, her shoulders slumped farther. "What kind of mother am I?"

Phoebe settled on the bed beside her. "You're a great mother. You always have been and that's what's got me wondering. The Becca I know would be there for her daughter, not cowering in her room. What's going on, Becca? There's got to be more than feeling bad about Simon."

Becca stood up and started for the door, but Phoebe grabbed her arm. "If you're going out there, you might want to do something about your hair and face. You're likely to scare her more like this." She eased Becca back down on the rumpled blue blanket and moved across to her own bed to face her.

"Now what's really going on, Becca? I've never seen you fall apart like this. After the kayaking trip you were all take charge and caring for everyone."

Becca looked away. Her face was pale beneath the tan she'd gotten on their trip so far. "Everyone was safe in Pirate's Cove. At least by the time I got there. I think I might have died if I'd been there when everything was happening. I like to think I'm as strong as you, but when I think about what you did, I'm clearly not. How do you do it, Phoebe? How do you keep on going and look so calm and in control even when the world is ending?"

Phoebe reached over and caught Becca's fingers even though Becca's assessment was a lie. Calm and in control were about the farthest thing from what she was feeling. It was more like part of her was frozen and the other part—the part she shoved down—was on fire.

Becca's hands were cold as ice and Phoebe wrapped her hands around them to comfort her younger sister. "First of all, it's teacher training. Never let them see you sweat because the little buggers will see your vulnerability and eat you up. It's the first lesson they teach you in teacher's school. You don't learn it, you die." She forced a grin at Becca hoping for one in return. "Figuratively, of course."

Becca only sighed.

"And we are safe, Becca. We're all here and together. None of us has done anything wrong, so we don't have anything to worry about except the money to pay for extra nights in these rooms and, in the end, getting home. We have return tickets, so even that's not a big deal. If we don't want the rest of our tour, well, that's nothing. We'll have had an adventure together like no one else. Understand? Together we can make anything a fun adventure."

Becca finally met Pheobe's gaze and straightened. "I should be mad at you for making me so desperate to keep you safe that I left Canada and came here. I put myself and my child in danger."

"You love me and I love you right back. But we are not in danger."

Becca closed her eyes a moment, then opened them and stood. "Okay. I will try to believe that. And now I'm going to wash my face and comb my hair and go apologize to my daughter."

Phoebe caught her hand again. "A nice idea, Becca, but you're avoiding my original question. Sure, Simon's death is upsetting, but I've never seen you like this. What's got you so upset?"

The tendons worked in Becca's neck and she looked as if she might yank loose and run. Then she sighed and sank down on the bed again. "Sometimes I wish you didn't know me so well." Her gaze got lost in the shadows in the corners of the high ceiling.

Phoebe squeezed Becca's hand, recognizing the signs. Becca was just looking for the strength and the place to begin.

"Last night I was with Simon," Becca said.

Phoebe had been expecting something, but not that. She hoped she kept her surprise off her face and simply nodded at Becca to go on.

"I was upset and I needed to talk to Simon about Zamir's behavior toward Alice. You see, he kissed her that night on the train from Goa. I knew Simon could make him stop. Heck, I suppose I wondered whether he might have put him up to it, the way I think Simon sicced Zamir on me when we joined the tour. You noticed, right? The way he was always trying to get me alone. The way he always sat too close to me? Well, when we first joined the tour, I was in the pool with Alice and I saw Simon and Zamir watching us and talking. Simon nodded toward me and the next thing I knew, Zamir was in a swimsuit and had joined us in the pool. He kept swimming too close to me and wanted to join in when Alice and I were playing. I finally told Zamir I wasn't interested and that seemed to be it, but then he turned his attentions on Alice. A married man!"

She shook her head. "I guess I've had misgivings about the tour for a while even though Simon was recommended. I actually wondered whether they were trying to compromise me somehow—you know, get me involved with them sexually. Maybe—maybe they thought a single mother would be vulnerable to Zamir's attention. Anyway, I'd thought about it and thought about it and finally I decided that I had to give Simon some feedback on the tour and tell him to make Zamir back off from Alice. I was just working up the courage. I guess her telling me that he kissed her on the train was the last straw. Apparently, he was waiting for her when she went out to the bathroom before bed the night before. The way she described it, he sort of cornered her and kissed her. She said it was weird—his lips were nice, but everything inside her said it was wrong."

She studied her hands in her lap.

"At least she knew to talk to you and not simply accept it. Alice's got a good head on her shoulders," Phoebe said softly.

"She's a good kid." Becca nodded. "That night I went to bed early like you and Alice, but I couldn't sleep, so I got up and threw some clothes on in hopes of catching him before he was asleep. Imagine my surprise when I found him getting ready to leave the Guesthouse. I grabbed some shoes and went after him.

"It was hard talking about it. I mean, how do you ask a person whether they're a sex tourism operator and expect the guides to sleep with the clients? I started off just giving him feedback on the tour so far. The hotels were mostly okay so far. The issues with meals and the kind of food. How we needed vegetables other than potatoes—that sort of thing. So, I walked with him as far as a parking lot by the ocean. The moon was out and I could see these huge contraptions that looked like dip nets I've seen pictures of. He told me that he had people to see and that we could finish our talk the next day, but I needed to get it out. I guess I just blurted out that Zamir was coming on to Alice and it had to stop now. He actually had the gall to suggest she liked it. I told him she didn't and that whether she liked it or not, she was barely thirteen, I was her mother, and I wanted it to stop."

Her eyes scrunched shut and her hands made fists in her lap. "The bastard actually laughed at me. Then he suggested that I was jealous that Zamir had moved on to Alice. And that's when I slapped him and pushed him."

She opened her eyes and drew in a long breath as if she'd just run a difficult race. "I realized that I was so furious that I couldn't talk to him so I turned around and found my way home. I'll tell you that wasn't fun. I got lost three times from taking wrong turns. Finally, I stopped a woman walking by and she showed me where to go."

"No wonder you wanted to sleep in the next morning."

Becca nodded. "I hardly slept a wink, thinking about the conversation and wishing that I hadn't hit him. You know I don't like violence."

Phoebe shifted beds so that she sat beside her sister. She patted Becca's knee. "Okay. The good news is that Simon probably died by accident. The trouble is that you *were* in the area where Simon died, but clearly you didn't kill him. However, when the police interview you, you need to tell them what happened." She caught Becca's hands in hers. "I think you need to stop worrying about what might happen and focus on having fun with your daughter. And your sister, for that matter. Isn't that why you're here? And as for Zamir, if you like, I'll have a word with him. Would that help? I think he's got enough to worry about."

Becca closed her eyes. "I hate the fact that I'm so weak, but would you talk to him for me?"

Phoebe pulled her sister into a hug. "Of course I will. And just so you know, you're not weak. You just hate confrontation, but when you have to, you get the job done. It was you who took care of me and helped me live through the aftermath of the school shooting. No one else could have got me through that."

"Thanks," Becca whispered and released Phoebe. "And now I *am* going to wash my face and brush my hair and go be with my wonderful daughter."

Leaving her sister to clean herself up, Phoebe went to talk to Zamir and to see whether Jeannie and Trevor had any news. She, Becca, and Alice needed to check in with their travel agent and travel insurance, too, so that was a task she could give to Becca. Something to take her mind off of Simon.

She crossed the lobby, smiled at Avni whose return smile seemed a little more forced than it had been, and stepped out by the pool. The lovely gray paving stones were covered in damp footprints—Alice's. She and the two Indian gentlemen had begun a rousing game of water polo. The edges of the pool were awash and the dining tables close to the pool had been abandoned except for the men's wives in their saris. Drops of spray glittered on the jasmine and bougainvillea. Zamir once more sat at the table they'd sat at for lunch. This time he was on the phone, two credit cards, an iPad, and an empty cup on the table in front of him.

Phoebe threaded her way past empty tables to him. "How is it going?" she asked as she sat down. "How do you like your new room?"

Zamir gave a head waggle that told her nothing. A waiter approached and she ordered two chai on their behalf and waited as Zamir spoke Hindi into the phone. He hung up with a sigh and a shake of his head. He picked up one of the cards and set it on top of the other.

"That is it, then. There is nothing more to be done. The tour is over."

"What did they say, Zamir?" she asked.

"Exactly nothing good. The first card they have frozen even though there is money credited to the account. The best they could do was honor any charges that went through today. They told me that the bill for our stay here went through, but that will be the last." He looked shell-shocked, his gaze uncertain as he looked from the cards to her.

"What are we to do, Phoebe? There is the tour, but there is also my family. Simon—he paid for everything!"

Phoebe didn't have the heart to tell him maybe he'd have to pull up his big boy panties and support his family himself. That was probably what had him so scared.

The waiter brought their chai and she sipped the sweet-spicy mixture. She'd been so concerned about dealing with fallout for the tour that she hadn't even thought of Zamir's family. Truly Simon had been the goose that laid Zamir's golden egg. She wondered what it had cost Zamir. In some ways he seemed no more than a child—a dependency Simon had promoted?

"Well… I suppose the first thing is not to panic. This is a business and it was this business that paid for things for your family. It seems to me that it's time for you to focus on maintaining *this* business. It might mean that you have to stop doing other things like acting and selling gemstones. Think about it, Zamir. Simon was training you, so he obviously thought you had the skills. Now's the chance to prove it."

God, this pep talk was so similar to so many she'd given students over the years. She'd even said something similar to Rick before everything went off the rails and the shooting started. The memories crowded in and she shuddered, suddenly cold.

"Phoebe? Are you there?"

She blinked and there was Zamir with concern in his eyes. She smiled. "Sorry. Haven't had one of those in while. I was a few thousand miles away." Not to mention numerous hours in PTSD therapy. "Zamir, I'll help you any way I can. I made sure Avni processed our bill, so we're okay for our stay here and she has rooms for us to extend our stay. Do you know whether Simon had a will? If he did and named you executor, you might have access to funds to deal with his commitments. Did he have a lawyer?"

Zamir brightened. "There is one, but he is in Chennai."

"Perhaps you should call him and advise him of what has happened. He might be able to advise you better than I can. Explain the situation."

His expression brightened. "I can do that!"

She smiled. "I know you can. Just like I have confidence that you can do everything else that needs to be done. You just need to pick off the tasks one by one instead of getting overwhelmed by everything that needs to be done. For example, we need to make plans about Simon's body. Is he to be sent back to Canada, or buried here, or cremated, or what?" She realized she hadn't a clue about Simon's faith. He'd shared very little of himself.

Zamir stood up. "I will make the call to the lawyer. If Simon didn't say how he wanted his body cared for, he must have a Tamil funeral."

"That's good then, but there is one other thing." She glanced over her shoulder at Alice, who was now huddled at the side of the pool talking to her mother.

"Alice," she said softly. "You kissed her."

Zamir sagged back into his chair. "She told you?"

"Her mother did." Phoebe nodded. "Alice is my thirteen-year-old niece. She is still a child and still trying to understand what being an adult means. If I *ever* hear that you, a thirty-something-year-old married man, have done or said anything to her again that is in any way sexual, well, then I will go to the police—or I will deal with you myself. Do you understand?"

He must have heard something in her voice or read something in her face, because his usually charming smile faded and his face paled.

"I understand. It will not happen again. You have my promise." He stood, with the iPad and phone in hand.

She hadn't seen him with an iPad before. "Is that Simon's?" She motioned to the tablet.

Zamir flushed and nodded. "When they told me to collect my things and move rooms, I took it. Simon always used it and I thought it might help me with the business."

"You know you'll have to turn it over to the police."

He nodded and she thought a moment about how Simon had supposedly been meeting someone. "May I take a look?"

"Help yourself. It is of no use to me. I don't know Simon's passwords." He handed over the iPad, half bowed to her before he rushed across the courtyard and up the stairs.

Well, the little discussion about Alice put the fear of God into him, at least for the moment. She just had to hope that it had no resulting fallout in how he treated Phoebe's family.

She glanced at Alice back in the pool and then flipped open the iPad. When she pushed the home button, the password keypad came up. A lot of people simply used 123456, but apparently not Simon. She thought a moment and angled the screen to the light. Instead of showing keystrokes, a zigzag streak crossed the screen. Simon had used a pattern instead of keystrokes. She tried the zig zag stroke in one direction, but was again denied access. She tried it in the other direction and the screen opened.

Knowing she had no right to do this and feeling like everyone knew what she was doing, she glanced over her shoulder. Alice and her mother were now lounging in chairs across the pool. The gentlemen had left with their female companions.

She gave herself ten minutes. After that she'd get the tablet back to Zamir. She opened the mail program on the tablet, scanning the emails. Most appeared to be male friends around southern India that he planned to visit when the tour was over. A few were those he planned to visit in the towns they would visit on the remainder of the tour. She closed the mail program and opened messenger.

Bingo. The last message, dated the day they arrived was a conversation with someone identified by the initials A.K. and a phone number. The conversation was brief: simply a statement of time and place: the fishing nets at eleven thirty at night.

She committed the number to memory, closed the messenger program and the iPad, and shoved the tablet across the table to Zamir's seat.

She closed her eyes and allowed the sunlight to warm her face. Just who was A.K. and why were they meeting so late at night? That didn't sound like any normal meeting. She was becoming less and less certain that Simon's death was accidental.

In the courtyard the only sounds were vehicles from the street and the muffled sound of voices from the kitchens. Her thoughts whirring, she listened to the buzz of insects in the flowers. It was peaceful if she could set aside what had happened and all the things that had to be done. It was a shame when the historic town of Kochi was just outside their door.

She heard footfall approaching and opened her eyes to see Becca rounding the pool from her chair. She had changed into a less wrinkled shirt and a knee-length skirt. Her hair was pulled back in a short braid and there was color in her face, though she still had signs of strain around her eyes.

"You okay?" Becca asked and settled into the chair she'd used at lunch. She glanced at the iPad but said nothing.

"Just taking in the sunshine. I should ask you the same."

Becca studied her hands in her lap. "Better, thanks to you. Thank you for listening." Her grin wobbled as her gaze wavered to Alice. "She took the apology pretty well."

"She would. You two have a good relationship."

Alice sat up, perhaps knowing they were talking about her. She stood and dove cleanly into the pool and stroked twice underwater to pop up at their side of the pool. "I forgot to tell you, you look good, Mom!"

Phoebe could have kissed the girl. It was exactly what Becca needed to hear.

Becca went to the side of the pool to crouch down. "Thank you. And I just want to say again how sorry I am for how I acted in the room."

Alice cocked her head as if thinking about it. Then she nodded and pushed back from the side of the pool. She splashed a little water in her mom's direction and caught Becca squarely in the face. "That's for making me feel bad."

Phoebe burst out laughing. The kid had her ways, that was for sure. She stood up from the table. "I've been thinking. Regardless of what happened this morning, we are in Kochi. We know our time won't be ours tomorrow morning because the police will be here. How about we spend this afternoon out in the stores like Alice wanted?"

"Really?" Alice asked, treading water.

"It sounds like a good way to take our minds off things," Becca said.

"Do you mind if we get in on some of that action?" Jeannie asked as she and Trevor crossed through the tables toward them. "We barely got any photos this morning. There should be some good opportunities for street photography."

Trevor stopped at the end of the table, his attention locked on the iPad. When he saw Phoebe notice, he looked away.

"The more the merrier, as far as I'm concerned," Phoebe said, but noticed a frown cross Alice's face. "Did you have any luck contacting the travel company back home?"

"We left a message on their answering machine, but we likely won't hear anything until tomorrow. Sixteen-hour time difference and all that. Our travel insurance company said they could repatriate us to Canada, but they couldn't cover extra costs for the tour. You might want to check with yours. Ours is kind of exclusive—for photographers like us."

"Good to know." Not good news, but good to know. "I've had our reservation at this place extended if we can come up with the money. And our payment for the original reservation has gone through."

Alice hurried back to the room to change and Jeannie and Trevor gathered their camera gear. Phoebe ran the iPad up to Zamir's room— just down the hall from the one he'd occupied with Simon—and told him they were going out. Then together with their map and a newly clad Alice, they headed out into the street.

As usual, the humidity off the ocean was extreme. Sweat beaded at the nape of Phoebe's neck and trickled down her spine. By unspoken agreement, they avoided the seawall and headed into a warren of narrow streets lined with small shops selling all manner of mementos. Alice regressed to the kid that she was, dashing between displays of brass bells and globes to others of ready-made clothing. Jeannie and Trevor took their time taking photos of bright displays of tika powders and ornate glass bottles of scented oils. The air carried the scent of sandalwood, frangipani, roses, and clove. Colorful window displays held brilliant patchwork purses, embroidered wall-hangings, and pillows.

"Look at that!" Becca stopped in front of the window of a larger corner shop with a broad open door that led into dim shadows and a hint of incense. A rack of many-colored, fluttering, silken scarves next to the doorway held Becca's attention. She fingered a crimson scarf.

"Come in. Come in!" A slim-faced proprietor came to the door. He was older, with distinguished gray hair, a hawk nose, and a small beard. He wore a cream-colored shirt with cuffs rolled up around his forearms and black trousers with knife-blade pleats. "You like the scarves?"

"They're very beautiful. I—I love the colors," Becca stammered. Even after two weeks in India, she still hadn't gotten used to the banter between vendor and shopper.

"Then you must come in. This is only a taste. I have many, many beautiful things." The man half-bowed to welcome them in.

The usual shopkeeper's lure.

Becca glanced helplessly at Phoebe and Phoebe waved her in. Becca enjoyed shopping and surely seeing beautiful things would help take her mind off Simon. Feeling like Gretel lured in with the promise of candy, Phoebe followed Becca inside into cool shadows. Alice and the others waited in the street.

The interior was a large shadowed space with high ceilings and slow turning fans that stirred wool- and incense-scented air. In one corner, a stack of richly colored burgundy and blue rugs lay stacked on the floor. Cloth-laden shelves covered two walls, while the others displayed Tibetan mandala tapestries or small, intricately patterned silken carpets. Glass display cases ran the length and sides of the room. The floor was covered with worn Persian carpets—or Indian as the case may be.

Becca had been lured up to one of the glass counters and had taken a seat—the universal sign that she was prepared to shop—as the proprietor pulled a stack of more silken scarves from under the counter. She'd be a while, by the look of it. Phoebe wandered to the other counters. Silver jewelry—much of it Tibetan-looking—filled one of the displays. Another held Tibetan-looking artifacts—a knife, a strange-looking thing shaped something like a hand weight but with the ends hollowed out, a pale bowl with silver-gilt edges, among so many other things, including what looked like a brown shawl folded up so that only a colored border of deep blue and crimson showed. There was something about the colors that held Phoebe's attention. So vivid. And the fabric looked immensely soft.

"Can I help you?" The voice came over her shoulder, and she spun around feeling guilty.

A young man faced her. Tall, thin, but with a round face, although his hawk nose told her who his father was. He wore clothing similar to the man assisting Becca.

"I was admiring the shawl." She looked back at the display. "There's something about the colors."

"The colors, yes. It comes from age, I think. And they are natural Tibetan dyes. Unfortunately, that piece is not for sale. Perhaps you are interested in Pashmina?" He looked at her from the tops of his eyes as if it was almost a dare. A test? Had she missed something?

Back home Alice had given her a pashmina for Christmas. It was a lovely blue scarf, but though it was warm and said made in India on the label, it was just as clearly made of polyester. A true pashmina wasn't polyester, but was made from the chest and beard hair of a goat. She'd heard about the scarves. In fact, she'd turned down many touts on this trip who offered to show her such scarves. A real pashmina *would* make a nice memento for the tour…

"Perhaps. Could you show me some? But only real pashmina, please. There are too many imposters back home."

He led her to a counter beside Becca's and—what the hell—she took a seat. In for a penny, in for a pound. It wasn't like she had to buy something.

He pulled out a stack of jewel-toned shawls, each wrapped separately in plastic. "Perhaps this, Madam?" He pulled a rosy-hued shawl out of its plastic and came around the counter to drape it around her shoulders.

It was—like air against her skin. So soft and light and yet warm, and smelled of wool and warm sunshine.

The young man pulled out a mirror. "You see? It is a good color for you. Where are you from, Madam?"

"From Canada," she answered distractedly as she wrapped the

shawl around her neck. The color was nothing she'd have chosen, but it *was* absolutely lovely against her skin. And totally impractical given she owned nothing that would go with a scarf that color.

"Oh, Phoebe!" Becca said, coming to stand behind her, a silken scarf of turquoise and blue draped around her neck. "That is simply gorgeous." She ran her finger over the rosy scarf. "Oh. Oh, my God! Why am I looking at silk? What is this?"

"Pashmina," Phoebe said, feeling suddenly overwhelmed by the beauty of the scarf and the stack of beautiful colors on the counter. "The real stuff."

The young man had returned around the counter and now held up a bright blue Pashmina for Becca. "It would go with your eyes, Madam. "And if you prefer, there is this." For Phoebe he held up a café-au-lait colored scarf with a lovely floral pattern woven into the fabric. Phoebe took it from him. The same softness of the rose scarf. She wrapped it around her neck.

Nice, but not the 'gorgeous' Becca had named the first scarf. She stripped it off and forced herself to remove the rose scarf, too, setting them both on the counter. Perhaps she could buy two. "How much are they?"

Becca was modeling the blue scarf and it was striking on her, bringing out her eyes exactly as the young man had said. The proprietor left his array of silk scarves and came to them.

"Very beautiful. Very beautiful, indeed," he said to Becca as she looked over her shoulder at herself in the mirror. The shawl was simply striking.

"I asked how much they are," Phoebe repeated. "In Canadian dollars." She was not going to fall in love with them. Not yet. In this life where life itself could be taken away so quickly, she couldn't afford to become attached.

The older man produced a calculator from under the counter. He punched in numbers and held it out to her.

A hundred and sixty dollars. She felt like choking, but kept her game face on. "For one?"

As if she paid that amount every day for a scarf. Heck, she'd never paid that much for any piece of clothing except her travel rain jacket.

"Of course, Madam. These are first quality pashmina, woven in Kashmir."

"Mom? Aunt Bee? Are you going to be all day?" Alice's impatient call preceded her into the store. Becca whipped the blue scarf off from around her neck as if she'd been caught red-handed.

"We were just doing a little shopping. These pashminas caught our attention," Phoebe said. "Becca, put the blue scarf back on." Becca did and Phoebe draped the rosy-hued one around her own neck. "What do you think?" She threw an arm around Becca's shoulders.

"Wow!" Alice stopped where she was and studied them. "I think I need to take your picture. Those colors are brilliant on you."

She brought her camera up and snapped away, then brought the camera down again. "Are you going to be long? Trevor and Jeannie have already left, but I wanted to stay with you."

She came up to them and fingered the edge of a shawl. "Nice."

"Very fine, Miss. The finest pashmina."

"Really?" She neither looked, nor sounded like she was impressed. She looked up at her mother. "So, are you going to buy it?"

Before Becca could say anything, Phoebe showed her the calculator. Becca visibly blanched. With reluctance, she stripped the blue scarf off and draped it on the counter.

"Too rich for my blood," she said. "But you should get yours, Phoebe. The rose one looks wonderful on you."

Phoebe stripped the rose scarf off, too, draped it on the counter, and in fond farewell, stroked its softness. "I'll think about it, but it is too much. Thank you very much for your time."

She, Becca, and Alice turned toward the door.

"But Madam, you must make an offer," said the older shopkeeper. "We wish to sell these scarves to those who will love them. What is your price? If you take two, surely we can make a good deal for you."

A good deal. She'd heard that every time she went to buy something. "I don't think you can make the deal good enough," she said and followed Becca and Alice to the doorway. "If I'm interested, I will come back." And be prepared to still walk away if she couldn't get her price.

Stepping outside was like stepping into a cauldron. The afternoon sun filled the streets, and even though the shadows were growing, the heat was unrelenting. She fanned herself and turned to Alice. "Where would you like to go?"

Alice turned and pointed down the street past myriad other curio shops to a shop with cute sundresses in the window.

"Then there we will go."

"They were beautiful scarves," Becca said with a last wistful look back at the shop they had come from.

"They were." Phoebe agreed, fanning herself. Not that it did any good. "I don't think I've ever seen anything quite so soft and fine. Don't you agree?"

Becca nodded.

Alice shrugged. "I've seen pashmina before."

Phoebe smiled at her. "And thank you again for the lovely gift at Christmas. These ones were just so expensive." It came out as a sigh.

"I've read about scarves that are more expensive," Alice said from where she walked ahead of them, clearly impatient with the 'old folks' stroll.

"Do tell?" Becca asked as she shook her head at her daughter.

"Something called a shahtoosh," Alice said. "They can cost twenty thousand dollars a scarf."

"A little outside of our household budget," Becca said.

Alice shrugged and surged ahead of them toward the clothing store.

"Hold on there, young lady! You will not go running off alone, you hear!"

"Mo—om." Alice rolled her eyes, but she slowed her pace to theirs.

I t was a scorching late afternoon by the time they straggled back to the Scandinavian Guesthouse. Alice had successfully scored a couple of sleeveless tops and a pair of linen trousers. Becca and

Phoebe had bought nothing, Phoebe still feeling shell-shocked from the beauty of the pashmina and guilty because she desperately wanted one. From Becca's distant gaze, she likely felt the same.

They all pulled on swimsuits and dunked themselves in the pool. That was where Zamir found them. If anything, his expression was even more desolate.

7

---

amir stood like an unhappy statue at the side of the pool, the afternoon sunlight placing a corona around his head and shoulders. His expression was despondent, his shoulders slumped.

"What is it, Zamir?" Phoebe asked from the sun-warmed pool.

"I spoke to Simon's lawyer. He was happy to be informed of Simon's death and told me that they were the executor of record for the estate." His voice caught. His eyes filled with tears. "I do not have control over Simon's funds!"

"Well…" Phoebe thought a moment. "If the lawyer is the executor, and the tour is part of Simon's business, his estate should ensure the completion of Simon's tour commitment, or a refund. They should also ensure your wages. You should phone them back. Tell them what you need."

He looked stricken at the prospect and she doubted that he would do it. Zamir wasn't the kind of person who would push the lawyers on anything. All of Simon's 'help' over the years seemed to have settled Zamir more into a dependent instead of encouraging independent business acumen.

The news stripped away the happy atmosphere at the pool and bled away her gentle yearning for a rose-colored pashmina. The rest of the afternoon and evening were taken up with worry about what the next day would bring.

T he next morning found them up early for some reason. Jeannie and Trevor had already gone out for early morning photos, but Alice, Phoebe, and Becca opted for a pre-breakfast swim. Jasmine scented the air in the guesthouse's inner courtyard. Early sunlight flashed and glimmered on rippled reflections of the pink and orange bougainvillea in the turquoise pool water. Phoebe floated at the side of the pool as Alice attempted to lure Becca into a water fight. Silver droplets flashed in the air and showered Phoebe's hair and face. Becca finally took the challenge, dove, and yanked a yelping Alice under.

Phoebe simply floated and hoped the sunlight would erase the chill that seemed to go right down to her bones.

Last night she'd had dreams of the rose-colored scarf and draping it around her neck to luxuriate in the softness. Until Simon ripped it off of her and ran away, leading her a merry chase through progressively narrower and darker alleys.

Weird dream. All she could put it down to was concerns about the cost of the tour. If they had to pay for extra days of hotels, the money wasn't there to make such an extravagant purchase.

Guests of the guesthouse began to straggle down for breakfast while she paddled in the pool and Becca and Alice swam leisurely laps. The catering staff busily set out urns of coffee and chai and platters of fresh fruit. She was just beginning to notice that her fingers had pruned from being in the water so long, and wondering whether she could stay in long enough to eat breakfast *in* the pool—when Zamir appeared on the stairs.

He trotted down to the pool area, looking like the night had erased a million years of worry. His dark skin was its old lustrous color, his damp hair combed back from his forehead, and his gaze clear. He wore a white golf shirt with open collar and black jeans.

When he saw her, he waved and hurried through the empty tables to the poolside. "Good news! I have some good news for a change!"

"That's great!" Phoebe hauled herself up onto the side of the pool and pulled a towel to her. "What's happened?"

"I did like you said and phoned the lawyer back. I explained what had happened and that we were stranded. At first, he said that you should use your travel insurance and go home, but I held my ground. This was Simon's business. This was his business commitment and it should be followed through with. I explained that some of the money was loaded on a credit card, but we could not access it to pay for the rest of the journey. He said that he would contact the bank and work with them to ensure that we can finish out the tour!" He punched the sky. "You see? You were right! And he told me that Simon named me his sole beneficiary. I am so happy I could kiss someone." He leaned down and pecked her on the cheek. "There! Done! It is a new day all around. I can tell." Then he colored. "Pardon, Madam. I should not have been so forward."

Phoebe patted his hand, not having the heart to remind him that she and the others might not want to continue the tour. "Don't worry. It was news worthy of a kiss on the cheek."

The news got Phoebe, Becca, and Alice out of the pool and dressed for breakfast. Zamir had settled at their usual table and they joined him there, happy that there was good news for a change.

"I wonder if we can keep to our timetable and leave tomorrow as planned," Becca mused over a second cup of coffee after her egg-white omelette.

Phoebe looked up from finishing her regular omelette with vegetables and paneer cheese, surprised that Becca would want to continue.

"But we've hardly seen Kochi," Alice said.

Phoebe nodded and sipped her chai. The cardamom and pepper was surprisingly calming. "That afternoon tour was awful and, well, you know how our early morning stroll ended. I don't feel like I've seen anything. I'd like to get out today."

She checked her watch. It was already close to nine thirty and Detective Mathias was due here at ten. His news would tell them whether they'd be able to leave. She prayed that the pathologist deemed Simon's death accidental.

Across the lobby, a sweaty but satisfied-looking Jeannie and Trevor entered the lobby, camera gear in hand. They spotted Phoebe and the others and crossed to them. "What a morning! The sunrise was spectacular beyond the Chinese nets. The shadows in the old city were inspiring."

Alice's mouth made a moue. "And I missed it."

"You will sleep in…" Phoebe said. The girl had a long history of having to be dragged out of bed. Phoebe had lived through it on their last adventure together. She looked back at Jeannie and Trevor. "Did you hear back from Simon's travel agency?"

Jeannie rolled her eyes and Trevor shook his head. "Apparently they have no responsibility for the tour once we've left the country. They were just a funnel for the money."

"Probably took a cut, too. Just gave this operation a smell of legitimacy it didn't deserve, so people like us would fall for it," Trevor said and settled at the table with a dismissive glance in Zamir's direction. "So, the money's gone and now we're on our own, right?"

"Actually, Zamir was telling us that he's spoken to Simon's executor and the estate will cover our expenses. This was Simon's business, after all, and Zamir is his sole beneficiary."

Trevor and Jeannie exchanged glances. "That's good news."

A movement in the lobby caught Phoebe's eye. A tall, male figure had gone to the desk. The figure turned and she recognized Detective Mathias's straight posture and his impeccable clothing. Three uniformed officers followed him inside and he motioned them toward the stairs—probably to search Simon's room. Her stomach flip-flopped as he started through the lobby toward them. Phoebe forced herself up to greet him, then noticed another uniformed police officer enter the guesthouse's front door and position himself as if blocking the exit.

"Detective Mathias," she said, her stomach sinking. Today he looked, if anything, more imposing, dressed in an impeccable navy-blue suit even in the day's heat. A white shirt so crisp that it had to have been washed at the dhobi khana laundry was buttoned to his chin with an elegant blue striped tie tied tightly. His dark hair had been newly cut over the ears and his expression was, impossibly, more reserved. He would not meet her gaze.

He ignored the offer of her handshake and scanned the table as if taking inventory. He named off their names as if seeing whether he could match name to face. When he got it right, he nodded. "You are all here, I see. Good."

"Is there news?" Phoebe asked. "Did the pathologist's report come in?"

"It did." He gave a perfunctory nod. "There was no water in Simon Roy's lungs and we have found his blood on the pavement on the seawall. We must assume his death was not accidental." His gaze slid around the table to each of them. "You will remain here, please. Ms. Clay, you will come with me."

No time to ask questions. No time to even digest his news.

He swung around as if he was on parade and then looked over his shoulder to check whether she was following. She looked back at the others.

"I guess I'll be back soon." She shrugged and followed.

Detective Mathias had apparently commandeered the hotel office for his interviews. It was a small, functional office with its door under the stairway to the second floor. Its air carried the faint scent of chai and a breakfast masala curry. Unlike the lovely mahogany-louvered windows in Phoebe's room, this room had a single functional window in one wall with warbled glass as if it was original to the building. The other two walls held shelves of ledgers and what looked like Wi-Fi equipment, a small green light blinking on and off. A plain wood desk filled the center of the room. It was piled with papers in neat stacks, most of which looked like bills with cheques attached just waiting to be mailed. An old oak desk chair sat behind the desk and a hard-backed wooden chair faced it.

Detective Mathias edged through the narrow space around the desk and motioned her to the straight-backed chair. She waited until he'd seated himself and sat. The chair was as hard and unyielding as Mathias's glance. He shoved the stacks of papers aside and placed his notebook on the table before folding his graceful hands over the notebook, much like a student awaiting a classroom lecture. She decided to wait for him to start instead of peppering him with questions.

His study seemed to want to strip layers of her away, but unlike some people, she was just Phoebe Clay all the way down. She'd had any artifice burned away in the court of public opinion after the school shooting. She allowed her lips to curve under his scrutiny. Let him guess why. In a game of wills, she had plenty of practice after years of dealing with high school students.

Like Rick Hames.

Her certainty wavered a little at the thought. Rick was a ghost she'd hoped she'd left behind with the school and the classroom. Hadn't she already gone through hell to forgive herself?

Not that she had or ever would.

She pressed her lips together and met Detective Mathias's gaze. Decided to take the offensive. "What kind of Indian name is Mathias? It sounds English."

The good detective's expression shifted from assessing to slightly amused. "French or Dutch, if you must know, though it came to me via the Portuguese. When they arrived in Goa in the 1500s, they began to encourage conversion to Christianity. With conversion came the taking of a new name. My family took Mathias. It is uncommon, but there you go. It is mine."

"So your family is from Goa."

A nod and a single forefinger tapped his notebook. "Colva area. A small village named Chandor."

Phoebe grinned and sat up straighter in the uncomfortable chair. "I know it! We visited to see the Braganza and Fernandes houses."

The huge old Braganza and Fernandes houses were molding vestiges of the glory days of the Portuguese colonial period, with ballrooms, treasured gifts from long-dead kings, swords, and secret passages all slowly collapsing under the sun and humidity of the coast. The owners of the old houses had now opened their homes to tours and were using the income to preserve the old buildings. The Fernandes house even had bullet holes in the walls!

He tipped his head. "They are cousins. Now. Are you finished? May I conduct this interview?" His voice had gone stern again and she sighed and leaned back in her seat.

"So it wasn't an accident."

"Correct. His death was caused by a significant blow to the back of the head. There was no water in his lungs indicating that he was dead before he was deposited in the water. Now may I?" He flipped open his notebook. "Yesterday you told me about your arrival in Kochi and what had occurred up until the time you found the body."

Phoebe shook her head. "I did no such thing. Yes, I told you of our first evening in Kochi and what had occurred the morning that the body was found. I did not find the body. Neither did Alice. We simply spotted it. Alice must have been one of the first to see it in the net." After her previous dealings with the law, she knew precision and accuracy were key to the truth. She was not going to admit to anything she hadn't done.

"I stand corrected," Mathias said. "Tell me again what you did that first day in Kochi."

Sighing, she settled back in her chair. "We arrived on the train and had breakfast at the Ernakulum Junction station because we were all famished—all except Simon, it seemed. He was in a rush to catch a ride to the hotel. It took over an hour to get to Kochi and we got to the guesthouse and had lunch. Then Simon excused himself saying that he had a meeting or something and Zamir took us on a tour. It was very hot and humid and the things we were expecting to see weren't open. We got back to the hotel, Alice and Zamir had a swim, we all had dinner, and I headed off to bed at about eight thirty p.m. I don't remember anything until the next morning." She finished and had to stop herself from folding her arms across her chest. If this was just going to rehash what she'd already told him, he was wasting both of their time.

He studied his notes. From outside the door she could hear the muffled voices of the staff, and in the dining room, presumably the voices of the tour members, too. From beyond the window came the rumble of one of the small trucks that delivered in Kochi's narrow streets.

Mathias glanced from his notes to her. He shook his head. "It seems that we have a small discrepancy with your story."

She sat up straighter and ran her fingers along the front edge of the desk. "What do you mean?"

"I mean what I said. We have a witness who places you at the fishing nets at half past eleven."

"That's impossible." A chill ran up her spine and her flesh turned clammy. "I was asleep."

"I have a credible witness who saw a woman matching your description in the vicinity of the fishing nets in the company of Simon Roy."

The room felt too small. It was difficult to breathe. It was all happening again—the blame of the blameless—except this time it was Becca who was going to be the center of the investigation. She wasn't sure how her sister would handle it.

She kept her eyes on Mathias and forced herself to inhale, determined not to volunteer anything. Exhaled and imagined her anxiety going with it until she was calm, like the therapist had suggested. Of course, it had never worked well. "Then your witness is mistaken. Ask the front desk. Ask Alice. Ask my sister. They'll all tell you the same thing. I didn't go out until the next morning once I entered the room."

Again, that index-finger tapped a single time. He leaned back in the chair and it squealed under him. "I intend to do exactly that." He nodded. "You may go, but don't leave the hotel. Please tell your sister I wish to see her."

"Her name is Rebecca and she has exactly nothing to do with Simon's death." Phoebe shoved to standing. She went out the door and closed it behind her, a little harder than necessary.

She stood there, feeling the sweat run down her scalp and between her breasts. She hadn't done anything. She *had* been asleep.

But Becca.

She needed to be protected, but what could Phoebe do?

She looked across the dining room to the tour group's table. Becca's pale face turned toward Phoebe and their gazes met.

Becca who was her sister. Becca who had always been there for her, including putting up with the media stakeouts when Phoebe had taken refuge in Becca's home after the school shooting. Becca who had still loved her even after Phoebe had almost lost Becca's beloved daughter.

Becca who was just as blonde as Phoebe, though her hair was longer.

Becca who had been seen with Simon just before his death.

It would be too easy for the Indian police to try to pin the murder on her, rather than look for the real killer.

8

The sunlight was unbearably bright in the courtyard, the reflections off the pool water almost searing Phoebe's eyes as she set out across the courtyard dining area. The spice scents of curry from the kitchens turned her stomach and her legs felt like water.

Breathe in. Breathe out. The sick feeling in her chest didn't loosen.

There had to be some logical explanation. There was no way in heck that Becca had killed Simon. It simply wasn't possible. Becca was gentle and kind. And even though she'd been upset enough to confront Simon about Zamir's actions toward Alice, she couldn't imagine Becca overpowering the older man.

Detective Mathias might not be wrong that Becca had been seen with Simon, but he was dead wrong if he thought Becca had killed Simon. That was all there was to talk about. At the table she smiled down at the others. "There. All safe and sound. Becca, Detective Mathias wants to see you next."

Becca had frozen like a deer in headlights. Her gaze leapt from Phoebe to the office's closed door and back again. And again.

"Becca?" Phoebe said. "You can do this. Just tell the truth." As long as Becca had told her everything, they could deal with the repercussions.

"Mom, are you all right?" Alice caught one of Becca's hands that lay limp as old flowers on her lap.

She seemed to come to herself and rally as she scanned the faces around the table. "Of course I am. I've just never been interviewed by the police before."

Which wasn't quite true. She'd spoken to the police when Phoebe was in the hospital after her last adventure and had seemed to get on with them well. But then, at that time Becca hadn't been seen talking to the murder victim just before he was killed.

Becca's metal chair scraped too loudly across the patio stone as she stood. Phoebe caught her hand. Becca's freezing fingers twined in hers and held on for dear life. A shiver ran through her.

"Nervous, huh?" Phoebe asked. "I'll walk you over." She led Becca through the tables and felt her holding back like an unwilling horse.

At the door she turned to Becca and nodded. "It'll be all right. We'll make sure of it."

Becca eyed the door as if all manner of terrors lay beyond. Then she looked back at Phoebe, sighed, and shook her head. "It won't be."

"It won't be what?"

Becca's lips firmed and her shoulders straightened even though she looked about to cry. She released Phoebe's hand and grabbed the doorknob. "It won't be all right, Phoebe. They're going to blame me, just you wait and see."

She turned the knob, pushed inside, and closed the door behind her before Phoebe could respond.

Leave, or go in with her sister? Becca hadn't been through the wringer with the police before. The school shooting and the subsequent inquiry had laid bare Phoebe's life and raised questions about whether she could have stopped the event. In truth she still had nightmares about it—both the shooting and what came afterward.

Rick Hames had been a decent kid, and when he'd finally divulged his fury about the incessant bullying of his sister, Phoebe had gone to Principal Murphy to no avail. School policy had said that it required an intimate to the bullying to make the complaint and Rick hadn't been prepared to do that. Seeing Phoebe's inability to stop the hazing, Rick had misconstrued Phoebe's urging to 'do the right thing' and had brought a gun to school instead. As a result, Rick and two innocent school mates died.

The inquiry had considered whether Phoebe's suggestion had incited the killing. They hadn't seemed to consider all the times she'd begged Principal Murphy to do something. Two years later, sometimes in her darkest dreams she wondered herself. The inquiry and the police had made sure that she doubted herself. Hated herself, too, until the therapy had finally unwrapped some of those self-inflicted bonds.

And now the police might do the same thing to her sister. She couldn't let that happen. Becca was Alice's mother and Phoebe's lifeline. There had to be other viable suspects.

She raised her hand to knock.

"Aunt Bee? Can we go back out onto the seawall this afternoon?"

Phoebe swung around and lowered her hand.

Alice frowned, then studied her bare toes in her sandals. "After what happened, I can barely remember the place. Jeannie and Trevor have been telling me about a fish market and all the Chinese nets and, well, I'd really like to get some pictures… Maybe at sunset?"

"Of course, hon. We can do that." Phoebe glanced back at the closed door and heard the murmur of voices beyond the wood. "But first I want to check on your mom. Make sure she's all right after the interview."

Alice's gaze darted to the door. "She's been acting really weird. All introverted and hyper concerned about me. Not like Mom at all."

Phoebe cocked a doubtful brow at her.

Alice shook her head. "Okay. She's always concerned about me, but she doesn't want me going anywhere without either you or her with me. And I can't go near Zamir without her."

Phoebe crossed her arms. "Did you ever think that what happened on our kayaking trip might have made her a little concerned about you? It certainly brought home for me the dangers of being a lovely young blonde girl—and having to watch out for one. We're in a foreign country and things can happen, Alice. I agree with her about that." She glanced back at the door. "But I also agree about your mom being out of sorts. I think I know why. How about you go back with the others and I'll see you in a few minutes."

Alice hesitated, but finally retreated to the sunlight. Phoebe raised her hand to knock again, but decided against it. Instead she simply opened the door and stepped inside.

A hard-faced Detective Mathias sat behind the desk, his pen in hand. Added to the desktop was a tape recorder that hadn't been there when Phoebe was in the room. She swallowed and glanced at Becca. She slumped in the lone chair, her face stained with tears.

"Ms. Clay. Just what do you think you are doing?"

She took a step behind Becca and placed her hands on Becca's shoulders before meeting the detective's gaze. "Supporting my sister. I should have been in here with her from the start. If what I think is happening in here is occurring, I think I should warn my sister not to speak to you until she's consulted a lawyer."

"There is no such requirement in Indian law. Your sister can be arrested and I can interrogate her in custody."

Phoebe stayed where she was, her hands resting on Becca. No way was she leaving her sister to fend for herself. That was what she'd done to Rick Hames.

"At the very least she should speak with a representative of the Canadian consulate."

Becca's hand came up to cover Phoebe's. "It's all right. He already knows that I was out with Simon that night." Her voice hitched as she spoke, but she took a deep breath and steadied herself, her hand holding tight to Phoebe's. "I told him how I followed him out because I needed to talk to him privately—without you or Alice around—and how we finally had our conversation in the parking lot just before the Chinese fishing nets. And how it didn't go well. But when I left him, he was very much alive."

Her voice died away and under Phoebe's hands Becca's shoulders slumped.

"So, you see, I did what you said. I told him the truth." She turned a bleary blue gaze up to Phoebe. Her eyes were an older, exhausted version of Alice's clear blue. "And now I suppose I'm a murder suspect."

"You can't believe Becca'd kill anyone," Phoebe said, even though it was probably what every suspect said. "This is a woman who has a hard time spraying the neighbor's cat when it poops in her garden."

Mathias sighed and leaned back in his chair. "There have been less likely suspects and worse reasons."

"What reason could she have to kill Simon? Sure, he was an infuriating little man, but that's not reason enough to kill someone!"

"A mother will do terrible things to protect her young," Mathias said softly.

Phoebe straightened. "Grizzly bears, maybe. Maybe orcas. I don't know. But my sister wouldn't kill Simon."

"I wanted to."

Becca's soft voice filled the room. Phoebe wheeled on her, suddenly furious at the way Becca seemed to want to take the blame. "Do. Not. Say. Anything else. Understand?"

Phoebe turned back to Mathias who this time had pity in his gaze, but no remorse for his questions. He stabbed a button on the tape recording.

"I think I have enough."

She could have launched herself across the desk at him. She could have snatched the tape recorder and smashed it against the wall. Those were the things she felt like doing. Instead she drew in a steadying breath. "I think my sister has had enough for one day. I am taking her out of here to rest and spend time with her daughter."

She caught Becca's wrist and half-dragged her out of the chair. Detective Mathias stood behind the desk. "May I remind you that your sister is now a suspect. We will continue to investigate, but none of you are to leave old Kochi, Ms. Rebecca Clay in particular. Now I would like to interview Alice Standish-Clay."

Phoebe shook her head. "Not going to happen. At least not today. You've upset Becca and a parent should be present for the interview of a minor. Becca's in no state to do it." At least that was the rule at home, but here? God, how was she going to protect them?

She opened the door feeling like a mother bear and pulled Becca into the blessedly cool air of the lobby. Then she turned back to the office and the detective. "Talk to Jeannie or Trevor. Or better still, talk to Zamir and find out just what he—a married man—was doing kissing a thirteen-year-old!"

With that, she slammed the door and dragged Becca toward their room, wondering just how much trouble they were in. Across the courtyard, Alice and the others turned toward them. Phoebe motioned them to stay away.

Inside the room Phoebe released Becca's wrist and whirled to face her. "What the hell have you done? What did you admit to him?" Then she caught herself and took a deep breath.

By the sunken defeat in Becca's shoulders and the tears in her eyes, she knew perfectly well what she'd done.

Becca crossed the room to perch on the edge of her bed. The slatted light through the louvered windows placed a dark band across her eyes. "I messed up, is what I did." She sighed.

Phoebe waited. Dust danced in the narrow sunbeams across the dimly lit room. The place smelled of Becca's cinnamon-and-clove hand cream and Alice's apple shampoo.

It was like this with her students. Waiting them out, the other teachers had called it. Phoebe preferred to think of it as allowing the other person time to collect their thoughts. Of course, it also allowed them to edit themselves. Or sort of out their lies, according to police officers she'd spoken to.

Finally, Becca straightened and nodded. She met Phoebe's gaze. "Sorry. I need to grow up and take responsibility. It happened like I told you. I was upset and I needed to talk to Simon about Zamir's behavior. But I need to tell you the rest."

Phoebe froze. The rest?

She settled herself on the bed beside her sister, fighting back a wave of anger that clenched her gut. "The trouble is that you *were* in the area where Simon was killed and you were seen having an argument in which you hit him. That doesn't look good. But you didn't kill him and that means someone else did—maybe the person or people he was meeting." She caught Becca's hands in hers. "When you were with Simon, did he mention where he was going or who he was meeting?"

Becca pulled her hands away and shifted on the bed. "Phoebe, just for once would you listen, instead of trying to solve my problem? I didn't tell you everything and I know that was really stupid, but I *know you*. I didn't want you running out there to save me and getting in danger again. You've been through enough." She scrubbed at her face and squared her shoulders. "You see, I did push Simon and I did leave, but I was so mad that I simply couldn't walk away."

The room suddenly turned cold as Becca rubbed her face with her hands. "I went back. I went back and found Simon on the seawall and we got into a great rousing argument and I pushed him and he fell. I was so shocked that I turned and ran, but I'm sure he didn't hit his head or anything. I'm sure I heard him laughing as I ran away. At least I think I did. I hope I did."

She swallowed. "I might have killed him, Phoebe. I just don't know."

Phoebe wasn't sure what to say. Instead she pulled Becca into a hug, but Becca pulled away. "I'm in a lot of trouble, aren't I?"

About as bad a trouble as possible unless Becca had been caught working the fishing nets that night. But Phoebe squeezed Becca's hands. "Nothing we can't get you out of. First off, did you tell Detective Mathias this?"

Becca nodded. "I was focused on the truth, remember?"

"Did you tell him all of it?"

"I said I did, didn't I?" Becca rolled her eyes.

At least that was something. She hadn't lied to the police. "Now think, Becca. I want you to think back to that night and I want you to tell me everything—all the details. You met him in the guesthouse and asked to speak with him, but he told you he couldn't. What did he say, specifically? Close your eyes and picture that you're there."

Obediently, Becca closed her eyes. She inhaled deeply and dug her fingertips into her thighs as if the effort would make it all come back to her.

"I'd just come out of the room in my flip-flops and there he was, headed down the stairs. He would have ignored me and walked right past, but I stopped him."

"Stopped him how?"

"I caught his arm." She frowned. "No, that's not right. I reached out and caught that stupid little poof of his because he'd stopped when you did it. He was *not* happy and demanded it back. I told him he could have it back when he showed me some courtesy and spoke with me."

And clearly that hadn't worked.

"What happened next? What did Simon say?"

"He demanded his poof back and tried to grab it out of my hand. I could see by his expression that he was furious. I told him he had to wait for me to put on some proper shoes. I ran back into the room and was sure I'd wake you up, but both you and Alice were out for the count. I put on my sneakers and headed back out. Simon wasn't there and I thought he'd gone without me, but he was waiting out on the street. I gave him his poof back then—it was probably the only thing that kept him waiting." She shook her head and then frowned.

"I asked him what his hurry was and he said he had an appointment. I asked him what sort of appointment you make after eleven at night and he said it was a business meeting and then kept walking. I don't think he expected me to keep following him, so at the parking lot he was trying to get rid of me. He was trying to put me off, I think. Anyway, after he laughed at my concern about Zamir and Alice and I pushed him, he stomped off toward the water and I rushed off to get home." She shook her head, but her hand slid across the bed cover to clasp hold of Phoebe's. Their fingers entwined and Becca held on tight. "But then I stupidly went back and the rest is history. After he fell on the seawall, I found my way home after getting lost a few times. Then I crept into bed and slept in. Then the news came that Simon was dead and I knew that I was in trouble."

Phoebe studied the window's chiaroscuro lighting across their clasped hands. From outside the room came the sound of people's voices from the street. The scent of chicken curry reached them from the kitchens. Someone was having lunch. Out in the world everything was so normal, but here in their room normalcy was gone and might never return unless she could figure out what had really happened to Simon. Detective Mathias might seem like a decent human being, but he was a police officer with a suspect, and even at home in Canada, the police too often zeroed in on a suspect and stopped looking at other possibilities. She had to make sure that didn't happen.

"Guess I'm not setting a very good example for Alice, am I? I'm so sorry I didn't tell you." Becca slumped sideways against Phoebe's shoulder.

"My God, Becca. You're an excellent mother. You were trying to protect your child. No wonder you lost it when he wouldn't even give an honest response to your concerns about Zamir. I'd have likely lost it, too."

"But you didn't and I did."

"Yes, but there are still things we can do to help your situation. If you didn't kill Simon, someone else did and you might be one of the last people to have seen him alive. I want you to think back to that night. You're walking with Simon toward the parking lot. Did you see anyone else?"

She felt Becca's head shake.

"Close your eyes. I want you to just relax and breathe for a moment."

Becca relaxed against Phoebe and her breathing slowed. Phoebe let her rest that way for a moment. She had done such exercises with students who had test anxiety. She'd spent time with them getting them to visualize being wherever they usually studied. "Becca, you're at the parking lot and you're mad at Simon. You're arguing with him, but you're aware of your surroundings. Was there anyone else around?"

Becca started to shake her head again, but suddenly sat up, her eyes flashing open in a band of louvered light.

"There was someone. I don't know who it was, but there was someone under one of the trees. I caught the movement of a shadow there. For an instant I felt nervous." She swung around to Phoebe. "That's it! Maybe that's the person who killed him! We need to tell the detective."

Phoebe held up her hand to stop Becca's excitement. "After you went back to Simon, you followed him up to the seawall. I want you to close your eyes and do the same thing. Was there anyone else around?"

Once more Becca stilled and only the sound of distant traffic and the omnipresent thunder of waves filled the room. Then Becca stirred with a shake of her head.

"I've got nothing. There was no one else there as far as I can remember."

"Okay. We'll update Detective Mathias," Phoebe said with a sigh. "But you're still the one who fought with Simon and you're the one who had a motive. The person you saw could be the police witness for all we know."

"You really know how to keep my spirits up, don't you?" Becca said, sagging a little from the resolve she'd shown. "So what now?"

"I want you to keep thinking back to that night and anyone else that you saw. Think about when you left and when you returned again and when you followed Simon up onto the seawall. Was there anyone who might have seen Simon after you left?"

"I don't know. I don't know." Becca ran her fingers through her hair and looked harried and frustrated with herself and oh-so-vulnerable. "I was upset. I was scared of how angry I was and what I had done. I was trying to figure out what to do. I was worried about telling you if I decided I was going to leave the tour and take Alice home. And I was trying to find my way back to the guesthouse—not very well. I finally realized that I was lost and had to pay attention. I asked a woman for help and she told me how to get home again." She shook her head and studied her hands as if seeing blood on them. "What am I going to do, Phoebe?"

Phoebe really wasn't sure how to answer. She wanted to wrap Alice and Becca up in cotton batting and pack them away, but that wasn't how life worked. Even if she wanted to, she wasn't sure she could do it alone.

"I think—I think maybe it's time to call the consulate," she said.

9

———

The louvered shadows shifted across the guesthouse room wall as Phoebe paced the linoleum floor and Becca hunched on her bed over her phone. Thankfully, Alice had remained with the others at the table by the pool. Regardless of the spinning fan overhead, the room smelled stale and the scent of cooking from the kitchens turned Phoebe's stomach. What had previously seemed like faint street noise now seemed to roar in her ears as she tried to hear the tinny voice on the other end of Becca's phone. Finally, Becca hung up and Phoebe looked at the time.

After thirty minutes, what they'd learned didn't amount to much. First, there was no Canadian consulate in Kochi. The nearest was in Mumbai, over fourteen hundred kilometers away. When they'd found the number and called them, it seemed like everyone they should talk to was on lunch hour. Finally, they were connected to someone who was the assistant to the assistant for citizens' services—who knew who that was?

"So? What did the assistant to the assistant have to say?" she asked, her knees cracking as she crouched in front of Becca.

Becca shook her head. "Not much. Until I'm formally charged, the best that I can do is retain a lawyer and cooperate."

Which left them no farther ahead than they already were.

Phoebe shifted to the bed across from Becca. "So, I guess we need to get you a lawyer."

Becca let out a deep breath. "How are we going to get through this? How am I going to tell Alice?"

"We'll tell her together, if you like."

Becca shook her head, her blonde hair falling across her face. "I did this. It's my responsibility. She doesn't need to hate both of us for wrecking the trip. What's she going to think if I'm charged? Oh, God!" The resolve to deal with her situation faded on her face. "What happens if I go to jail?"

"We'll get through this together. We always do. Just like you helped me hold it together after the shooting, I'll help you."

Her head shaking, Becca scrubbed at her face. "This is too much."

Too much trouble? Too much effort? It was Becca's life and her daughter! Wasn't that worth whatever the fight? Heaven knew the price Phoebe had been prepared to pay to save Alice. Wasn't Becca prepared to do what was needed to save herself?

A tight knot of anger caught in Phoebe's throat. She stood. "Get up."

Becca shook her head.

"Get up, damn you! Don't you dare give up! You get up and you be prepared to fight because you've got more to fight for than anyone." She grabbed Becca's arm and hauled her up. "I'm not going to be the one propping you up, trying to do everything. You have a daughter and she needs you to protect and reassure her. You damn well get up and start working with me or, so help me God, I'm going to slap you! I will not have you go all helpless on me."

She froze, shocked at the anger she felt at her sister, whom she dearly loved. She was just so damned tired of everyone expecting her to take charge and respond to tough situations. Didn't they understand the toll it took? Didn't they understand that people had to take responsibility for themselves?

But didn't Rick Hames do exactly that? He took on the personal responsibility, and made all the wrong decisions because she'd pushed him to 'do the right thing.' She'd pushed him to do something instead of just harboring his anger and hadn't understood just how angry he was.

By her own admission, Becca had been angry, too. And she *had* tried to deal with the situation between Alice and Zamir…

Angry enough to kill Simon?

Was this helplessness the result of a guilty mind?

Becca ripped loose from her grasp and stood there, wide-eyed and panting, as if she was afraid of what she saw in Phoebe's expression.

Phoebe fell back a pace, shocked that she could even consider such a thing. That she could say such things to her sister. She retreated to the window across the room, trying to catch her breath. Outside the three uniformed officers she'd seen go up to Simon's room were climbing into two Kochi police vehicles. She ran her fingers through her close-cropped hair and wished for someone to come along and make things better.

"I'm sorry, okay? I didn't mean what I said." But she had. With every fiber of her being. "But we can't simply sit here and wait for the police to do their worst."

Sighing, Becca shook her head. She closed her eyes and her shoulders squared. Then she looked at Phoebe. "No. Every damn word of it had to be said. I think everything was so overwhelmingly horrible that I just wanted my big sister to take over running the ship. But that can't happen. I got myself in this mess. Now it's up to me to get out of it. So what do we do now?"

Finally. Becca was looking forward and trying to be proactive. Phoebe's gut unclenched.

"You need to write down everything that happened that night. It will help your lawyer when we get you one and might indicate new evidence. You can't afford to leave anything out. Any noise, everything you saw, heard, smelled, etc. You need to write it down. You need to do that now while the memory is fresh. Can you do that?"

"Of course. I've got paper." She craned over the end of the bed for her suitcase and came up with a ringed journal and pen.

"Good. We need to find the police another suspect. From what you've said and what I know, I think there are some other things we can do, too. Are you up for it?"

Becca swallowed and nodded, the louvered light catching in her eyes.

"Good. We need to get a look at Simon's room. I know the police are searching it, but they don't know Simon like we do. There might be something in there that can tell us something. He and Zamir were fighting the day we arrived. Maybe that was enough to cause Zamir to kill him—especially given Zamir is Simon's sole beneficiary. He acted surprised at the news, but that could have been an act. And there's something else. Zamir had Simon's iPad and I managed to get into his email and messages before Zamir turned the machine over to the police. There was nothing interesting in his email, but there was something in his messages. He was meeting someone with the initials A.K. at eleven thirty last night. I memorized the number. Maybe there'll be something in the room to tell us what they were meeting about."

"You think Zamir killed him?" Becca's horrified expression spoke volumes of just how unprepared she was to believe the worst of anyone.

"I don't know who killed Simon. That's the point. Everyone is under suspicion."

Becca nodded again and shoved her loose hair behind her ears. "So how do we get into Simon's room?"

Phoebe went to the door and checked outside. Reception was busy with a new group of tourists, but across the lobby in the courtyard, Zamir, Trevor, and Alice were seated talking, so Detective Mathias must be speaking with Jeannie. Phoebe pulled her head back into the room.

"Here's what we're going to do. You're going to go out to the table and keep Zamir and Trevor talking. Try to lead Zamir into discussion about Simon not being an easy guy to be around. See how he responds and see what he says. If he doesn't say much, mention that you heard him and Simon arguing and see what he does. In the meantime, I'm going to try to snag the second key to Simon's room from the front desk and take a look-see. Sound good?"

Swallowing back any uncertainty, Becca nodded and stood. She took a quick detour to the washroom where she washed her face and brushed her hair. Then she smoothed her blouse and capris. "I'll keep the others down by the pool until you're back."

"Good woman." Phoebe gave her an affectionate squeeze. "I knew you had it in you. You only needed to figure it out for yourself."

Becca slipped out the door and Phoebe waited for her to reach Zamir, Alice, and Trevor before leaving the room herself. From the direction of the table came laughter as Becca settled to her task and Phoebe sidled up to the front desk and Avni, who nodded at her distractedly as she continued to check in new guests milling around her desk. In the crowded area behind the desk, Avni's small work counter was full of papers. Behind her on the wall was a grid of cubbyholes, each containing extra room keys.

She waited until Avni was in the middle of something on her computer. "I just need to grab a key, okay?"

Avni glanced at her and nodded, so Phoebe took advantage. If her and Becca's room was 102 and the argument they'd heard was overhead, it made sense that Simon's room was 202. She hoped. Thankfully, the police hadn't confiscated the keys.

Clutching the key she'd pilfered, she nodded at Avni and glanced in Becca's direction. She had Zamir and Trevor tied up in conversation and Alice was sitting with her feet in the pool, probably getting sunburned. Phoebe hurried up to the next floor.

Room 202 was at the end of a short hall with red tile floors and cream walls. The doors of the guestrooms were plain wood panels set in wooden door frames, but the door to room 202 had was lusciously carved with wooden flowers and vines. Phoebe listened at the door briefly to make sure no one was inside, then checked over her shoulder. She quickly unlocked the door and slipped inside.

The room was larger than she'd expected, but then perhaps it was the single king-sized canopy bed rather than three smaller beds that made the space appear larger than the room downstairs. Open louvered windows allowed in sunlight and the scent of the jasmine vines. The faint scent of shower gel and aftershave—Zamir's—still lingered in the air even after twenty-four hours. Two chairs on either side of a small, bare table sat against the far wall under a second window. Instead of a separate washroom with a door, this room had a half wall that separated the sink, toilet, and an open shower from the main space. Not exactly a place for privacy, but then this was likely a honeymoon suite.

She started her search with the suitcase set against one wall. Simon's three cotton safari shirts were immaculately folded in his carry-on sized suitcase as were two pairs of Bermuda shorts and one pair of trousers—each folded to preserve appropriate creases. The police had left things surprisingly neat. A few pairs of neatly folded underwear. Two t-shirts that celebrated pride parades from back home in Vancouver. Three pairs of white athletic socks that actually looked like they'd been ironed and folded instead of rolled in a ball like she preferred. At the bottom of the clothing was what looked like a folded shawl. She picked it up and it was at least as light as the pashmina she'd admired and every bit as soft except this one had soft hairs protruding from the weave. Probably not as good quality as the rose-colored pashmina, but a good way to stay warm on some of the colder nights in the hill stations. She set it back in place and moved on to the night tables.

On one side of the bed, the table held only a half-finished bottle of water. On the other side lay a book opened and face down. She recognized the book that Simon had been reading on the train and circled the bed. A box of tissues. Simon's reading glasses. Another bottle of water, this one filled. A small metal vial that when she opened it and sniffed, made her eyes water. The label read amyl nitrate. She'd seen some confiscated in a drug search at school once upon a time. Apparently it was used to produce euphoria and enhanced sexual pleasure, especially in the gay community. Nothing else. She went into the bathroom and found only soap, shampoo, toothbrush and tooth paste, and a single prescription bottle made out to Simon for something named Vasotec. She made a note to check what it might be for and moved on, conscious of how much time she was taking. She hoped Becca was okay.

There really wasn't anywhere else to check. Simon's phone had obviously been lost with him. Perhaps the police had it in their possession and that meant the information on the phone was beyond her.

She pulled up the blankets and checked under the mattress. Nothing there. The single drawer in the night stand was empty as was the alcove under the drawer.

A noise from the hallway made her glance at the door. Voices, but they were Trevor's and Jeannie's, not Zamir's. That meant that Detective Mathias was probably interviewing Zamir, which meant she had no idea how long Zamir would be, but there was a good chance Detective Mathias would come to inspect this room when he finished his interviews. Hopefully Zamir turned over the tablet so that the police would see the message and know that there was another viable suspect.

She gave herself two minutes before she had to be out of the room.

She took one more scan of the room and noticed the wastebasket by the door. Oddly, it hadn't been emptied. With one of Simon's tissues to cover her hand, she sorted through used tissues, orange and banana peels, chocolate bar wrappers and potato chip bags. Nothing much there other than a magazine. She pulled it out to examine. An old issue of the Canadian news magazine, Maclean's, that she remembered seeing Simon reading on various occasions. She flipped the magazine open, hoping that use had created a place that the magazine naturally opened.

No such luck. She considered the magazine. Did she dare take it? Why bother? It was obviously garbage. But it was also something that had likely been tossed out by Simon on his last day alive. Given how most travelers traded reading material rather than throwing such things away, and given that the issue was six months old, maybe there was a reason Simon had still had it. On the other hand, maybe it was simply an old magazine someone had given him.

But there was a chance there might be something there that she could learn.

Quickly she folded the magazine in half and tucked it into her trouser waistband, pulling her loose t-shirt over top. She paused at the room's door long enough to sense that there was no movement in the hall and silently let herself out. She started down the corridor toward the stairs.

"It's all gone to shit," Trevor's voice came from his room. "I don't understand why we're sticking around."

Phoebe stopped. Were Jeannie and Trevor considering leaving even though the police had instructed them to stay? Jeannie's response was muffled by the heavy wood door.

"I know it was a good plan, but the man is dead." Trevor sounded fed up and tired.

"We're still here. Might as well use the opportunity. Maybe make his connections," Jeannie said.

Jeannie's voice was just the other side of the door. Phoebe turned and hurried down the hall. The door opened door behind her.

"Phoebe?" Jeannie's voice stopped her.

Phoebe swung around. "Jeannie! Hi! How are you? How was the interview?" Make it look like she didn't have a care in the world. She started back to Jeannie.

Jeannie shivered. "I don't want to go through that again, even though I'm not a suspect. That detective asked hard questions, though." She grimaced. "I hate to say it, but he was asking about your sister."

Phoebe's heart sank. "Becca? What about her?"

Shrugging, Jeannie shook her head in a movement that was reminiscent of the Indian head-waggle. "You know. How did she get along with Simon? Had there been fights or tensions? That sort of thing."

So, the good detective was trying to add strength to his theory that Becca killed Simon.

"What did you say?"

Jeannie's gaze drifted over Phoebe's shoulder. "Oh, you know. That there were tensions for all of us with Simon. That sort of thing."

"Had you seen anything specific between Simon and Becca?" Phoebe pressed.

"Well, no. But she clearly didn't like him because she rolled her eyes an awful lot behind his back."

To the best of Phoebe's recollection it was Jeannie and Trevor who had done most of the eye rolling—and complaining behind Simon's back.

"I see," Phoebe said, feeling frigid in the heat. "Did you provide anything else as helpful to the good detective?"

Jeannie shook her head. "I just told the truth."

"As you saw it."

"Well, of course," Jeannie said.

"Thanks for letting me in on it," Phoebe said and walked away instead of grabbing the taller woman by the collar and shaking her. Didn't she realize what she'd done? Poor Becca could end up in prison all because she was protecting her daughter. And just what was the conversation between Trevor and Jeannie about? Connections to what?

Down the stairs, Zamir must still be in the interview. Becca sat at the table, but now she had her open notebook before her. At least she was keeping her end of the bargain, though at the moment she was talking to Alice, who was still dabbling her feet and legs in the pool. The girl was going to turn into a prune at this rate. Becca noticed Phoebe and waved Phoebe over.

The sun beat down and radiated back at Phoebe from the courtyard stone as she shook off the chill of her conversation with Jeannie. She suddenly felt weak as the adrenaline from the search leaked from her system. She sank into the chair beside Becca and nodded. There was half a page written in Becca's notebook.

"Sorry. I couldn't think of an excuse to keep Trevor and Jeannie here any longer. You find anything?" Becca asked softly.

"Only this." She hauled the magazine out from under her shirt and flipped it open. The cover showed the Canadian prime minister on the cover. The date was from six months ago, so old news, whatever it was. "It's an old magazine. Either Simon was desperate for something to read or there was some reason he kept it. I just need time to go through it."

"What are you talking about?" Alice hauled herself away from the pool, her wet feet leaving footprints over the stones. "Can I help? Mom told me what's happened, Aunt Bee. I'll do anything I can to help." She leaned over the table, her wet hands dripping water across the magazine cover.

"Hey!" Phoebe brushed her away. "Don't ruin the evidence."

"Evidence?" Trevor's voice came from behind them. "Of what?"

Phoebe's stomach flip-flopped. Given the conversation she'd heard upstairs, she wasn't sure she trusted the photographers. There was something about what she'd heard that was—off. Why would they be concerned about Simon's connections? She turned to him and Jeannie as they crossed through the tables. She definitely didn't want them knowing where she got the magazine.

"Evidence that Alice can read something other than a George R.R. Martin fantasy novel. She found this old magazine and was going to read it. It proves there is hope for the next generation." She found a smile to paste on her face.

Trevor settled at the table with Jeannie beside him. His gaze found the magazine and lingered, then swept away.

Had he looked at it too long? Had that been a glimmer of recognition? They'd all seen Simon reading it at one time or another.

Phoebe had to be imagining things. As far as she knew, Trevor and Jeannie had no more reason to kill Simon than Becca did. Less, perhaps, given Becca's concern about Alice.

"What's the plan?" Trevor asked. "Now that we've got our interviews done, are we free to go our own way? See this burg?" He grinned. "If so, we've got a couple of thousand more frames of images to shoot. You with us, Alice?"

Alice looked up from putting truth to Phoebe's lie about the magazine. She had the magazine open and had actually been reading an article. "Nah. I think I'll stay with Mom and Aunt Bee today."

"You don't have to, you know. You can go use your camera. It's a great opportunity to learn from more experienced photographers," Becca offered.

"I know." The kid looked at the magazine and then caught her mother's hand. "Maybe I just feel like hanging out with you."

It was a lovely bit of mother-daughter sentiment, but the slight frown around Alice's eyes spoke more of worry than a simple Hallmark moment. Alice wasn't stupid. If Becca had told her what happened, she could figure out how serious the situation was.

"Then I guess we'll be off." Trevor lurched to his feet and Jeannie followed, but not before Trevor glanced again at the magazine in front of Alice. Then they disappeared up the stairs only to return a few minutes later with their camera equipment. "Tell Zamir not to wait dinner for us," he called. "We'll catch something ourselves and probably not be back before dark."

Tripods clattering, they headed for the front door. Phoebe watched them go and then realized that she was almost holding her breath, that her heart was pounding, and even her palms were sweaty. She even felt a little shaky.

"I need to get out of this sun," she said and stood. "I'll leave you to your writing," she said to Becca. "Alice, can I take the magazine?"

Alice stood up from the table. "I'll come with you. I've had enough pool for the day." She relinquished the magazine to Phoebe. "Actually, this is interesting. You remember those expensive pashminas I told you about? There's a little article about them here."

"Interesting." They left Becca writing her recollections of the night Simon died and headed across the lobby toward their room. The registration desk was empty, Avni nowhere to be seen. Phoebe took the opportunity and stuck the key back in Zamir's room cubby and was just entering her room as the door to the guesthouse office opened.

Zamir stepped out, followed by Detective Mathias. Phoebe stepped back into the shadows of her open room door as the two men shook hands. Then they started up the stairs and her knees went weak. If she'd been ten minutes longer, she'd have been found in Simon's room. She closed the door softly behind her and sank down on her bed.

"What's the matter?" Alice asked from where she sorted through her clothing and then headed for the bathroom.

"It looks like the good detective is about to visit Simon's room." She looked down at her hands and they were shaking. In fact, her whole body trembled. The last time she'd felt like this was after the school incident. But then she'd been numb. Now she wasn't. Now she felt exactly how terrified she was. It had been ridiculously close.

"Auntie Bee?" Alice paused in the bathroom door. "You're investigating again, aren't you? Like with the whale. You're not going to stand by and let Mom be put in jail."

She didn't know what to say. Investigating the whale mutilation and murder of a youth had almost ended in disaster for Alice and almost killed Phoebe. She shook her head. "I honestly don't know. I'm not Nancy Drew. I'm a retired schoolteacher with my own issues."

Like the nightmares and the anger that seemed to strangle her throat so easily these days.

"Auntie Bee, you have to help Mom. You're smart and you don't get afraid. You do what needs to be done. Please, don't let anything happen to Mom!"

Alice was thirteen and trying so hard to be strong in the face of everything, but there were tears in her eyes and her lips trembled.

Phoebe crossed to her and pulled her into a hug. The little-girl scent had been replaced by green apple shampoo, and the childhood softness was being replaced by adult muscle, but she would always be the baby Phoebe had held like a precious gift on the day Alice was born.

"Of course I'll help your mom. I love her, too, you know."

Alice nodded into her shoulder and pulled away palming off tears. "Sorry about that, but I worry about her, you know. She's not as strong as you and me."

"She's stronger than you know. Now go get ready and maybe we can still get out into the city for a bit this afternoon."

Alice disappeared into the bathroom and Phoebe sat down on her bed to leaf through the magazine. She really should turn it over to the police, but they'd already made the choice to leave it behind. She thumbed through to the article that Alice had mentioned and read about shahtoosh scarves and endangered Tibetan antelope. The world really was going to hell. Abandoning the article halfway through because she really couldn't stomach another horrible tale, she left the magazine on her bed. Instead she went in search of Avni. If Becca needed a lawyer, then Avni might be able to recommend where to start.

The telephone book Avni provided to Phoebe didn't so much help as overwhelm her. Finally she found a phone number for the Ernakulam Bar Association and, back in her room, made the call on her cell. A man with a mellifluous voice answered the phone and she explained her problem.

After too many "Very good, Madams" and "Of course, Madams" and "Our very best and brightest, Madams," she came away with three names and phone numbers that she prayed would yield help for her sister.

She hung up and felt herself under Alice's regard. She'd changed into khaki capris and a cool white blouse.

"So? Did you get her a lawyer?"

"Possibly. It might be best to interview them so Becca can decide who she trusts."

Alice spotted the magazine on Phoebe's bed. "Did you find anything?"

Phoebe shook her head. "I read a bit of that depressing article on the scarves. Maybe we should go through it together. We might recognize something that might be relevant." She thought a moment. "I think we probably need to go talk to people down at the fishing nets, too. See whether anyone saw anything beyond your mom arguing with Simon. We might find something the police missed. And there was a text message that looked like it arranged Simon's meeting…"

She was about to suggest that they call the number to see who they would get when she realized she was talking to Alice.

Thirteen-year-old Alice.

Alice who she had nearly lost during her last misadventure.

There was no way she dared involve Alice in her investigation, and while Becca was trying, Alice was right in her assessment of her mother's bravery.

As with her other investigations, in this one Phoebe was alone.

10

The street outside the guesthouse wasn't dark when Phoebe stepped outside at eleven o'clock that evening. Instead, streetlights placed an amber glare across the road and black jasmine shadows against the guesthouse wall. The cool night air was filled with the flowers' perfume twined with the salt scent of the sea. The street was quiet; no one walked or drove, though she heard a car engine a few streets over. In the guesthouse, light showed through Zamir's second floor window, but everything was dark in the room she shared with Alice and Becca.

She and Becca had argued about Phoebe going out on her own. First Becca didn't want Phoebe going at all. Then she'd been determined to accompany her. It had only been after Phoebe argued that Alice might be thirteen but she still needed someone to stay with her that Becca acquiesced. When Phoebe left the room, Becca had been awake. Her whispered "be careful" had followed Phoebe out the door. Alice, on the other hand, had seemed out like a light, still able to sleep with the innocence of the young regardless of all that had gone on in her short life.

They'd kept busy all afternoon, Becca completing her written recollection of the night Simon died, then leaving messages with all three of the lawyers. Phoebe tried the phone number associated with the message to Simon from A.K. It was answered by a man who spoke in Malayalam so Phoebe hung up. She'd also looked up Vasotec—the name of the drug she'd found prescribed to Simon. It was a blood pressure medication, which made sense given how intense Simon was. She'd also read over Becca's statement, but there didn't appear to be anything new or helpful in Becca's recollections.

Just before dinner, they'd gone out shopping, touring old Kochi, including a route that Becca had quietly said retraced her walk with Simon that fateful night—as best she could remember. After a good dinner at a restaurant in town, Alice had fallen into bed with the magazine for company, but soon enough her head nodded. Becca had retrieved the magazine and had thumbed through six-month-old domestic and international political commentary, bad news about the economy back in Canada, and doom and gloom about environmental tragedies. Phoebe had lain in the darkness, breathing slow deep breaths to contain her nerves.

It hadn't worked. Even in the cool night breeze she felt heated and ready to jump at the slightest noise. But she had work to do. Finally, she'd climbed out of bed, dressed, and slipped out the door.

Cell phone and mini flashlight in her pocket, she set off toward the water.

The streetlight had swiftly faded behind her and the next light ahead was a good distance away, in front of the office building cum dormitory where the ATM gleamed like a searchlight in a well-lit cubical. She turned toward the seawall as she had done the first day with Alice, Jeannie, and Trevor, but her path diverged there. Instead of walking the seawall, she followed a street that wound past a soccer pitch, various parking lots, huge old moldering houses smothered in spreading banyan tree branches, and a few open-air restaurants where the servers were just upending chairs onto the tables. The air still carried the pungent scent of hot oil, fried fish, and spices.

Something made Phoebe stop. The restaurants might not be right near where Simon was found in the fishing nets, but perhaps they had seen something.

She brought out her phone and found an image that included Simon and Becca from earlier in the trip.

"Excuse me," she said to a woman busily wiping tables before the chairs were lifted onto them. "Could you help me?"

The woman looked up, neither welcoming nor turning away. She was young, with long dark hair braided down her back and unusually clad in a t-shirt and jeans instead of a sari.

"We are closing. What do you need?"

"To ask you a few questions. A man was killed the night before last and I wondered whether you saw anything."

"I did not work that night." The woman's gaze wavered to one of her coworkers, an older man in a plain white shirt with the sleeves rolled up over the elbows and dark trousers with a white towel tied as an apron overtop. The woman spoke to him in rapid-fire Malayalam. In the midst of the barrage, Phoebe caught one word.

Simon.

"You know him!" Phoebe cut in. She held up her phone with the image showing. "How do you know Simon?"

"Excuse me, Madam," the man said with that ubiquitous Indian head-waggle. He had refined features, a square jaw, and a luxuriant moustache that matched his thick hair. "Mr. Simon—he has—brought his friends here many times over the years."

The woman spoke sharply to him, still in Malayalam, until he barked back at her. She shook her head and went back to her tables, muttering under her breath.

"Please excuse her, Madam. She is my daughter, but today young people are not always respectful. She should have been married long ago, but refused. It is my family's shame." He shook his head.

The daughter clearly felt strongly about something related to Simon, but she wasn't sharing, though she kept glancing up from her tables to glare at Phoebe.

"Did you see him the night before last? I believe he walked past here at about this time. He would have been with a woman." She held up her camera and tapped the image of Becca. "This woman."

The man looked from the image to Phoebe and back again. Finally, he nodded. "She is your family. You have similar faces and coloring. I saw them. They were talking intently. She," he nodded at the image. "She did not seem happy, but then it was rare for people to be truly happy around Simon."

She frowned. "But you said he came here with his friends…"

He half-bowed his head in acknowledgement. "There are unhappy friendships, too, it seems. Simon introduced them as his friends, but I never got the sense that those accompanying him were happy—even though they smiled."

Smiled for him. Still not certain what he was trying to say, she waited for him to continue as the staff finished their work and the lights at the front of the restaurant were turned off. The amber light from the streetlamps filled in the blanks.

"That night was the first time I saw him with a woman. That is more why I remember than anything."

She nodded. "So, Simon only brought male friends here."

"Young male friends. Yes." The head waggle.

"May I ask how young?" She held her breath.

"In their twenties, I think. Or perhaps older teenagers. I knew some of them were weightlifters from near the seawall. Others were from elsewhere. I didn't know all of them."

She nodded and took a deep breath. "I see. Did you see Simon with any of these friends that day or night?"

"No, I did not."

But the man's head waggle was far less definitive.

Phoebe thought a moment. "I want you to think back to the night you saw Simon and my sister. Did you see anyone else that night? Someone who was headed in the same direction or someone who might have been following them?"

"I think not," he said, but again his head waggle made her doubt him.

"Think hard, please. The police suspect my sister killed him. I need to prove it wasn't her."

The man caught her hand and patted the back. "Madam, there were many people who would have liked to see Simon come to an end. Your sister would not have been the first or even the fifty-first. As to your question, there were still people out but I cannot tell you who or describe them. We had had a busy night in the restaurant—a pre-wedding dinner—and we were busy with clean-up. I was surprised to see Simon. With a woman." He patted her hand again. "And now I must go, but I wish you well in your search."

He released her and turned to the rear of the restaurant where his daughter waited. She once more peppered him with rapid-fire Malayalam, but he waved her away and flicked off the last of the restaurant lights.

Phoebe stood there in the amber streetlight considering what she'd learned. There had been people about. She just needed to find someone who could describe them.

The restaurant staff deserted her amongst the empty tables and chairs. The night hummed around her with the song of night insects and the not-so-distant rumble of waves. The streetlights turned everything to a sepia color as if all vibrancy had run out of the world and she wondered whether that was how Becca had felt as she stumbled after Simon, trying to get answers to the questions she had never in her life expected she'd have to ask.

Well, Phoebe's questions weren't exactly anything she'd ever expected to ask either. Did you see anyone other than my sister who might have killed Simon?

Nope. Hadn't expected to ask that one at all.

She set out down the paved street and turned into the parking lot that Becca had pointed out earlier in the day. To either side of the lot stood homes and expensive guesthouses and restaurants with tall, stout walls. The streetlights didn't reach far enough to illuminate the parking lot. The uneven dirt expanse held only shadows seeping in from spreading banyan and other trees she had no names for that acted as a border between the homes' and restaurants' tall brick walls and a low brick barrier that separated the parking lot from the trees. The space under the trees would provide shade in the middle of the day. At night it would be a place to sit and watch while remaining unseen. Had someone been sitting here the night Simon was killed? Had the killer been waiting there?

Swallowing back her unease, she turned, slowly scanning the darkness under the trees. A ripple of nervousness ran up her back. People could be watching her right now and she would never know.

Unless she went closer.

Did she really want to engage with someone who stayed out here in the middle of the night? Back home, those kinds of people were the ones you avoided. She couldn't imagine it would be much different here.

But if she wasn't going to pursue the people who might have seen whoever really killed Simon, then why was she here?

Ignoring all the alarms in her head, she crossed to the wall on the left of the parking lot. The tree here was tall and spreading, like the ones set just inside the seawall. There were benches and upended crates under the branches and a small table set up next to the wall— probably the stall of one of the daytime vendors selling mango pickles or ices. There was no one there now.

She followed the wall toward the ocean sounds. The seawall was only about twenty feet away beyond another band of trees cutting across the night just beyond the parking lot. Beyond the trees was the star-dusted sky and the huge silhouettes of the slumbering fishing nets. She had stood up on that wall and on the beach barely thirty-six hours ago feeling like a criminal simply because she knew Simon and hadn't liked him. The guilt was striking, just as the guilt over surviving the shooting had been.

If she had been stronger, more firm with Principal Murphy. If she had been more supportive of Rick. If she had been braver.

She might have walked him down to the principal's office. She might have made sure the bullying stopped. She might have helped Rick deal with his anger. Heck, she might have confronted Rick and taken his gun to protect the other students.

She might have done so many things to help Rick and the others. She hadn't even been able to help herself—except to survive. A part of her hated herself for that.

She wasn't going to leave so many things undone when it came to Becca.

She had to explore every avenue in finding a witness who had seen something beyond Becca and Simon's argument.

Her breath felt like a bellows as she continued along the low barrier, trailing her fingers along the rough stone. A slight tremor in the darkness stopped her. She turned to scan the abandoned table and benches again. There was nothing and yet she was certain that she'd seen a movement from the corner of her eye.

A dog? A rat? There were enough of them in every Indian city she'd been in.

She stood there, inhaling the sea scent, the leaves of the trees fluttering gently above her head.

No… they weren't fluttering with the breeze. Instead a branch swayed and was far too large to be stirred by the passing light wind.

She peered up into the branches, wondering what she had missed. A night bird? Did Kochi have any? Rats could climb trees, couldn't they? Especially long, narrow, almost horizontal limbs like these.

Her gaze skimmed the limbs of the trees, but nothing caught her eye until she looked back to the center of the tree where the base of the branches formed an open cup around the twisted trunk. Something was there. Two eyes peered out at her.

She almost turned and ran, but the darkness in the tree slowly coalesced into a boy. He had a straight nose and mouth under a mop of hair that stood out from his head like a wild animal pelt. He wore filthy trousers the color of the dusty brick in the shadows and a tattered t-shirt of the same shade so that he seemed to melt into the mottled bark of the tree trunk.

"Hello?" she said softly, but her voice seemed too loud on the still night air.

The boy didn't move, so for a moment she doubted her eyes. Were her regrets about Rick creating another boy who looked like he needed help?

"My name is Phoebe—Phoebe Clay. Can you help me?"

She stayed where she was. The boy's expression reminded her too much of a feral animal that could turn and disappear into the darkness at any moment. Swallowing back her fear, she eased herself down onto the top of the stone barrier. "Would you talk to me? Please? It's terribly important."

"He does not talk to anyone. He cannot speak," came a male voice out of darkness.

Phoebe leapt up and stumbled back. She spun around, seeking the owner of the voice, but spotted no one. Her sudden movement sent the boy leaping down from the tree. He scrambled like a monkey up and over the high brick wall beyond the trees and into someone's garden, disappearing as if he had been an apparition.

"Perhaps that is the way most people like it." The voice spoke again as a shadow detached itself from the trunk of the neighboring tree and came toward her. "He cannot tell tales."

Phoebe backed up a pace as the shape materialized into a slight man about the same height as her. He was older, his hair graying at the temples so it caught the little amber light from the streetlights, but it was long and caught behind his head in an uncommon male pony tail. He had a round face that belied his slim stature and he walked with a limp as he came toward her. He wore cut-off dark trousers and a shirt that had long ago been washed into a dust-toned gray.

He stopped several paces from her and looked her up and down. "You do not belong here."

As if she didn't already feel that with every inch of her body.

She nodded. "I—I'm hoping you can help me."

"You said that to Chandu." The man nodded to where the boy had vanished. "What help could you need?"

As if a western woman could ever need help.

"Help that requires me to put myself at risk walking alone on such a dark night," she said.

He studied her a moment and then tipped his head. "A real need, then." He looked back to the shadows under the trees. "One with value. Perhaps I may be of help."

He turned away to return to the darkness of his original tree, then turned back to her. "Come."

She didn't have a choice. She sat down on the low barrier and swung her legs over, then dropped down to the ground. It was lower here than in the parking lot. She followed him to an area where the ground had been swept clean of leaves. Five benches huddled together near the base of the tree. He settled himself on one and motioned her to another, but she stopped at a stirring in the shadows at the base of the tall wall. She blinked and realized that what she'd thought was a pile of garbage blown against the wall was actually a person sleeping. No, make that three—four—no—six other people sleeping.

Or perhaps not. She felt gazes on her, but none of the people shifted from their spots along the wall. Swallowing back her disquiet, she settled on a bench across from him and then wished she hadn't, for the parking lot loomed wide and dangerous behind her and she could not see any danger approaching.

She pushed the fear away, though she knew her hands trembled. She held on to the tops of her thighs to hide it from this man's too seeing eyes.

"My name is Phoebe Clay. Two nights ago my sister walked this way with a man. They were arguing. In the parking lot there," she nodded at the lot behind her. "My sister slapped him and pushed him and then turned and walked away. The next morning the man was found dead in one of the Chinese fishing nets and now the police think my sister may have killed him. Where you here that night? If so, did you see anything? Anyone else?"

The man reached into a pocket and pulled out a cigarette. He lit it with a match, but pocketed the match rather than drop it on the ground. Drawing in a long inhale, he then exhaled a cloud of tiny *o*'s that lifted above him to catch the breeze and then were gone.

"Why should I help you?"

"Because it's the right thing to do? My sister is innocent. She would never kill anyone."

He arched a brow at her. "Give someone enough reason and they can do almost anything."

Phoebe stiffened. "Not my sister. She couldn't. You sound like the police."

He took another puff and released another string of *o*'s. "You hear that, brothers? I sound like police."

Quiet laughter came from the not-so-slumbering figures and she knew that these men were aware of everything around them. They could be an important information source.

The smoking man eyed her. "You sound like a sister who cannot believe in reality. Your sister pushed him, not once, but twice."

She closed her eyes and took a deep breath. He had seen Becca and Simon. That was something, though this man could be the police's informant. "I am trying to find people who might have seen something that night. Something beyond the argument that Becca had with Simon. Were you here?"

"My brothers and I sleep here every night." He inhaled deeply on his cigarette.

"So, you already told the police what you saw."

A fit of coughing took him and he released smoke in a single, formless cloud. He gasped and coughed and then caught himself.

When he looked back at her, she realized he might have been laughing.

"What's so funny?" she demanded and stood.

The man wiped his eyes and motioned her back to her bench. "Sit down. Please. It is just that we do not speak to the police unless we are forced. We are quite skilled in avoiding them."

"They haven't interviewed you?"

He shook his head and seemed to assess her. "How badly do you wish to know what we saw?"

"It's my sister—family." She let her words hang in the air. This man had to understand family. Family relationships were the heart of everything in India.

"I saw your sister and the man. I saw her shove him and walk away so angry she dared not stay. But she came back again and followed him there." He lifted his chin toward the water.

Phoebe's pulse quickened. This was a man who might know what happened after Becca pushed Simon down. She could clear Becca. She pulled out her cell phone and brought up Simon's image. "This is the man you saw?"

He nodded.

If he'd seen Becca push Simon twice, he must have followed them to the seawall.

"What did the man do after Becca left? Did you see him get up? Did you see anyone else?"

The man's gaze was huge, liquid, and too-knowing. The way he puffed his cigarette, he reminded her of the caterpillar in Alice in Wonderland.

"That is valuable information, is it not?" He eyed her up and down, his gaze coming to settle on her phone.

She shoved the phone in her pocket. "What do you want?"

He took a final puff on his cigarette and threw it on the ground, grinding it out with the heel of his plastic flip-flop. "I am a businessman. I buy and sell what is valuable. From what you say, such information is of great value to you."

Her stomach clenched and, very much wanting to get up and walk away, she clenched her hands together.

"How much do you want?" She bit out the words.

"I am thinking a hundred dollars would be fair."

Phoebe fell back on the bench. "A hundred dollars! I don't have that kind of money on me! In fact, I have even less chance of coming up with that kind of money given everything that's happened. All the money we spent on this tour has been frozen and we're not even sure how we're going to pay for our hotels." Which was only a little stretch of the truth. "Please. Can't you help me for less?"

He studied her again, considering her request as overhead a dove cooed sleepily and insects hummed. "There must be people in your home country who will help. A hundred dollars is not so much."

Hot anger overwhelmed the cold fear in her gut. She wanted to grab this man by the neck. She wanted to shake him and demand his information. But that wouldn't work. So she tamped down the looming explosion and shook her head. "There is no one. We are single women. Our parents are dead. We have no other siblings."

A vehicle went by on the road, its headlights momentarily lighting up the empty expanse of the parking lot. The light didn't reach the darkness under the trees.

"Fifty," the man said. "That is my final offer." He stood and left her, going over to the base of a tree and retrieving a thermos. He produced a mug from somewhere and poured himself a cup of what smelled like chai tea, but didn't offer her one. He returned to his seat and faced her again.

Phoebe did a quick mental calculation. She had that much on her and this was for Becca's future. Even a hundred dollars would be cheap. She pulled out her travel wallet from around her neck and felt his gaze as she pulled open the section that held her everyday emergency fund—useful when she found something unexpected in a store that she absolutely could not live without. So far on the trip she hadn't needed it. Now she did.

She pulled out two crisp US twenties and a ten-dollar bill. That left her secret stash empty and she made sure that was obvious to him. She held out the money, but closed her fist on it before he could take it. "Tell me and this money is yours. Otherwise it goes back in my wallet."

Her words carried more bravado than she felt, but the man dug in his pocket for another cigarette and offered her one.

She declined and he lit himself a smoke, inhaled, and blew out a long straight stream of smoke into the air. "It was warm that night. Warmer than now and I could not sleep. I was sitting here, much like this, when I saw them arrive—your sister and the man. Sister looked afraid—her voice sounded like she was pleading. The man laughed at her and she became angry. She slapped him and pushed him and then left." He puffed on his cigarette and Phoebe wanted to grab him by the throat and shake him, just as she'd wanted to do the same to Principal Murphy when he wouldn't do anything to address the trouble she'd known was brewing in the school.

Why was it that people were so addicted to power, but when they had power, they refused to use it for the good of all? No, mostly it was used for personal gain and to be in control.

Her teeth clenched together and she tensed at all the years she'd had others lording their power over her, all the decisions she couldn't make or that had been unmade. Guilt because at times frustration had led to moments where she'd reveled in the control she had over her students. Had they known it, seen what she was? Was that why Rick would never fully reveal himself to her, why she missed what he was planning?

"Then Sister returned and followed the man to the water. They argued again and she pushed him down and left once more. The man was angry. He stood up. It was after Sister left that another man came."

The words fell like stones into water, disturbing the whirlpool of her thoughts and the distant thunder of waves. For a moment she felt trapped in a net like Simon had been. Trapped and sinking, to drown in her own guilt and anger.

But the man had said Simon was still alive when Becca left. She hadn't killed him!

She fought her way back to the moment and heaved in ocean-stained air, aware of the night noises of distant traffic, the creak of the old wooden nets and the tree branches overhead. For the first time since she'd arrived in Kochi, the breeze was cool against her skin.

"They spoke for a time and the new man carried a package with him." Her informant said. "They seemed to know each other well." His mouth downturned in distaste.

"What do you mean? What did the man look like?" Phoebe asked. She brought out her phone again and brought up an App. She began to take notes.

The man considered a moment. Then he shrugged. "They embraced. Then they kissed, not as friends, but as a man and a woman might." He waved his disapproval away. "Who am I to judge? As for what he looked like—he was young. Darker skinned." He shrugged again. "That is all I could tell. It was dark."

"What was he wearing? What did they do? Where did they go?" Adrenaline surged through her. She was getting somewhere, because the description could easily be Zamir. There *had* been that argument she, Alice, and Becca had heard when they first checked into their room...

Puffing his cigarette, the man reclined sideways on his bench and brought his feet up onto the wood. "You want a great deal from me, Phoebe Clay. I am not so sure your few dollars are worth the effort."

She was tempted to push him off his bench simply to get the smug expression off his face. He knew he had information she wanted. He had proven that. Now he wanted more.

"We have a deal," she said.

His brows raised slightly. "Deals can be renegotiated. I am tired and it is late. It is not a safe time for a woman like you to be out. I think you should come back and we will continue our conversation. When you come, you will bring more money. I think perhaps five hundred American dollars will suffice."

He leaned back until he laid on the bench and stared up through the tree branches, exhaling streams of little circles toward the stars.

Still seated, Phoebe followed his gaze. Up, up through the spreading branches to the sea of Milky Way stretched across the heavens. She wondered what he saw there. Probably riches spilling across his future from milking the woman across from him.

And there was nothing she could do about it, given he had the information she needed.

Unless he was lying to her. He could string her along even if he hadn't seen a thing. "How do I know you're telling me the truth?" she asked.

He shrugged. "You don't. You must have faith. Now leave. Come back at eleven o'clock tomorrow morning. The banks will have been open. You can get my money."

He closed his eyes and ignored her.

There was nothing more she could do here. Not now. Fighting the need to scream her frustration, she folded the bills she still held, stood, and shoved them in her pocket. Keeping an eye on him and the slumbering figures, she eased her way over to the hip-high barrier and then started toward the seawall. There might have been other people who saw something. Perhaps they would speak to her and not be so expensive.

"You should go back the way you came. There are dangerous men on the seawall at this hour." The man's voice floated over to her.

From the parking lot she eyed the darkness of the seawall. Beyond it and the fishing nets and the open channel, the lights glittered on the refinery across the harbor, but the illumination did nothing to relieve the darkness of the paved walkway along the water. It would be very easy to kill someone and roll their body into the water for the tide to take them away.

Not that anyone would have a reason to kill her... but there were people who didn't need a reason to kill.

And she was a rich westerner. Her phone could cost her her life and so could the fifty dollars.

She turned and started across the parking lot away from the water, unwilling to thank the man for his caution.

He was likely simply protecting his investment.

11

P *hoebe ran through the dark down a long hallway, the only light occasional amber sconces that stood in alcoves along the otherwise unmarked walls. At first it had been a street with streetlights and tall spreading trees to either side, but gradually the street had metamorphized into this unmarked hallway. Terror gave her feet flight. Who was after her, she couldn't say, but she knew she was running for her life. Running for Rick's life, too, if she could only find him. Only save him from whatever was chasing her.*

Her breath tore in her throat. Her pulse pounded in her ears in the same rhythm as the heavy footfall behind her. He was coming. It was coming. They were coming. She didn't know who. She just knew she had to get out of here. Maybe she could lead them away. Get them away from Rick and his sister. If she could just find a door. A window. Anything that would let her out of this place, because she wasn't sure how much longer she could keep running.

She came to a corner where the hallway turned either sharply right or left. She had to choose but was unable to make a decision. She couldn't go on like this. Couldn't keep running. Instead she'd stand and fight or die.

That was it, she'd try and she'd die, but at least she'd do something. She drew in a ragged breath, prepared to turn back to her pursuers, but a hand gripped her shoulder.

Phoebe screamed and bolted upright in bed, the scream still tearing at her throat. The darkness had lifted and light streamed through louvered windows. Alice stood with her hands pressed to her mouth, her back against the wall beside Phoebe's bed.

Alice. Alice was here. The room.

Kochi.

Phoebe swallowed back her keening fear and scrubbed at her face. Her heart hammered in her chest. Her pajamas were sweat soaked. So was her bed, the sheets tangled into knots around her limbs. She looked back at Alice.

"Are you all right?" Phoebe asked. The girl was white as a sheet, her eyes glassy with tears.

"Auntie Bee?" Alice whispered and then she took a step before her knees folded under her and she was in Phoebe's arms. "Mom told me to come wake you because breakfast was ending. But when I came in, you were tossing and turning and moaning in your sleep. I—I touched your shoulder and you screamed."

Phoebe folded her arms around Alice's trembling body, trying to remember what had caused her so much fear. It was all a dark blur, but her heart still raced and her body felt tender as if she'd been beaten. She knew Alice needed comfort, but it was almost as if she didn't care. Or couldn't. Still, she went through the motions.

"There, there, sweetie. It's all right. I'm sorry I scared you. It was a bad dream, is all."

Alice lifted her head from Phoebe's shoulder. "I'm sorry, too. I guess I shouldn't have touched you."

From somewhere, Phoebe dragged up a smile. "Better you woke me than left me in a nightmare. I don't know why I was so frightened..." But she did. Oh, God, she did, for the helplessness still rode her. She frowned and pushed the feeling away. She needed to be strong for Becca. "Thank you for coming to get me. What time is it?"

"Almost nine thirty. Mom was getting concerned 'cause you nearly always beat us up and today you slept longer than anyone."

Phoebe untangled her legs from the bedclothes, suddenly recalling what she needed to do today. She'd spent the dark walk back to the guesthouse deciding whether to get the money and whether or not to tell Becca about it. She'd made and changed the decision too many times. At first she'd wondered whether the guy was simply stringing her a line, but when she thought of what he'd told her, it held the ring of truth. It matched too closely with what Becca had told her. So there wasn't any choice about the money. She had to get the information. As for telling Becca, well… she still hadn't settled on an answer. "I'd better get a move on."

Alice untangled herself and Phoebe glanced up at her niece. "How about you go and tell your mom that I'm up, but I won't be joining everyone for breakfast. There's something I have to do."

Alice hesitated, her expression one of concern, as if she didn't quite believe her Aunt Bee was fine. But finally she nodded and excused herself, the door clicking shut behind her.

Phoebe stood up and swayed. Her heart still raced and her hands still trembled. Tottering like an old woman, she grabbed clean clothes and crossed to the washroom. Thankfully, the shower helped settle her. She felt confident enough in her decision to go through with paying for the information—she had to get it somehow—and the sooner she could get the information, the sooner Becca would be cleared and they could leave this blasted city. She hadn't seen much of Kochi, and in different circumstances she might have liked it, but their situation was dredging up too much of her past.

Dressed in khaki capris and a cap-sleeved blue t-shirt, she combed out her short blonde hair and shoved her bangs out of her eyes. Good enough for negotiating for information. She stepped out of the washroom and found Becca waiting with her arms crossed on her chest.

"Okay, sister. What's going on? You spooked Alice real good."

Phoebe sighed. "I'm sorry, all right? I had a nightmare and when she woke me up, I screamed."

"That's what Alice told me." But Becca didn't budge from where she stood. The light through the louvers placed black and white horizontal stripes across her slim form and for a moment Phoebe had the sense of steel bands around her, gradually tightening until Becca wouldn't be able to breathe. That was what this place was doing to them—what it was doing to their family. "So, what gives? Where are you going in such a rush? For that matter, what did you learn last night? You retraced my steps, right?"

Phoebe glanced away from Becca's determined expression. The glint in her eyes said she wasn't going to be placated with generalities. So why was it so hard to tell her? It was Becca's life, for goodness' sake! It was all about her. But getting her hopes up until they actually had the information wasn't going to help, either.

Sighing, she looked back at Becca and nodded. "Sit down. I wasn't going to tell you in case it didn't work out."

When Becca sat on her bed, Phoebe perched across from her.

"Last night I talked to a couple of people. A restauranteur who indicated that Simon was fairly well known for showing up with young male 'friends'." She hooked her fingers in quotation marks. "I suppose one of those 'friends' could have killed him, but he couldn't give me anything concrete other than he saw you and Simon and was surprised to see Simon with a woman."

She shook her head. "Then I went to the parking lot and ran into a man who had seen a whole lot more."

She told Becca the conversation, leaving nothing out.

When she finished Becca nodded. "But that's all good for me, isn't it? He saw Simon was alive after I left and he saw him meet with someone else. All we have to do is get him the money and have him talk to the police."

Phoebe bit her lip. "I'll get him the money, but how reliable will the police consider his evidence if they know we paid him? And what if he just absconds with our money? Without his testimony, we'd be right back where we are now and five hundred dollars US poorer."

"What do you suggest we do?"

"Well." Phoebe caught Becca's hands and smiled. "I figure my only sister is worth five hundred bucks. I was about to go to the bank and take the money to him and I suppose we should call the police, too."

Becca's eyes closed and her lips trembled, but then her expression firmed and she smiled. "That's the nicest thing anyone's said to me today." She nodded. "Okay. I'm coming with you." She grabbed her brimmed Tilley adventure hat she'd left hanging on the corner of the bed.

"I'm not sure that's a good idea," Phoebe said, stopping Becca from placing her hat on her head.

Becca turned to look at her. "And why not?"

"If the police see you, it might look worse than if it's only your sister. You could be trying to cover up your crime."

Becca shook her head. "That's a pretty weak excuse. I'm coming, or you're not going either. Why don't we just tell that detective what you learned and let him do his job like he's supposed to?" She grabbed her purse and headed for the door.

For a moment Phoebe almost decided that it might be better to go to the police as Becca suggested and leave the investigation to them. The trouble was, she just didn't trust the Indian police to work to clear Becca.

Sighing, she gave in. "You have to come up with an excuse so that Alice doesn't come."

Becca grinned. "You forget. I'm a mother. I can be totally boring. It's natural to a teenaged daughter."

Outside the room, Phoebe nodded at Avni, as usual an exotic, sari-clad figure behind the counter. Today Avni was bent over files, with two fine lines etched between her arched brows. Becca headed for Alice and the others while Phoebe asked Avni for the closest banks. Becca was laughing when she returned.

"We lost out. Alice chose learning about portrait photography from Jeannie over a walk with her aging aunt and mother." She feigned an ancient crone's shuffle and led the way out the guesthouse door.

Sunlight fell like a hammer on Phoebe's head and shoulders the moment she stepped from the shade of the guesthouse into the street. Regardless of the cooling shower she had taken, she felt bowed by the heat, as if her limbs were too heavy for her body.

"Where to?" Becca asked.

"I asked Avni about banks. She confirmed that there's a bank machine down by the seawall. I thought I'd go there."

Becca motioned her to lead on and Phoebe headed down the street.

The building housing the ATM didn't look anything like the banks back home. There was a sign that indicated it was a bank, but otherwise the place looked more like dormitories than a financial establishment.

"What do you think?" she asked Becca.

"Not exactly promising. But I don't remember seeing any other banks where we've been in Kochi."

"It's a tourist center. Avni said there are two banks' branches in Kochi, but they're quite a distance away. Mostly people here use ATMs, while the banks are in Ernakulum."

Becca backing her up, Phoebe stepped into to the ATM cubicle. There was no air conditioning and sweat ran down her face as she pulled out her bank card and inserted it in the machine. She wasn't even sure that she could get the money she needed. She knew her bank had a limit on how much could be withdrawn through the ATMs on any single day, but she wasn't sure what the limit was.

For a moment nothing happened, then the machine beeped and asked her for her preferred language. She chose English and went through the process of requesting the five hundred dollars in US funds—something that would equal closer to eight hundred Canadian.

The machine continued to hum, but the transaction didn't complete. Then there was a click and the screen changed. No money came out. It took a moment for her to comprehend the message displayed on the screen. *Due to irregularities of this transaction, this card has been held. Please contact the bank administration.*

She read the message. Read it again. She pressed the buttons that would cancel a transaction.

Nothing happened. The transaction had already been cancelled. Every muscle in her body tightened.

She swung around to Becca almost unable to speak. "Did—did you see?"

Becca shook her head.

"It ate my card."

"Um. Maybe we should try mine," Becca said, already reaching into her purse.

"No! Dammit. We can't afford to lose both of our cards." She swung back to the machine wanting to curse at a world that apparently conspired against her. Wanting to hit something.

She breathed in deep, but it didn't help. It was as if all the frustrations of the past few years rose up and clenched everything inside her, frustrating her more when she JUST. WANTED. TO. HELP. HER. SISTER.

Gasping for control, she swung around and pushed past Becca, turning toward the ocean. She needed to walk, needed to move to get rid of this anger threatening to explode.

"Phoebe?"

What the heck was she going to do now? Her card was gone and she had no more money than what she'd shown that beast of a man last night. He certainly wasn't going to give her the information out of the goodness of his heart.

She stood in the dust at the side of the street and looked back the way she'd come. Sunlight filled the street as if that was a good thing, but all the brightly lit flowers, the bougainvillea that draped over tall stone walls and the lilies blooming outside of fences couldn't dispel the way the world closed in.

"Phoebe, we need to talk to the bank to get your card back. There's a sign there that points to an office just around the corner of the building."

Of course there was. What was wrong with her? She stuffed the anger down once more and turned back to Becca. "Sure. Of course. This's just one more thing that's gone wrong with this trip."

She followed Becca around the corner of the building to a glass office door and stepped inside into a tiny white-walled office that was about as far from a bank as Phoebe could comprehend. There were no counters, no tellers, no line-ups, and no patrons. Becca crowded in behind.

A pretty, young Indian woman in a crisp white blouse sat behind a lone desk and looked up from reading a magazine.

"May I help you?" she asked and stood, revealing an equally western slim-cut navy skirt. She motioned Phoebe to the chair in front of the desk and reclaimed her seat.

"Your bank machine ate my debit card," Phoebe stated.

The young woman nodded and brushed a hand at an imaginary hair that had escaped her exquisite chignon. "This is most unfortunate, indeed. Our manager with the key is not available this morning. Perhaps you could come back this afternoon?"

Frustration seemed to clog Phoebe's lungs. She was afraid to speak.

Like a savior, Becca leaned over her shoulder. "Maybe you could take our name and the bank card number so you can hold the card for us?"

The woman didn't look too sure, but she took the information down and Phoebe managed to thank her before they left the building.

"You'll have to phone your bank, of course, and tell them what's happened," Becca said, hurrying after her. "In case you can't get your card back."

"Of course," Phoebe said, not really listening. She checked her watch. It was almost eleven, when she'd agreed to meet her informant with the money.

Phoebe turned away from the street and toward the water. The seawall lay there, the source of all their problems. Well, she was never one to shy away from a problem. Besides, the ocean had always been calming and she definitely needed calm before they met with her informant.

Sweat ran between her breasts and down her neck and back. Water would help, but she was not going back to the guesthouse. Swallowing back her thirst, she crossed the paved area next to the muscle beach weights. Two well-muscled, young Keralan men worked bench press weights, one spotting for the other.

For a moment she could imagine Simon standing where she stood and watching, then approaching the lifters before selecting the young man who was most attractive. What did Simon do? Wave his wealth at the young man? Offer him the world in exchange for the use of his body?

She shook herself to rid herself of the image. The groans of the lifter carried across the pavement as his arms bulged and pushed the weight skyward. Then came the clang as the weight came down, each time.

The groan and clang sounded like she felt—it was all too much effort, and no matter what she did she would only have to lift again. There was no end in sight.

"Phoebe? You all right?" Becca came up beside her and offered an open bottle of water. "You look like you could use this. I brought it along in case." She patted her oversized purse.

Phoebe managed to find a smile as she gratefully accepted the bottle. She took a long pull of the cool liquid and sighed. "Sorry. For a moment everything got to me. I thought I might explode."

"Nice to know I'm not the only one who has those episodes." Becca caught her hand. "Now you checked your watch and then bolted over here like there was some place you had to be. Where are we going?"

"The meeting. We might not have the money, but we still have a chance of getting this man's help."

She drew in a deep breath and looked—really looked at the scene like waking up out of a deep sleep. Deep blue waves rolled in, gradually turning turquoise as they reached shallower water, only to collapse into white rollers as they spent themselves on the sandy shore. Beautiful, eternal. Powerful.

A light haze of evaporating water hung above the waves and softened the sun's glare. Across the water a huge ship was entering the harbor, blocking the view of the refinery's forest of tanks and piping. Closer to shore, small open boats headed out onto the water to join a flock of similar boats spreading nets beyond the wide harbor entrance. She recalled how Kochi's harbor—one of the best in the world—had been created by the collapse of an earthen barrier that protected a large lake. The ocean water had rushed in and the lake had died. She wondered what would rush in to take her place when she passed away and if the result would be so picturesque and lovely.

Most likely not. Nature made tragedy beautiful. Humans did not.

With Becca at her shoulder, they followed the seawall northeast along the water. If not for Simon's death and its aftermath, she could almost imagine enjoying this place. It was hot, yes, but the ocean breeze was refreshing and the people out walking the seawall mostly smiled and nodded at them.

She came to the jog in the seawall where Jeannie and Trevor had paused to take their photos and where Alice had gone ahead toward the Chinese fishing nets. This late in the morning the nets sat motionless against the sky, the waves running past them into the harbor. There were apparently clusters of them all over the waterways along the Malabar coast, but these were the best known.

And now they were the scene of a murder she was involved in.

"Even now, they're amazing, aren't they?" she said to Becca.

"A little less spooky than they were in the middle of the night."

"There is that."

A fish market was underway, with what might be tuna fish and other fish with bright yellow fins laid out on the sand. Town men haggled with the fishermen, but eventually boxes of large fish were carried away balanced on the men's heads, probably to restaurants and guesthouses like her own.

Just beyond the market she turned from the water and seawall to step down the few stairs into the parking lot where she'd met her informant the night before. At this time of day it was no longer the abandoned, haunted place she'd been last night. The gravel area was filled with cars and small tour vans bringing people to see the harbor and the nets. Glaring sunlight on windshields and chrome replaced the distant glow of amber streetlights. The trees from the night before were neither as tall, nor as spreading as they'd seemed last night. She hurried between the cars across to the spot where her informant had told her to meet him.

The space under the trees held the same circle of benches she remembered from the night before and there were blankets bundled against the taller rear stone wall, but otherwise the place was deserted.

She checked her watch. She was exactly on time.

"This is it? Where we're supposed to meet them?" Becca asked.

In answer, Phoebe sat down on the three-foot stone barrier, swung her legs over, and dropped down onto the bare ground under the trees.

"Hello? I came back like you told me." Cautiously, she crossed to the benches, half expecting someone to leap out at her from behind the broad tree trunk. Or from above? The boy could climb. She had to believe the others could, too. But the branches were bare of people. Just wood and fluttering leaves that blocked the worst of the sun and dappled the earth with shadow. From the parking lot behind her came the sound of car doors opening and closing, the voices of tourists, and footsteps crunching across the dirt and gravel.

Oh, God. Had she got it wrong? Did they somehow know that she hadn't gotten the money? Had they left for good or would they be back? Perhaps they'd gone for a meal or to the market and had been held up for the meeting.

And who was the fool, now, if she believed her own wishful thinking?

"Damn it. Damn it all to hell!" The anger she'd been tamping down all morning surged up her throat. She wanted to kick something. Most of all she wanted to claw this feeling of futile anger, helplessness, and hate out of her chest.

It hurt so much, how could she possibly contain it?

She clenched her fists to her sides, fighting the tightness and the tears. There was no reason to cry. The man simply wasn't here now. It didn't mean that he wouldn't be here later. And maybe it was better that way given she didn't have his money.

A throat cleared behind her and she whirled around to Becca, praying it was the man with the information.

A figure stood in the parking lot beyond Becca, who had paused at the barrier wall. The late morning sun etched a blazing corona around them as if they were both afire.

"The sisters Clay. My, my. Returning to the scene of the crime, are you?" Becca whirled around. Detective Mathias glanced down at Phoebe and then trained his considering gaze on Becca. She stepped back and stumbled against the barrier.

Oh crap, no.

"Detective Mathias," Phoebe jumped in. "What a surprise. I thought you'd already solved your case." She couldn't keep her bitterness from her voice.

He cocked his head at her and stepped forward so that the sunlight wasn't quite so blinding. His enigmatic expression hid whatever he thought about finding them here, though she could guess it wouldn't be anything good.

She glared up at him. "Unless you know something I don't, I believe the body was found in the water."

His gaze held uncomfortably steady on her, but then he nodded. "True, but this is the last place he was seen alive. And for your information, the death of Simon Roy remains under investigation. I do not like to charge someone based only on circumstantial evidence. I prefer a solid case."

So he was still looking for someone who had seen Becca actually kill Simon. Phoebe mulled over how much she should show that she knew and decided to throw caution to the wind. Besides, it wasn't her habit to hide information. She'd always tried to help the police. "You're forgetting that Becca left him alive down by the water. You said you had a witness who had seen Becca argue with Simon. But there could be other witnesses who saw him alive after she left. Did you check?"

His lips pressed into a hard line. "You think I don't know my business? We had police canvassing for witnesses as soon as the body was found. They've continued doing so since then. Perhaps the reason I'm here is to leave no stone unturned."

She glanced around her. "Well, there's no one here, is there? Maybe sitting here in your car in broad daylight isn't conducive to finding people who might have been here at night."

He inclined his head again. "There is that. But most of Kochi's nighttime denizens are less active in the day. I often find them sleeping. One in particular I often find here—if he doesn't see me coming." He nodded. "Tell me, Ms. Clay, what brings a retired schoolteacher and the main suspect in a murder into the empty camp of one of Kochi's most notorious gypsy thieves?"

12

———

The shadows under the spreading tree pulsed around Phoebe. The distant rumble of ships' engines vibrated through her. The calls of the fishermen came along the shore and the tree leaves whispered overhead. The scent of dust, sweat, and urine filled her nose and over it all hung the too blue sky that went on and on and on like Becca's vulnerable gaze that begged her to tell, just as the silence went on and on as Detective Mathias awaited her answer.

"I met the man last night when *I* was out looking for witnesses. He had seen something but only told me part of what he knew. I was to come back today at this time." Sighing, she scanned the packed earth around the benches. From the packed earth and the debris piled along the base of the parking lot wall, the place was well-used. "Apparently he never intended to meet with me, or he saw you and decided to leave."

"And how much did he expect you to pay for this information?"

"Five hundred dollars?" Becca said.

Phoebe sighed. She hadn't been sure she'd divulge that fact.

She frowned up at Becca, then turned to Mathias. *He* was the problem. *He* was most likely the reason her informant wasn't here.

Mathias scanned the parking lot, turned back to her, and shook his head. "I hope you realize that you are meddling in a police investigation and that it reflects poorly on your case?" He looked pointedly at Becca.

Phoebe's back went up. She placed her hands on her hips. "Don't tell me. You're going to arrest us both?"

"I suppose that I could." And the hard line of his lips said that he might. He easily vaulted the parking lot barrier and dropped down beside her. He looked up at Becca. "Is she always like this?"

Becca glanced at Phoebe. "Pretty much."

"Most difficult for you, I think."

"Hey!" Phoebe crossed her arms over her chest. "I'm standing right here."

Mathias looked down at her. "Yes. You are. Where I was hoping to find a possible suspect or a witness."

"A suspect? You're looking for someone other than Becca?"

His jaw worked as he glanced from Becca to her. "Ms. Clay, you seem to be under the misconception that the Kochi police don't know their jobs. I do not jump to conclusions about a case or its suspects, which is more than you have apparently done about me. Yes, Rebecca Standish is a viable suspect and apparently one of the last people to see him alive, but I have checked on this victim, this Simon Roy. He was disliked by many. My challenge is finding the witnesses I need, beyond the one witness who places your sister at the scene."

She had to tilt her head up to look at him, which gave him the advantage. It was worse because she felt the flush of embarrassment color her cheeks. "I—I didn't think you didn't know your job. I just wasn't sure you'd do it. Police have been known to decide on their suspect early on and then focus their investigation on that person, instead of looking at all possible suspects."

"If I recall, there are some famous Canadian cases with those circumstances."

"Yes. There have been." It was surprising that he knew.

"India and Canada are both in the Commonwealth. While our due processes may be different, we have been known to occasionally look at each other's case law. But until I find more evidence against your sister, I am prepared to investigate her version of events and look for other suspects." A mocking smile played on his lips again. He was making fun of her. "Tell me, Ms. Clay, is this how you treat everyone? As if they are your enemy?"

"I don't think she means to, but she does," Becca said softly from her vantage above them.

Dammit, what was she talking about? "I know who my enemies are, Becca. Maybe I've just learned that everyone is out for themselves." But Becca was her sister and Phoebe had almost treated Becca like she was the enemy when she had gone all helpless after her interview. Phoebe had treated Alice badly, too, for that matter—she'd just wanted her out of the way. The realization left her shaken. Was she really that kind of person?

She suddenly felt exhausted and just wanted to return to the guesthouse. She stepped up to the barrier to leave.

"You should know that Ijay Das is not a good person. Nor is he reliable. He will lie to you to get your money and once he has your money, he will not follow through on anything he has agreed to."

Phoebe stopped. "I haven't given him anything and still he talked to me. He gave me information that cleared Becca completely. He or his men saw Simon alive after Becca shoved him and Simon fell."

"But he wanted money. That is why you've come back."

She swung back to him.

He nodded at her. "I have dealt with Ijay Das before. He has bilked a great deal of money out of desperate tourists in the past. Most notably from a mother whose son had disappeared in Kochi—or so she believed. Ijay said he had contact with a kidnapper and would act as a go-between, but once he had her money, he disappeared for many months. The young man has still not been found."

"Perhaps his body didn't get caught in a fishing net. Perhaps it got swept out to sea," she said.

"Possible." He bowed his head. "Tell me, Ms. Clay, what did he say that made you believe his story?"

"Maybe it was what he did, more than what he said. He didn't take any money."

He gave that charming head waggle again and the sunlight flashed in his brown eyes. "He is skilled in setting up a larger payoff. He is a patient man. What did he tell you?"

She'd gone this far.

"Tell him, Phoebe. Please. He needs to know for his investigation."

She turned back to Mathias. "All right. I know this is all hearsay, but maybe it will help you clear Becca. That's all I want."

Standing in the dust and shadows under the spreading trees, Phoebe told him about her meeting with Ijay Das. "You see, I knew he was genuine because he knew Becca had left and come back. He knew she'd fought with Simon here and on the seawall and had pushed him down. He knew she'd run away, then, and he knew Simon was alive after she left and that he met with someone else—a young man carrying a package and that there seemed to be some kind of relationship between them. He wouldn't tell me more than that until I brought him the money."

Mathias listened intently, periodically glancing up at Becca as if some of the information from Ijay Das might be new to him. When Phoebe was done, he nodded at Becca. "By your expression, the story Ijay Das told fits with your recollections?"

She nodded.

He studied Becca and then shook his head. "You are either a very unlucky or very lucky woman. Unlucky for what has happened, but lucky for walking away on the seawall at night without mishap and perhaps for having a sister who will do so much to clear her. How many are devoted enough to risk themselves for the truth?"

He thought a moment. "Now that you have told me, you must leave finding Ijay Das to the police. We will redouble our efforts to bring him in. As I said, he is well known to us, though slippery as an eel to apprehend. Now, dear ladies, may I suggest you return home, or better still, may I drive you?"

Phoebe was all for rejecting the offer—she'd had enough of the detective for the day and wanted time to digest what had been said, but before she could demur, Becca accepted.

It seemed a long way home, crammed in the back seat of his Tata sedan while Becca chatted with the detective from the front seat. Becca seemed so relieved, almost as if she believed everything would be all right now that she'd handed everything over to the police.

The trouble was, Phoebe knew better. The police weren't in it for justice. They were in it to *appear* to do justice, the same as they'd appeared to help when they'd shared information with the school board investigation into the school shooting and placed doubts about the advice she'd given Rick Hames. The sharing of information might not be proper, but it had been done in good faith; but unfortunately, all it had allowed was for her to be blamed.

She prayed something similar wasn't about to happen to Becca, but every part of her didn't trust that it wouldn't.

13

———————

The white front of the guesthouse and its garden of vivid flowers was a welcome sight when Detective Mathias dropped them at the guesthouse. They thanked him and Phoebe watched him leave, the little Tata toddling off down the narrow street amid a flock of school children heading back to school after lunch. Had she ever been so innocent?

Becca had been. Still was, judging by the happy smile on her face. She caught Phoebe looking at her.

"What? Things are better, right? He knows and can take care of things. Don't you go telling me I'm wrong!" She held up her hand to stop Phoebe's comment and left Phoebe for the cool shade of the guesthouse's interior.

Phoebe hadn't been going to tell her she was wrong, exactly. Just not to get her hopes up. After all, Phoebe had thought the authorities would make things better after she'd spoken to her principal about Rick Hames. She'd found out differently.

With a sigh, she followed Becca inside expecting to see Alice in the pool and the others loitering in the area. Instead the pool had barely a ripple from the light ocean breeze. There was only the thrum of the lobby's overhead fans and the hum of the insects around the bougainvillea. Becca had disappeared into their room. The lobby was dim, but behind the front desk, Avni sorted through documents of some kind. Phoebe nodded in her direction and went to her room.

Becca was flaked out on her bed. Alice's pack looked like it had exploded in her portion of the room. All normal.

She'd thought she wanted to lie down, but now restlessness demanded she keep moving. Do something. Frowning, she stepped back to the lobby. "Where is everyone?" she asked Avni.

Avni glanced up at her, clearly distracted. "They went out, of course. Your niece went out with Trevor and Jeannie. I believe they said they were going to the old town. They were hoping to find spices to photograph this time. Zamir, I'm not sure where he went." She turned back to her papers.

"Avni, I hate to interrupt you, but I'm hoping you can help me with something. Have there been any messages left by the lawyers we called?"

The woman looked up again. Today she wore a vivid yellow sari that made her skin seem to glow in the gloom. Her black hair was pulled back in a bun and a red dot decorated her brow.

"I have taken no messages. You must give them time. They must be very busy."

And the lawyers hadn't called back on Becca's cell phone either. Busy, like heck… Didn't anyone care how important this was?

Phoebe bit back her frustration and went to the counter. "You told me that Simon had stayed here before."

Avni nodded. "Two or three times, that I recall."

"Good. Good." Phoebe framed her question. "During those times, did Simon ever bring anyone local back here? A business associate, perhaps?"

Avni's gaze stilled. "Why is this important?"

"Well…" Phoebe leaned both hands on the counter and smiled. "I'm trying to get a sense of who Simon's friends were. Perhaps one of them spent time with him that night after my sister was seen with him."

"So, you seek another suspect in Simon's murder." Avni looked away, shuffling the papers on her counter into no observable order. "You wish to find someone local to blame."

Phoebe frowned at Avni's response. The cool air from the ceiling fan brushed over her head and shoulders. "All I want is for the real killer to be found, whether he or she is local or foreign. That's all. To find the truth."

The trouble with truth was that every person had their own version. Certainly, Rick had had a different version from that of the bullies. So had Principal Murphy when he had testified in front of the School Board enquiry. He'd claimed that no one had come to him with concerns over Rick—totally refuting Phoebe's testimony.

The memory snarled inside her. She looked back at Avni, hiding behind her mahogany counter. "Were you Simon's friend?"

"No! I manage the guesthouse. That is all."

Avni's vehemence was not what Phoebe had expected. Phoebe eyed the woman across the registry counter. "But you know something. Why else would you be so frightened? Please. Help me help my sister. She and Alice are all that I have."

Her papers seemed to take all of Avni's concentration. Phoebe followed her gaze. Avni's hands were shaking.

"I need to know why you're so scared. Has someone threatened you? Even if I go to the police, if possible I'll keep your name out of it. Whoever has you so frightened never has to know that you talked to me."

Avni nodded her head the barest amount, but she looked around the empty lobby as if assessing whether anyone might overhear.

Reaching over the counter, Phoebe caught her hand and dragged her out from behind the registry and to a pair of comfortable chairs under one of the blessed fans. "What is it that you know? Who were Simon's friends?"

Inhaling, Avni twined her fingers in Phoebe's as if seeking strength. "Simon," she began. "Simon was a regular customer. He would come through once or twice a year with his tour groups or on his own. When he was here, he always asked for the same room.

Sometimes he brought someone with him, like now. Other times he was on his own—at least for a short while."

Her voice steadied as she spoke. She still clutched Phoebe's fingers, but her words came faster. "Simon is the kind of man who seeks out young handsome men. He has western money. The young men like it and they get to experience a different kind of life when in his company. I see other westerners do it as well. The Germans. The Dutch. The Englishmen. The Americans. And Simon, the Canadian."

She shook her head and sat as if to sort through her thoughts.

"If it helps, I'm sorry that he did that."

Avni shook her head again. "They knew what they were getting into when they met him. Sometimes it was a way to earn money for something important—a medical bill, schooling, their wedding. Still, it was hard to see young men that I knew accompanying him." Her gaze fell to her silk-covered knees and stayed there.

"So you know these young men?"

She nodded. "Some. From school. From college. Some from walking with my friends on the seawall."

"Can you give me their names?"

Avni's gaze jerked up and steadied. "They will not talk to you. They will be too embarrassed. Contrary to the image of the Kama Sutra, sexuality is rarely talked about in India and homosexuality even less so."

Phoebe released her hand and sat back in her chair. The throw cushion was soft Indian cotton in rich shades of terra cotta and green. She sorted through what she now knew. Simon had had a variety of male lovers when here in Kochi. He had brought them back here to the guesthouse in the past, but this time he did not. This time he had Zamir with him. If Simon had gone out to meet with one of his previous lovers, how would Zamir have reacted? Was that what the fight she and Becca had overheard was about?

Ijay Das claimed to have seen Simon with a younger man. A man who had shown personal familiarity like Avni was describing. And wasn't the embrace Ijay had described a sign that this was someone Simon hadn't seen for a while? Zamir had been with him throughout the tour. And they'd had that argument. The chances of them embracing like that were very small.

She looked back at Avni, who was eyeing the registration desk as if it was her security blanket.

"Who were the most recent men Simon had been with?" Because there were probably many of them Simon no longer saw.

Avni shook her head. "I—I can give you a name or two, but I need to think about it. Over the years, the faces run together. Could I provide that information to you tonight?"

Phoebe nodded just as Alice, Jeannie, and Trevor sauntered through the guesthouse door. All wore sweat-soaked t-shirts and shorts, but the redolent scent of cloves and turmeric came off of them.

"Aunt Bee!" Alice said. "We found warehouses of spice. It was amazing! I took so many photos. And I bought some spice!" She fished in her camera backpack and brought out a fist-sized bundle wrapped in white cloth. She crossed to the chairs and Avni excused herself and retreated to her desk. Trevor and Jeannie headed for the stairs to their room, while Alice stuck the bundle under Phoebe's nose. "You've got to smell this! I could bathe in that smell."

Phoebe inhaled and the fragrance of cardamom, cloves, cinnamon, and pepper filled her nose, sweet and spicy—like the best of Christmas memories or the best cup of chai.

"Oh, my goodness, that's good." She inhaled again, holding the bundle in place. Cotton cloth had been used to make a small, ecologically-friendly bag for Alice's purchase. She released the package and smiled up at Alice. "I might have to get the address."

"Trevor has it. He wants to go back for more photos when they're bagging the spices for sale."

She watched Jeannie and Trevor lug their camera bags up the stairs and was reminded of the odd conversation she'd overhead outside their rooms.

She stood up and crossed to Avni again. The woman looked decidedly less friendly this time.

"I just had a thought. Do any of the young men you know have the initials A.K.?"

Straightening from her papers, Avni frowned. "A.K.? Not that I can think of." She thought a moment and shook her head. "No. Where would you get such initials?"

Phoebe shrugged. "Just something I thought I heard. Thanks. If I could get the list of names later today?"

"After lunch it is," Avni said with a forced smile and turned back to her papers.

Phoebe went into her room with Alice, but she felt Avni's gaze on her. Perhaps she'd asked the busy woman for too much.

Inside the room, Alice had thrown her camera bag onto the disaster that was her bed. She'd plunked down beside Becca and was regaling her with stories of the spices and her photos.

"Dibs on the shower," Phoebe said and grabbed clean clothes. She reveled in the shower, gradually changing the water from hot to cool, then toweled off and dressed in a pair of white Bermuda shorts and a blue tunic top. When she exited the bathroom, Becca was still on her bed, but Alice was tapping her foot impatiently with an armful of clothing. Quick as a wink, she ducked into the bathroom behind Phoebe and closed the door. The sound of the shower running filled the room.

It looked like Becca really was napping, so Phoebe grabbed a pen and paper and went out to the restaurant table in the shadow of the bougainvillea. She ordered a chai and settled herself. It might be enough for Becca that Detective Mathias was on the case, but that didn't mean Phoebe had to trust him to get the job done. There was too much at stake.

She went over what she knew: it wasn't a lot. Simon had gone out, with Becca following along at eleven o'clock, apparently because he had an appointment with someone with the initials A.K. Becca and Simon had walked to the parking lot by the Chinese fishing nets and there they'd gotten into an argument. Becca had slapped him and shoved him twice so that he'd fallen down, but then she'd walked away, leaving Simon apparently alive—at least according to Ijay Das. He also confirmed that Simon met a young man carrying a package and that their meeting indicated a familiarity beyond simple friendship.

Avni confirmed that Simon had a number of young male 'associates' here in Kochi, and so had the restauranteur she'd spoken to. The number belonging to A.K. had been answered by someone who sounded male.

Had Detective Mathias found that message and traced that call? Had Simon's death been the result of a lover's spat? It could have been, but she kept coming back to the package. Why would a lover bring a parcel to a midnight meeting?

A gift? For some reason she just couldn't make that fit. So the meeting was more than an assignation.

Of course, the young man in question could simply have picked up his laundry before the meeting and not had the chance to drop it off at home. Or he could have been bringing Simon's laundry to him. Simon had said that he was dropping laundry off at the dhobi khana. But she didn't actually know whether the package the young man carried had been for Simon. It hadn't been found with the body. Had it been washed away like his poof had been? Or had the killer taken it? Ijay Das and Detective Mathias had both said it was dangerous on the seawall. Maybe a stranger had killed Simon for the package.

Which meant the suspect list had increased to the entire Kochi population.

Oh, God, she was getting nowhere other than identifying more questions. Her thoughts ping-ponged around in her brain. She closed her eyes and turned her face up to the sun filtering through the bougainvillea. Jasmine scented the air. The sun's heat was luscious on her skin. She slowed her breathing and tried to still her mind as the therapist had shown her, bringing her attention back to absolutely nothing again and again, each time her brain tried to take her down a rabbit hole of worry.

The sound of footsteps brought her eyes open. Alice stood there.

"Is it okay if I swim?" Her hair hung in long damp strands from her shower, but she wore her two-piece swimsuit. Trust Alice to have her shower *before* she went swimming.

"Of course!" Phoebe motioned her to the pool and watched as Alice left her towel on a chair by Phoebe and then made a clean dive into the blue water. She stroked across the pool and then floated back to Phoebe on her back.

"Oh, my God, that feels so good." She hung off the side of the pool and grinned up at Phoebe. "You really should have been with us today. The spices were so neat."

"I'm sorry I wasn't." Phoebe glanced down at her pad. "Other things got in the way."

"How's Mom doing? She seems better, but I'm not sure." Alice glanced worriedly toward their room.

"I think she's really just trying to nap. I don't think she's been sleeping very well with all that's been happening."

"And you're sitting out here trying to make sense of what we know." Alice flipped water in Phoebe's direction. "I have eyes, you know. I'm not some stupid eleven-year-old. Besides, I remember when we were in Johnstone Strait. You'd look distracted and would sit down and make lists of things you knew."

Grinning, Phoebe looked down at her page. "It helps me sort my thoughts. And speaking of that, you seemed to have something to add to the conversation the other day. You mentioned hearing or seeing something?"

"Yeah. I did." Releasing the poolside to tread water, Alice thought a moment. "It's probably nothing—or a couple of nothings. Things I hear when people talk to each other. I think, because I'm a kid, they forget that I'm around. Anyway, when we were in Goa, I overheard Simon on the phone. He was talking to someone about a shipment or something. Simon was all about it had to be first quality, not the garbage he got last time. Whoever he was talking to must not have fully convinced him because Simon ended the conversation with 'We'll see.'"

She pushed off and swam across the pool and back. "Like I said, probably nothing, right?"

"Not necessarily. The night Simon died he was met by a man carrying a package." A package that probably didn't contain Simon's laundry. A little thrill of excitement pulsed through her belly. Could

Simon be running drugs? There had been that vial of amyl nitrate in his room…

"Aunt Bee?"

Phoebe pulled herself back from her thoughts.

"There's something else." Her fine features screwed up in a frown. "I'm not sure what it is, but I don't think Jeannie and Trevor are really photographers."

"What? They've got all that camera equipment. We've been with them when they've been taking pictures. They've helped you learn—" God she had no idea what exactly it was they'd helped Alice with. "—stuff. They've helped you learn camera stuff."

"Well, sure. They take pictures, but the other day I asked Trevor who he liked best, Freeman Patterson or Galen Rowell. Those are two iconic photographers and Trevor stumbled around saying he liked them both, but when I pushed him he didn't even seem to know that Galen Rowell was dead and *everybody* knows that. At least anybody who knows anything about photography."

Phoebe didn't have a clue about the photographers Alice had mentioned, but Alice's observations fit too well with what she'd overheard outside Trevor's room. They'd discussed having the opportunity to meet Simon's contacts. Trying to move in on Simon's operation to create one of their own? That could fit.

But if they wanted Simon's contacts, what was to stop them from killing Simon to get them?

The warm day froze at the terrifying thought. How could she and Becca have entrusted Alice to them on more than one occasion?

They truly couldn't trust anyone.

14

———————

Once she'd recovered from the chilling thought, Phoebe added what Alice had told her to her list of facts. Maybe it was time to allow Detective Mathias to interview Alice. Overhead, the bougainvillea rustled in the breeze and placed shifting shadows on the glass table. She sifted around what she knew of the case. Ijay Das had said that Simon had met a young man. Maybe he'd been lying, but maybe not. What he hadn't said was whether the young man was Indian or white. All he'd said was that the man was darker skinned. Could it have been Trevor? His skin was very dark with tan…

That could open up a whole new avenue of investigation.

But Ijay Das had said the man had sounded like he was from Kochi, but with an accent. Surely that left Trevor out of the equation. But the comments she'd overhead and Alice's observations suggested she couldn't simply eliminate Trevor and Jeannie as suspects. The young man who'd been seen might not have killed Simon either. She really didn't know about Trevor and Jeannie other than what they'd told her at the start of the trip.

Groaning, she looked up from what she'd been writing.

Zamir stood on the other side of the table watching her. Alice had left the pool and was presumably in the room with Becca. How had she not noticed?

"You were out," she said.

He nodded and settled in the chair across from her, the sun turning his brown eyes almost golden. "I have a question for you. The police allowed me back into Simon's room. I was going through Simon's things trying to decide what to do with them. I realized that his small pocket cloth isn't amongst them—you know, the woven cloth with rainbows on it. Do you recall whether you saw it amongst his effects when his body was found?"

He looked away as if he could not quite meet her gaze. Perhaps it was emotion evoked by going through Simon's things.

She shook her head. "It wasn't there when he was found. It was one of the first things I noticed when—when they brought his body up."

When it flopped like a dead fish onto the boards at her feet, his face bloated and white, his eyes already partially gone.

The heat went out of the afternoon for a moment.

"It wasn't in his pocket?"

She shook her head.

Zamir scanned the sunlit dining area.

There was no one around, though Phoebe could do with some lunch and Becca and Alice were likely hungry, too. There was no evidence of the other guests either. Presumably they were exploring the town or on a tour.

He turned back to her, his face concerned. "That is—unfortunate. I thought perhaps I could claim it from his effects. It was—important."

Light glared off the pool and the glass tabletops so she shaded her eyes with her hand. "Important how?"

"Simon had it with him for a long time. It was expensive. Something he bought himself as a special gift, he said. I thought—I thought if it was here, I might sell it so that I could send the money home to my family."

She thought about it a moment. It was hard to believe that the odious little bit of rainbow cloth she'd touched could be of much value.

"Even the lovely Pashmina scarves Becca and I saw were only worth a little over a hundred Canadian dollars. That's not going to help your family very much."

"It was bigger than it looked…" He stopped, looked as if he was about to say something more, but then he nodded. "You are probably right."

He left her for his room, but he had disturbed her quiet contemplation, and all the negative stuff from earlier in the day came blowing in like a gale.

She needed to move to quiet the storm. She stood up, thinking to go for a swim, but decided on a walk. She went back to her room to claim her purse and thankfully Becca was in the shower. She told Alice she was going for a walk to clear her head and would stop at the bank to reclaim her card. Alice offered to go with her, but Phoebe demurred.

It would be good to be alone with her thoughts.

The afternoon sun was a hammer on her bare head, but she headed toward the water where there would be a breeze and stopped at the bank on the way.

The ATM kiosk gleamed, an incongruous bit of plastic and chrome amongst the old stone buildings and flowering plants. She followed the path around the building to the office she and Becca had visited what seemed like an eternity ago. She pushed inside the glass door into the cool of the fan whirring on the ceiling. The same young woman in western clothes sat at the desk reading magazines. She looked up at Phoebe as if surprised she'd returned.

Phoebe reintroduced herself. "I'm here about my bank card. Your ATM machine ate it this morning and you said the manager with the key would be here this afternoon."

"Yes. Yes. I recall. You will have a seat please, while I get the manager."

The woman waved Phoebe into the single hard-backed chair. While Phoebe sat, the woman knocked on a narrow side door, then opened it and poked her head inside. She spoke in rapid-fire Malayalam, then returned to Phoebe and her desk.

"He will be with you in a minute."

The young woman returned to her reading as one minute stretched into five, then eight, and Phoebe's patience began to simmer. She kept reminding herself that this wasn't Canada and, from what she'd seen of India, nothing worked quickly here. She settled back in her chair and focused on her calming breathing exercises.

At ten minutes, the narrow door opened and a slim-hipped, young man entered the room. He was dressed in the ubiquitous pressed trousers and crisp white shirt, though his sleeves were rolled down and buttoned at the cuffs.

"Yes, may I help you, Madam?" he gave a slight bow.

Phoebe stood and explained about her card being eaten and how she wished to get it back.

The young man nodded through her story and even after she finished.

"There is—was—a problem with your card, Madam. Our computer said it was stolen and the card was to be destroyed."

"What?" Her frustration threatened to boil over from the froth of anger in her gut. "That card was never out of my possession!"

He held up his hands as if to ward her off. "Please, Madam. Please. The fact that you immediately reported the problem to our office and left your name and contact information suggested there might be an error. I retrieved your card from the machine this morning and managed to contact your bank. They assured me that there have been no reports of the card being stolen. I have just contacted my head office to advise them of the irregularity and to seek permission to return your card." He gave that little head waggle and as his words sank in, the action was charming.

He was helping her.

"So you have my card?"

He fished in his shirt breast pocket and produced a familiar gray and red card. "But first there is the matter of confirming your identity and the paperwork."

It took another ten minutes, but it didn't matter. Something had gone right today. Something had gone right in Kochi. Now if the police could just interview Ijay Das, Becca could be cleared and they could get on with their lives.

When the young man returned her card and asked whether there was anything else he could do for her, it took only a second of thought. "I'd like to withdraw five hundred U.S. dollars."

"Of course, Madam."

Fifteen minutes later she left and turned toward the water, the money in her travel safe feeling like a too-conspicuous wad under her shirt.

This afternoon the great nets were in use, dipping down into the water and then up again, like gigantic deformed herons. Beneath the dipping monstrosities, small boats were pulled up on shore, their crews sorting through turquoise nets that caught the sunlight. Small fish glittered as they were tossed into buckets. Crows lined the ropes of the Chinese nets and leapt into the air like flotsam on waves as they dove to feed on discarded catch. Shoals of tourists took photos from the net's walkways, while other more intrepid photographers went down among the beach garbage to photograph the fishermen. She passed the open-air fish market with its fresh fish lined up on the ground and men swiftly bartering their prices.

She stopped.

The parking lot lay just beyond the line of trees. Should she go through with asking Ijay Das for more information and to give a statement to the police? Detective Mathias had said the man was dangerous and untrustworthy, but as far as she knew, Ijay Das was the only one who could completely clear Becca.

Who was she kidding? The only reason she had five hundred US dollars in her possession was to do exactly that. It was daylight. The parking lot would be busy. She'd be safe. Maybe she could escort Ijay to the police station. Or she could call Detective Mathias to join them here.

It all depended on whether Ijay Das was even here.

The dusty parking lot was once more crowded with small tour

busses and private vehicles, and the scent of exhaust battled with the salty ocean air. Dust rose at her footfall and heat reflected off the metal vehicles.

Sweat beaded Phoebe's forehead and ran through her hair and down her neck. Lovely. Just lovely when she was hoping to be cool and collected when she met Ijay Das again.

Movement at one side of the lot stopped her dead. Trevor and Jeannie stood in the sun, Jeannie's red hair gleaming over a dark green t-shirt. Trevor's shaved head gleamed darkly and his khaki shirt was stained dark with sweat. They were talking to someone hidden in the shade of the trees.

Phoebe stepped back into the shadow of a bus. Clearly the photographers were deep in conversation with someone, and from the location, Phoebe could guess who. Trevor reached into his breast pocket and brought out his wallet. He handed the unseen person what looked like folded cash or maybe a business card. She couldn't be sure. Then Trevor reached down and the unseen person came into view. Ijay Das shook Trevor's hand.

The photographers then walked away to the street beyond the parking area. Phoebe stayed where she was as she watched them go. They turned toward old Kochi and sauntered away as if they hadn't a care in the world.

What the hell? Were Trevor and Jeannie meddling in the investigation? Or, given what she'd overheard, were they trying to find Simon's connections or make their own? From what Detective Mathias had said, Ijay Das would likely have many criminal connections.

Her legs felt weak at the betrayal by people who might not be bosom buddies, but they'd at least been new friends. At least she'd thought so.

Until she couldn't any longer.

Maybe paying Ijay wasn't such a good idea. If Detective Mathias had already interviewed the man, then there was no need for her to do this…

She edged through the parking lot using the busses and tourist vans to mask her location until she had a view of the shaded area under the trees.

Ijay and his men were packing up their scant belongings—blankets, a pot or two, perhaps a bundle of clothing. Ijay yelled something up at the lad who stretched on a branch in the tree. He scampered down like a monkey only to huddle amongst the motley band.

Four of the men each hefted one of the benches. Then the whole group shuffled off along the wall under the trees and into the street. With the sun beating down, they headed toward the main Kochi port and the old town. The fact that they took the benches with them suggested they weren't coming back.

Even in the bus's shade, the heat and humidity were insufferable. Sweat poured down her back and between her breasts.

What if Detective Mathias hadn't interviewed Ijay Das? What if he hadn't been able to find him?

She hauled out her phone, found a number for the Kochi police station, and dialed. When someone answered she asked for Detective Mathias, but was told that he was delayed at a meeting. He was expected back momentarily. She gave them her number and told them it was urgent. Please have Detective Mathias call her.

She thought a moment. "Listen. I'm calling about the murder of the man found in the fishing net. There is a man—Ijay Das—he has important information for the case, but he is leaving his camp. He has packed up his belongings and left his camp by the seawall. Someone needs to stop him—bring him in for an interview."

The person at the other end of the phone paused. "That is Detective Mathias's case."

Phoebe looked heavenward and took a deep breath. "I know that. But if Ijay has left when Detective Mathias arrives, there'll be no one for him to interview. I'm asking you to send someone to follow Ijay Das until Detective Mathias is available."

"Thank you for your call, Madam. I will see that appropriate action is taken."

She could almost hear the head waggle of the person at the other end of the phone as her connection was cut off. She didn't think there was much chance the Kochi police were going to arrive, which meant she had to wait for Mathias to call her back. If he got the message.

When she looked back to the street, Ijay and his men were gone.

Behind her the ocean roared and the Chinese nets creaked and groaned. The street was empty, the parking lot full of sunburned vehicles. Given Ijay and his men had taken all their belongings, they could be leaving Kochi for good.

She hurried across the parking lot and out to the street. She couldn't let Ijay simply walk away… If she followed him a little way, at least she could tell Mathias where he was headed.

Narrow as all the other streets in Kochi that she had seen, this one curved through tall, spreading trees that laced shade over the pavement. Looking at the old walled homes and churches, she could almost imagine the clip-clop of horse-drawn carriages and the soft laughter of ladies with parasols and long dresses from the heyday of the Raj.

She rounded the curve. Still no sign of Ijay. If she'd lost him, she'd never forgive herself.

Panic sent her running down the road, checking the side streets as she went. No group of men down any of them. Heck, there was barely anyone except a few tourist busses releasing their load of passengers in front of a guesthouse or some tourist sight that Phoebe had missed.

She ran faster, the afternoon sun like a forge overhead, sweat running down her face, her arms, her legs. She rounded another curve of road and there, ahead, sauntered the group of men with Ijay at their head. He was using a cell phone. She stopped and hung back behind a swell of orange bougainvillea hanging over a wall.

In the sliver of shade, she caught her breath and watched the men down the street. When they turned a corner, she left her refuge and dashed after them, only to spot them still ahead, taking another turn like a procession or parade. First went Ijay like a drum major. Behind him was the boy, gamboling like a clown, running up to tourist storefronts and grabbing small items. If he was spotted, he'd drop the item. If not, he'd run back and give whatever he'd taken to Ijay, like a dog returning a ball to its master. Behind them came a gaggle of six other men, others joining them, as if appearing out of cracks between the white and gray buildings. In their faded dhoti or shirts and trousers, Phoebe was sure she'd probably passed them unnoticed against the walls.

She spun around to check behind her, but there was no one there.

When she turned back, Ijay and his crew were disappearing around another corner. She hurried after them.

The tourist town of bright storefronts gradually fell behind and the buildings grew older. She could smell the ocean, but also the potent stink of fresh cloves and open sewage that made her eyes water. The buildings were taller, some three and four stories, some painted in bright purple or yellow or brick color. An open sewer ran along the side of the road. Trucks blocked the street as spindly-legged men unloaded backbreaking bags of rice brought in from the mainland. Traffic backed up behind the trucks and huge tour busses came up behind to apparently stopper the end of the street. Ijay and his men threaded through it all and kept on going.

She looked at her cell phone. Where was that damned detective? Should she call him again? She shouldn't be the one following Ijay Das and she wasn't sure how much farther she should keep going, especially given what Mathias had said about the dangers of the man. Heck, she wasn't even certain she could find her way back now.

The rumble of huge diesel engines said they were near the harbor. Between the buildings on her left she caught glimpses of a large ship steaming past. Was Ijay leaving by ship? Had he used his mobile phone to arrange passage?

The last of Ijay's men disappeared around the latest truck blocking the road. Laborers bent double under heavy rice bags unloaded into the dim interior of a warehouse. She shoved around the mess of vehicles, dodged the two wiry men who unloaded the truck's bags, and pressed into the shadows around the side of the huge, brightly painted truck. The stench of metal and diesel and ocean salt was almost overwhelming. She turned sideways to slip past the truck's cab when suddenly the cab door opened.

Ijay's boy leapt down at her. She jerked back. From behind strong arms caught her and a hand covered her mouth. The other arm wrapped around her shoulders, hefted her off her feet, and dragged her back as she fought—kicked—elbowed—tried to stomp on his foot. The world reduced to salt-stained, white walls, a narrow strip of dappled sunlight above, and the receding side of the truck as Ijay's boy gamboled after her. Her captor dragged her into shadows where the buildings were so close her shoulders touched both sides. Then a small door opened in the white wall to her left. Two stairs led downward into darkness. She fought to stay where she was, grabbed for the door frame. Kicked her captor again. Again.

Once she was inside, no one would see her. No one would be able to hear her.

She bit his palm. Ripped her head free and screamed.

He swung her around, slammed her into the wall, and punched her in the stomach before shoving her through the opening. She stumbled down the two steps and the door slammed behind her.

More arms caught her and dragged her farther into darkness as if she was drowning. She kicked and scratched and felt her feet connect. Hands grabbed her arms and shoulders. More hands rifled her pockets.

They pulled out her phone, pulled the lanyard with the cotton travel safe that held her money, bank card, and passport from around her neck.

Then a single bare lightbulb flared to life overhead and she found herself facing Ijay Das. She felt like retching. Her stomach throbbed.

"What do you want?" she managed around the pain. She strained at the hands that still held her arms.

Studying her, he lit a cigarette and exhaled his signature line of *o*'s. "I believe I should ask you the same thing, Phoebe Clay. Why are you following us?"

"Because you looked like you were leaving before you'd given the police your information."

He chuckled and set free another line of smaller *o*'s.

One of Ijay's men exclaimed in Malayalam and Ijay turned to him. The man held up the wad of US dollars. Ijay took them from him and stuffed them in a pocket.

"So you were bringing me my money, were you?"

She shrugged, not knowing what to say.

He grinned at her, his teeth dark yellow in the incandescent light. "What is it you would like to know, Phoebe Clay?"

She felt like a cornered mouse facing a cat. Plead to be released or ask what he knew? He had her money anyway and Ijay Das didn't strike her as a man who listened to pleading. But at least if they were talking he wasn't killing her. Maybe they could make a connection. Maybe he would let her go.

Swallowing, she thought back to her information and what she still needed to know. "The man who met Simon. You said he gave Simon a package? What can you tell me about that?"

"It was about this big." Still grinning as if he played with her, he held up his hands to show a package under a foot square. "But it was only about six inches deep."

"Was it a box?"

He shook his head. "A parcel wrapped in white cloth like other parcels." He frowned. "I—I think it was soft, bendable."

"So the two of them meet. They embrace and the young man has a parcel. You said the young man had an accent. If you could hear that, you must have heard what they said."

"Aah. Now we come to the heart of the matter." Ijay smiled, this time as if he almost meant it. "I had not expected you to come back to that. Most people would not have."

"The police would," she said, her heart rate slowing slightly. The fact he was answering was good, wasn't it? Maybe he would let her go.

His head gave a little wobble and the light bulb carved deep shadows into his eyes and around his mouth. "Perhaps. There was the usual 'good to see you' and other such salutations. The young man stroked your Simon's arm and the fabric he had in his pocket. There were enquiries after family—the young man's father and sister both doing well, but apparently unhappy that Simon was here. And more enquiries after school. Then your Simon asked if there had been any difficulty and the young man patted the parcel. He said the Kashmiri had delivered it only that morning. It was first quality and just as well camouflaged as Simon's own.

"It was then that they walked away down the seawall." Ijay sighed and the light caught his yellowed teeth, but left his eyes in shadow. The interior of his mouth was too pink and hungry by half.

Phoebe looked away from the unsettling sight. "Did you see anything else? Hear anything?"

"It was dark. I did not follow them, but after a short while there were raised voices. One of my people said he saw someone running. That is all I know."

Or all he was willing to tell her. By his bored expression, that was the case. He nodded at the men who held her and they dragged her across the small room to an open door.

"Wait! Please! You spoke to two other people today. Westerners. The woman had red hair."

Ijay held up a hand; the men held her where she was.

Ijay crossed the room to her and leaned in too close. "Were you watching me, Phoebe Clay?"

He released a puff of fetid smoke directly into her face and suddenly she was very afraid. This man could answer all her questions, but it was clear he had no plans to 'connect with her', no plans to let her go.

"N-no. I came into the parking lot and saw them talking to you. They're on the tour with us. What did they want?"

"They wanted information on people who deal with Kashmir. I told them to check in the market as there are many there."

Kashmir. Trevor and Jeannie had been asking about Kashmir, and Simon's contact had also brought a package with a product from Kashmir. Didn't they grow poppies there?

Heroin?

If so, she'd gotten herself mixed up in something very dangerous, indeed.

She drew herself up as straight as she could and nodded. She would not look cowed to this man though she was as frightened as she'd ever been in her life. "That's all I want to know. Now, you have your money. Surely you can let me go."

Ijay Das barked a laugh and the men suddenly shoved her backward through the open door and into darkness. The door slammed shut behind her blocking all light and she heard the snap and slide of a metal bolt.

Then she was alone. Lost in Kochi.

That was when she started to shake.

15

Inky darkness. Phoebe's rough breathing and the wild pounding of her heart almost masked the muffled voices from the room outside her prison and the more distant rumble of ships' diesels. The air hung musty and damp against her skin. It smelled of seawater and she was drowning in the darkness and her hopeless situation.

She wanted to scream. At the men who had abducted her. At herself for following them. At Detective Mathias, who hadn't returned her call. If she could just get out the screams, maybe she'd stop shaking.

Her knees shook. Her shoulder throbbed from when she'd hit the wall during her struggle with the men. Her stomach still pulsed with pain. Shudders ran through her. But damn it all, if she gave in to the terror, she'd never get out of here. At least not alive and sane.

She had to keep her wits about her. She inhaled against the tight feeling in her chest. Screaming wasn't going to help. From what she'd seen, these old buildings had thick walls, and she was pretty sure Ijay Das wouldn't have put her anywhere anyone could hear her shouts.

At least he hadn't killed her. That was something, right? Something to hold on to? And the floor seemed dry underfoot. At least she wasn't standing in water. All good, wasn't it?

As if there was anything good about her situation. But hadn't she lived through worse?

Still trembling, she put her arms out in front of her and took a tentative step toward where the door should be.

Her fingers brushed rough wood and a surge of relief ran through her, though she wasn't sure why. But the door gave her situation solidity and something she could deal with. She traced the edge of the door—barely taller than her head, but broader than doors were back home—perhaps five feet. By the feel of the wood, she'd say it was old. Probably as old as the old town that she'd been walking through. Not that that information helped her get out of here.

Beyond the door, the voices had stopped. Had they abandoned her here or were they listening to her. She didn't know which frightened her most.

She pressed her ear to the crack at the edge of the door but still heard nothing. "Ijay! Ijay Das! Are you still there?"

Was that a slight scuffling sound? Was someone out there?

"Why are you doing this to me, Ijay?" What could she say that might influence him? "I'm sorry I followed you. My sister and I don't have much money. We're not rich, but I'll give you more if you'll just let me go." It was a hollow offering. He already had her five hundred dollars.

Still no response, even though she could hear the desperation in her voice. Surely any listener would respond.

So they'd left her here.

She fought down a new surge of panic. Keep busy. Keep moving. Don't curl into a ball.

In the darkness, she traced the wall away from the door. Two feet away it turned at a right angle. She paced ten lengths of her feet along, so about eight feet on this wall. Around another corner, she paced another ten lengths of her feet. They'd put her in an eight-by-eight holding cell and left her. To die?

It would be easy enough to do...

The flutter of panic took wing in her chest. She chose not to believe it—had to keep her wits about herself so she could take her chance whenever it came. That meant that she had to keep up her strength. She settled herself to wait on the floor opposite the door. The stone was cold and chilled her back. Her shoulder throbbed. Her stomach ached. She focused on the door and checked her watch. Its antiquated glow-in-the-dark dial read five forty-five p.m.

Surely Detective Mathias would have received her message by now. Surely he would have tried her phone and had no response. Surely he'd be looking for her and Ijay Das.

Or he could ignore her as a meddling fool. She prayed that wasn't the case.

Meanwhile the others would be getting ready for dinner. Becca and Alice would be beside themselves with worry, being consoled by none other than Trevor and Jeannie. Dear God, she'd placed her entire family in danger this time! Did Trevor and Jeannie know that she'd seen them? Had they arranged for her to be taken? It would be easy enough for them to do something to an unsuspecting Becca and Alice, too.

And here she was helpless to help them.

She banged her head back against the wall. Again. Again.

The pain helped her forget the way her heart was racing.

The rumble of the huge diesel engines of the ocean-going ships reverberated through the thick walls. With its great deep-sea harbor, Kochi would be the perfect place for Ijay and his men to take ship. It was also a great place to lose a small parcel of something valuable off the side of a boat.

Or a body.

Hers? Why did she keep getting herself into these situations? What was wrong with her? The shivers returned with a vengeance. She wrapped her arms around herself. She must have closed her eyes at some point for she woke with a start.

Voices came from beyond the door. She stood, listening, but the voices were too indistinct to hear the words.

She used the flat of her palm on the door and the sound echoed hollowly through her cell. The voices stopped. A stir of movement came from beyond the door and then metal-on-metal scraped and snapped as the door bolt was opened. The door pulled open and Phoebe blinked in the blinding brilliance of the single lightbulb in the outer room. The people were dark blurs to her light-deprived eyes, but gradually resolved into Ijay Das, his men, and a sari-clad woman.

She turned toward Phoebe, the light catching the turquoise of her sari and placing highlights on her black hair.

Avni.

Surprise froze Phoebe. Then dismay. "Avni? What are you doing here?" She looked from the silent Avni to Ijay Das. "What's going on?"

Avni's gaze searched Phoebe's face. "It seems that troubles follow you, Phoebe Clay. I was asked to come and ensure that it was you."

Asked to come? Surely, that could only mean Becca had sent her. Relief surged through her.

But why send Avni? And where was Detective Mathias?

She frowned. "Are Becca and Alice okay? They must be worried sick. Is this…is this a ransom or something?"

Avni glanced in Ijay's direction and back at Phoebe. She smiled. "Your sister and niece are fine. At the moment. They are at the guesthouse."

At the moment? What did that mean? Phoebe stopped.

Avni's smile never neared her eyes.

"You have seen enough," Ijay said, stepping between them. "It is her with the questions. She continues asking. I suggest that you return with the money or surely there will be more trouble." He lifted his chin at Phoebe and two of his men grabbed her shoulders.

"No! Please! Don't hurt them! Leave Becca and Alice alone! I won't try anything." Oh, God, no! She'd put them in danger by asking her questions.

They shoved her back into the dark room. She stumbled against the far wall and the door swung toward her.

She lunged for the opening. "Leave my sister and niece alone!"

The door slammed shut. The bolt shot home.

Blocking all light.

All hope.

16

———————

S he pounded her fists on the door until the room outside went silent again.

Then she slumped to the floor, the door at her back. She had to get out of here, but her explorations before had shown that there was no way out. Helplessness filled her and she thought she might be sick.

Why was Avni doing this? She always acted like she liked them. She'd even offered to introduce Alice to her daughter. But that was before Simon died…

Could she be involved with Simon's murder?

The chilling dark pressed in around Phoebe. The stone walls weighed her down and her breath came in short, sharp, desperate gasps as if she couldn't quite feed her lungs.

But it made no sense. Avni had been working the night Simon was killed. Becca had mentioned seeing her the night she and Simon went out. How could she be involved? Was she part of the smuggling ring Phoebe now suspected Simon was involved with? Had Jeannie and Trevor made the connection and enlisted Avni to come and check that Phoebe was contained before they took over the network? What would they do with her? With Becca and Alice?

She shivered in the cold.

She couldn't think of another reason for Avni to be here.

And, she couldn't think of a single reason Avni might be meeting with Ijay Das that would be good for the welfare of one Phoebe Clay.

Feeling incredibly alone, Phoebe shook her head in the darkness. Ijay had said the last person he had seen Simon with was a young Indian man who delivered a parcel. So how did that relate to Avni? Was she the young man's wife?

But that didn't make sense given the greeting Ijay described between Simon and the young man.

But then, Zamir had a wife and children and was still with Simon…

Or was Avni a sister? That could be right, too, but regardless of whether Avni was somehow related to the young man, there was still the question of why she was here. Either she was here on behalf of Becca to pay off a ransom Ijay demanded—an option that seemed less likely the more Phoebe thought about it—or she was part of the crime and had paid Ijay to keep Phoebe quiet and contained.

Unfortunately, that made way too much sense.

And suggested an ending to Phoebe Clay that she really didn't care to think about.

The frustrating afternoon ticked away into desperate evening. Eight thirty by the watch they'd left on Phoebe's wrist. The chill through the stone floor eventually forced her to her feet. Listening to the regular thrum of the passing ships' diesel engines, she paced the room, rubbing her arms and legs for warmth and, ironically, desperately missing the heat of the day. At one point she'd been forced to use a corner of the cell as a washroom, so the acrid stink of urine cut through the smells of the sea. Of course, the day was passing. Dusk came quickly this close to the equator and by now the shadows would have flooded the streets and the flutter of moths would be around the streetlights. The jasmine would sweeten the air around the Scandinavian Guesthouse but Becca and Alice wouldn't notice. They'd be too busy worrying about Phoebe's absence if they hadn't been taken hostage themselves.

She winced at the thought. Alice had already been through the horror of being abducted. Becca had lived through the terror of not knowing whether her daughter or sister would survive.

There was no way Becca would know what to do if her situation got dicey.

No, that was selling her sister and niece short. Alice was smart as a whip—a trait she'd inherited from her mother. Becca had simply never been placed in a situation such as this. She wasn't prepared. But then Phoebe hadn't been prepared to deal with a school shooting, either, but in the face of that reality, she'd managed.

Well…actually, she'd bungled helping Rick just as she'd bungled her attempt to help Becca.

The knowledge sat more leaden than a bullet in her chest.

Restlessly, she circumnavigated the room until the lock suddenly screeched and the old wood door swung open. She fell back from the blinding light, but two men entered her cell, grabbed her arms, and yanked her into the adjoining room.

They pulled her arms behind her back and tied her wrists. Then they stuffed a twist of fetid cloth into her mouth and gagged her. A bag stinking of onions was yanked over her head. The men dragged-carried her up two steps and set her down. Blessedly warm evening air moved across her skin. She was back in the alley.

They turned her and pushed her to get her moving. A firm hand held her biceps and guided her along. Then she was stopped and stood there swaying. The mild ocean breeze blew full on her body. Waves lapped a nearby shore. Together they said she hadn't been brought to the street. She stood beside the ocean, the warm wind damp against her skin. The hollow sound of water on wood suggested a boat or wharf was waiting.

She backpedaled into her captor's hands. No way in heck was she getting into a boat. Who knew where the hell she'd end up if she did?

Drowning with the fishes came to mind.

Was another body going to be found in Chinese fishing nets tomorrow?

The rough hands on her arms kept her from backing away. She

fought them—kicking, stomping on feet she couldn't see. Throwing herself sideways and back until both handlers pushed and released her. She fell.

She landed on her side in shallow water and came up gasping against the sodden onion bag. The cloth plastered her face. It was hard to breathe. She rolled and struggled, trying to stand, but her feet sank in deep mud. Floundering, she went down again.

Rough hands found her arms and shoulders and wrenched her up out of the water and out of her sandals, only to drop her with a thud. Her shoulder exploded in pain.

Hollow wood under her. The boat. She'd try to get off, but at the moment, breathing was her first concern.

She shook her head and the bag parted from her nostrils. She sucked in onion-scented air and coughed, choked, spluttered.

Someone shoved her aside and the surface under her shifted. An old outboard motor came to life and the boat lurched and began to rock under her.

They'd left shore and she was likely in one of those rough wooden fisherman's boats she'd seen beached by the fishing nets.

The small boat turned away from the wind and set a course that set it running up onto the waves and then pounding down into the trough between them. Each time the boat dropped out from under her hip and shoulder, she thought it was the last, and then she crash-landed on the slatted hull. Over and over as if she was a piece of meat being tenderized. Against the battering she clung to the fact that she didn't think the boat was headed for open water. In fact, she was pretty sure that they were traveling deeper into Kochi's massive harbor. That suggested that maybe they weren't going to drop her overboard to kill her.

She could hope.

But if not kill her, where were they taking her and why?

The boat motor's roar lessened a little. The craft angled into the wind and the constant rise and fall subsided. Phoebe huddled on her side, her knees brought up to her chest, her forehead down to her knees as the boat's keel scraped bottom. A lurch and the sound of splashing and spray of water on her arms told her that someone had leapt off and was dragging the boat up into shore. Then more hands grabbed her shoulders and lifted her up. The side of the boat scraped her muddy shins, and then she was dropped unceremoniously into the water.

17

P hoebe landed hard on her side. A wave washed over her head, plastering the bag to her head once more and filling her nose. She tried to sit up, but with her hands tied behind her and mud underneath, she couldn't get any purchase. Another wave shoved her under again and then someone grabbed her and dragged her toward shore. She lay on her side, coughing and hacking around the gag. Her lungs hurt. So did her body—everywhere—but her shoulder burned as if she'd done something more. It came to her then, why Avni had been there with Ijay.

She felt old, tired, and desperate, not to mention foolish.

If any money had changed hands, it was to get rid of her and maintain Ijay's silence. The man was, after all, a businessman. And if Ijay had information, he was likely to try to sell it to the highest bidders—the people trying to solve the crime and the people who committed it. The murderers wouldn't want anyone knowing what they'd done or anyone drawing connections. Phoebe had obviously been getting too close. And by doing so she'd put all of them at risk because clearly these were desperate people.

Rough hands dragged her up and sent her stumbling, barefoot, up a slope. Sharp stones cut her feet. The scrape of stone on stone, a twig snapping, the squeal of gravel all told her that the person gripping her arm wasn't alone. The wind off the water chilled her sodden clothes, but then the ocean smell dissipated and she smelled the cool of trees. Heard leaves rippling overhead as she stumbled, dripping, through the darkness, the firm hold never leaving her arm.

At first the path was rough gravel and crushed grass. Then they crossed pavement and followed a rough path with more tall grass that swished against her legs. The sound of vehicle traffic came from off to her left. If she could only see, maybe she could get away and run. Surely someone would help if they saw a bound woman running.

Rocks bruised her feet. At one point she stepped on glass. They didn't stop, just pushed her, limping, on a circuitous route that traveled through narrow spaces and under trees until suddenly they must have come out in the open for the air felt different on her skin. Dry grass brushed her lower legs and crackled under her feet. The smells changed, too. Distant jasmine mingled with the onions of the bag over her head. And something else that she couldn't place.

She was shoved forward and tripped over a doorsill, fell to her knees, and the door closed with a well-oiled click behind her.

Swaying with fatigue and afraid to move, she stayed on her knees, head bowed. Then she sat down on her heels and felt the door behind her. She banged her head against the door hoping to get some attention. The door rattled loosely in its frame but there was no reaction from beyond. They'd left her wherever this was and were gone.

Which suggested that even if she could get her gag off and scream, no one would hear her. Defeated, she settled herself to wait with her head back against the door. She had to pee again and she was pretty sure there was no way she could get her capri's off without using her hands to undo them.

It was hard to think. The onion-scented bag seemed to compress around her head, muffling sounds and smells and keeping her blind. It felt like it smothered not only her senses, but also her mind. Just what were they going to do with her?

More importantly, what was happening to Alice and Becca?

Ijay must have gone to the killer immediately after Simon was killed. He must have asked for hush money with the intent of continuing to milk that source over the years to come. Then along came Phoebe asking questions.

That would give Ijay more than enough motive to lure her in and then take her captive. Frankly, it was surprising that they hadn't killed her already. They were likely trying to decide just how much Becca and Alice knew, too.

Her hands shook at the realization. Then her arms joined in, and then the rest of her body spasmed in wracking tremors. She was in serious trouble, and bound like this, she couldn't see how she was going to get out of it. Because from her read of the situation, Simon's killer had no choice but to kill again.

She wasn't going to simply lay here and wait for her fate!

Using the wall for support, she awkwardly climbed to her feet. Then she started pacing the walls, running her shoulder and arm along the wall. The walls weren't stone this time. Instead, the outside walls were closely-spaced smooth boards over a frame of two-by-fours. Sturdy enough if you want to store something, but not necessarily strong enough to hold a determined woman.

She returned to the door and ran the side of her sack-covered face around the frame. The woven sack caught on something at about elbow high. A hinge? A nail head?

She went to her knees and ran the sack over whatever it was until the sack caught again. She put her weight on the sack and heard fabric tearing. Was that a patch of slightly less dark?

Invigorated, she repeated her action. Maybe she could get the sack off. Heck, maybe she could come up with a way to get her hands free, too!

The world reduced to the something sharp on the inside of the shed and the sack on her head. Gradually, the sack shredded until it was a loose bag of threads that pooled across her head and around her neck. But through them she could see. The shed was dark, but between the boards and through a narrow space between the roof and the walls came an amber light that could only be streetlights. So she wasn't in the middle of nowhere.

Having the bag off her head not only gave her light, it dissipated the scent of onions. There was another scent present that she couldn't quite place, but it reminded her of her basement back home.

She turned back to the blessed nail—yes, it was a nail head—and stood to try the same fraying method on the ropes binding her wrists. She caught them on the nail and leaned forward, trying to either stretch the rope or tear it. She didn't care which. If she could stretch it, she might be able to get a hand free. If she could tear it, she might get free, too.

A few strands of the rope gave way each time she pulled. Unfortunately, the nail loosened. So much so that she was afraid it would pull free and she'd lose it in the darkness. She twisted the nail in the wood and without much work it came free.

She sat down and, sweating with effort, used the nail tip to tear at the ropes. Whoever wrote about doing so in mystery books didn't really know what they were talking about. It was awkward and almost futile unless you had wrists that were a heck of a lot more bendy than hers. She was swearing by the time she finally collapsed, still bound, against the wall.

At this rate she was going to be exactly where they'd left her when her captors returned. Tearing the hood to shreds didn't mean a thing. Neither did frayed ropes as long as they held.

If she could just get out of here, there was a chance that she could sneak away. Her legs were, after all, free. She eyed the patch of darkness that was the door and stood. If it was built as simply as the rest of the building, then there was every possibility that it wasn't built for security. The open space between wall and roof suggested that theory. That meant the door and lock probably weren't the heaviest material.

She worked her shoulders and winced at the movement. She couldn't afford to baby her injury. She was strong from the daily kayaking she'd enjoyed recently. Fraying the ropes on her wrists might not have freed her, but it had loosened her bonds so they no longer dragged her shoulders so far back. If she could hunch to protect her neck and use the weight of her five-foot-seven frame, maybe she could bull her way out of here.

Then she could find help and call 911 or whatever the equivalent was in Kochi.

She blew out a breath, knowing there was a slim chance of success, but at least it was something.

Setting her shoulders and taking a breath, she drove herself across the shed, leading with her left shoulder. The crash broke the night's silence.

The door flexed under impact and sent her reeling back. Her shoulder screamed in protest. She held her breath, listening, praying that there was no one close enough to hear.

Like Avni or Ijay or one of Ijay's men.

Or the killer.

When nothing happened, she drove into the door again.

Was that a groan of the wood? She was groaning herself. Her shoulder throbbed so badly tears filled her eyes, but she had to use this time as a gift and do everything she could to help herself and Alice and Becca.

She tried three more times until she collapsed in the shed's back corner, sobbing at the unbearable pain. The damnable door was looser, she was sure. It rattled more on its hinges, but the lock still held on the other side of the door.

Damn it, she couldn't even wipe her eyes or nose. She couldn't even use her shoulder. Finally, she cleared her nose by blowing outward and was disgusted at the satisfying plop of snot on the floorboards. Desperate times, desperate measures, and she was darn well not giving up.

She returned to the door. If the lock wasn't giving but the hinges were, well then, she needed to focus her efforts on the hinges.

She kicked sideways, trying to channel her inner ninja and project all her energy through her foot and into the door.

It didn't quite work because she stumbled and landed on her bum on the floor.

She awkwardly regained her feet and shook her kicking leg to clear the pins and needles, then drove another blow into the door.

The sound of metal ripping through wood was the most beautiful sound she'd ever heard. Her hip and knee shot pain when she put weight on them, but she went to try the door. Something had ripped free, but the door still held, though it rattled more. When she felt the hinges, it was clear that the lowest hinge had ripped loose. The middle one was twisted, but the top one held. So did the lock holding the door on the other side.

She repositioned herself because putting the force of impact on the middle hinge was going to require a higher kick. She drove the bottom of her foot into the door next to the hinge. Did it again and lost her balance, tumbling onto her side. Her leg was on fire. So was her hip. She wasn't sure whether she could stand, which would be a good laugh on her if she wanted to get out of here.

Hauling herself up to sitting and wincing against the pain, she crawled to the door to see what she'd accomplished. When she rattled the door, the whole thing swayed on a pivot between the top hinge and the lock.

Maybe… She used her good shoulder to shove the freed bottom corner outward. She pushed farther until there was a wedge-shaped space about ten inches high at its tallest and running the full breadth of the door's bottom.

Big enough for a woman to slip through.

Maybe.

On her belly, with her hands still tied, she wriggled forward, using her head to push the door ajar. Her head and neck poked free and then her shoulders. Her bare toes scrabbled on the shed floor as she forced her hips through the opening and then fell-rolled-slithered the rest of the way out the door and down the step to lay on brittle grass that smelled of dew and life and sunshine even in the darkness.

She was free. Sort of.

She rolled onto her back and above was a net of stars that even the lights of Kochi couldn't dim. Most of the constellations were unfamiliar, but Orion was still there, with his mighty sword ready for action. She could do with a sword like that to cut her wrists free.

Fighting her way to her feet, she scanned her surroundings.

Streetlights sat beyond a low wall and tall trees that bounded rows of sheds and an open field. The shed that she'd fought her way out of was located in the row of sheds farthest back from the street, presumably so people couldn't hear any fuss she made. The sheds backed onto an open field that separated the sheds from the nearest house by the length of at least a football field. Dry brittle grass rattled in the breeze, but it was the ranks of poles and sagging rope lines that told her where she was—that and the scents that she now recognized as detergent, scorched fabric, and rice water.

Dhobi khana. She stood at the edge of the field that in daylight would be filled with gleaming sheets and shirts. At this hour, the row upon row of poles and lines reminded her of the product of a giant spider.

What the hell was she doing here and how could she use it to her advantage? Clearly Avni was connected to this place. A relative of one of the workers perhaps?

She could figure that out later. At the moment her task was to get away. She scanned the way to the road, but she was not going any closer to the main shed. From what she'd seen in other parts of India, there could be people sleeping there even though the noise she'd made breaking out of the shed surely should have brought them here. She turned toward the field. That would be a better option, but it was going to be tough slogging ducking under and over the ropes with her arms still tied. With the gag still on, she couldn't even yell for help.

She needed to get rid of her bonds. She crept back against the row of sheds. From this side, the shed that had held her wasn't even locked. It simply had a metal bolt rammed home to keep her captive. This was only one of the sheds, so perhaps she could find something to help her in one of the other buildings.

The next shed in the row had a similar closure. Using her shoulder, she slid the bolt open and peered inside. The air was close with the scent of wool and incense. Odd. Wool wasn't something usually laundered like cotton. She stepped inside. In the corner sat a hip-high, sheet-wrapped bundle like she'd seen in the ironing shed of the dhobi khana. Hung on the wall above the bundle was a shelf that held a clear bottle, a small brazier complete with the stub of an incense stick, and—praise the deity that had brought them here—a pair of shears.

She hurried to the shelf and used her teeth to haul the shears off the shelf. They tumbled onto the top of the bundle and she fumbled for them with her bound hands.

It was hard to hold shears with bound hands. It was even harder to cut the bonds that held her wrists—like downright impossible. She finally gave up that idea, sank down on the floor, and opened the shears. Then she started running the ropes over the cutting edge. The trouble was, the shears kept falling over. She needed a way to prop them firmly in place.

Scanning the walls of the shed, there really wasn't any likely place. Propping them against a two-by-four didn't work. Propping them between the door and the door frame seemed to work for a moment, but they slipped repeatedly even when she braced herself on the cloth bundle.

Her eyes flooded in frustration. She was really getting tired of swallowing all the swear words her gag stopped her from saying. At this rate she was still going to be here in the morning. She should make a run for it and take the shears with her until she got some place safe.

Fumbling the shears out of the door, she struggled to stand. She could tell she was getting tired because even getting to her knees was a problem. She finally backed herself into the bundle and got her elbows planted in its side as high up as she could. That helped her lift her bum so she could get her knees under her. Of course, that was when she dropped the shears.

Almost in tears, she sank down on the floor again and repeated the process. From there, it wasn't too hard to climb to her feet, but she was sweating and mortified that it had been so difficult. She sank, shivering, against the bundle to catch her breath.

The darn thing sank under her and she scrambled up. All her efforts had pulled the cover askew to release a scent of incense and reveal a stack of plastic packaging. She used her hip to nudge the sheet cover further aside. Stacks of pashmina scarves were tied into bundles that were stacked four bundles deep and two-by-two across. So, the dhobi khana was expanding its business. It made sense. They knew cloth and the hand laundry business had to be under threat as more individuals and businesses turned to automation with their own washing machines and driers.

Well, she was cold, and after what she'd been through, she needed a scarf more than they did. With her bound hands she dragged a pashmina out of one of the tied stacks and, shears and pashmina clutched in hand, she left.

The air was cool and damp as she headed across the field. Just in time, too, for in the east the sky was lightening. The pitch black over the trees had given way to pale streaks of apricot and blue. Somewhere, a lone dove had started cooing. Taking care not to stumble, because she didn't have a pile of pashminas to help her up again, she hurried between the rows of drying lines until she reached the low wall that separated dhobi khana from surrounding homes.

To climb it, she was forced to lay on her belly on the top and swing her legs over. When she was done, she stood in the street and eyed the houses around her. This close to the dhobi khana, there was too good a chance that this was where the laundry washers lived. She struck out along the narrow road that ran along the wall. On her right the drying racks were skeletal in the predawn gloom. Another narrow road that was barely more than a lane ran off between the homes to her left. It looked like it might parallel the main road. She winced at the sharp stones underfoot, but turned to limp down the lane. She wasn't sure, but she thought that when Simon had stopped at the laundry the first morning, they had left in this direction.

That meant that Fort Kochi and the old city and the Scandinavian Guesthouse had to be in this direction. Becca and Alice were there and safe.

She hoped.

She just needed to make it back before Avni and whoever she worked with took Phoebe's escape out on her sister and niece.

The lane stretched farther than she'd imagined it would. She tried to jog, but jogging with both arms tied while holding a sharp set of shears didn't work. The fading adrenaline surge that had kept her going so far was being replaced by pain and exhaustion that threatened her determination to keep moving. Finally, head down, she just kept putting one foot in front of the other. She gave up on swallowing because her gagged mouth was a desert. The sky faded to gray and the sound of a car engine came from ahead.

She stumbled out of the lane and found herself on a paved street, with light standards gleaming. A car came slowly down the street. Caution stopped her from seeking help. Her captors could have discovered she'd broken free. They could be looking for her.

On the other hand, so could the police.

With regret, she slunk back into the lane before the car's lights found her and collapsed against a wall. She had to get the darned ropes off. If she could do that, there was hope. At least she would be able to walk and run and speak and breathe like a normal person. And scream.

The relatively brightly lit street was nowhere to do anything, so she retraced her steps farther into the lane. In her fatigue she hadn't noticed the stout stone and stucco walls to either side, separating the houses and their small yards. Closed iron and wood gates barred the way inside. By daylight it was probably a very nice area. The kind of area where people might call the police if they spotted someone stumbling around. Which wouldn't be a bad thing if she could trust that would happen. Unfortunately she was still too close to dhobi khana.

So, she was going to have to be very quiet no matter what she did.

She located a chink in a wall suitable to hold the shears and a stone that might help to hammer them into place—not an easy task when her hands were bound behind her and she couldn't afford noise.

The results were the shears bent but braced in place, and an abundance of stone bruises on her knuckles and fingers. Praying that this time it would work, she left the pashmina on the ground and worked her wrists back and forth along the blade.

The shears held.

It took longer than she'd thought it would.

When her hands were finally free, she almost cried from relief and the pain in her shoulders. She was drenched with sweat and her arms shook from exertion. She threw off the ropes and gingerly rubbed her raw wrists, then yanked off the gag. She was going to throw it away, but decided to keep it and the ropes as evidence. The shears she yanked loose from the wall and kept as a weapon. Just in case. The pashmina —a periwinkle blue one—she wrapped around her neck and shoulders hopefully to disguise herself and her condition.

Overhead the sky had lightened to pale blue. Streaks of gold cut through the trees as the sun topped the horizon. From the houses came the sounds of voices and people moving.

Wincing, she worked her shoulders and set out walking. The gravel lane hadn't been kind to her feet. The pavement was better, but not much. She had too many cuts and bruises on the bottom of her feet.

In the increasing daylight she looked down at herself. The lusciously soft pashmina hid a multitude of sins, but not everything. Her body was covered in a layer of dried mud. Scratches on her lower legs had bled, leaving behind black scabs like leeches down her shins. Her grimy hands only loosed more grime when she ran them through her hair. She needed a bath. She needed a shower. No, she needed a bath *and* a shower and thought longingly of the shower at the Scandinavian Guesthouse. That and a long soak in the pool.

If she could get there. If Becca and Alice were safe.

She hurried her pace, the sun heating up the air around her and traffic increasing in the street. No one slowed at the barefoot woman in the periwinkle shawl. They must get tourists of all kinds here. She just wished she knew where she was and where she was headed. If she could only find the harbor, then she was pretty sure she could find the guesthouse, but wandering around in Kochi's interior streets told her nothing. The only good thing was that Kochi was an island. Eventually, she'd reach water and hopefully be able to find her way home.

The sun had lifted over the trees and drenched her in sweat by the time she reached an area of white-washed buildings that she thought they had passed the first day they entered Kochi. Up ahead should be the harbor and off to the side the shopping streets she'd explored with Becca and Alice.

She could have cried when she spotted a shop with brass platters heaped with colorful pyramids of tikka powder in vermillion, saffron, fuchsia, blue, and every other vibrant color of India. She *was* where she'd thought. She could find the guesthouse from here.

She turned doggedly up the street, checking over her shoulder for any pursuers. Ijay Das's men had detached from these walls like supernatural sentinels when she'd followed them yesterday. Were they back today? Would they come after her? There was no way she could outrun them, but at least she could scream.

If they didn't cover her mouth.

She kept to the center of the narrow street, passing the lanes with caution. Shopkeepers were still placing their wares outside their doors. She passed the shop where Alice had bought her clothes and the pashmina shop she and Becca had lingered in. Just a few more blocks and she would know Alice and Becca were safe. She could call Detective Mathias and tell him what she knew. It would be over and they could all get on with their lives—maybe catch the next flight out of here.

"Phoebe?"

The voice came from behind her and she spun around. Jeannie and Trevor stood in the entrance to the pashmina shop.

"It *is* you!" Jeannie said and hurried down the stairs.

Phoebe turned and ran. Trevor and Jeannie were involved in this whole thing somehow. She didn't dare trust them.

"Phoebe, wait!" Trevor's voice and footfall pounded behind her as she spent the last of her strength. Rounded the corner toward the Scandinavian Guesthouse before a strong hand fell on her shoulder and spun her around. She ripped away leaving the pashmina behind, but Trevor caught her arm and hung on.

"Phoebe? What is it? Where have you been? What happened to you?"

She knew she couldn't outrun them, so she held her ground, ripping free of Trevor again. "You know damn well where I've been. Ijay and

Avni have been holding me prisoner. I managed to escape this morning. What have you done to Becca and Alice?"

The two photographers frowned and looked at each other. Both shook their heads.

"Becca and Alice are fine, Phoebe," Trevor said. "At least they were when we saw them at breakfast. They're staying put at the hotel hoping for good news from the police. We've all been looking for you for the past twenty-four hours. The police have, too. All we knew was that you'd gone out for a walk and didn't come back."

"I don't believe you. I heard you talking. You were all about taking over Simon's contacts." She left what Alice had heard out of it.

Trevor and Jeannie looked at each other again. Finally Trevor nodded. "That's true about wanting to locate Simon's contacts, but not for the reason you're clearly thinking."

She still couldn't believe him.

Sighing, he fished in his shirt and pulled out a white cotton travel safe. From inside he produced a slim wallet and flipped it open. A badge and RCMP ID caught the sunlight.

Her legs felt weak. She didn't know what to say, so looked from him to Jeannie.

She nodded. "I'm RCMP, too."

"Aren't…aren't you an awfully long way from home?"

"We are. We're tracking a smuggling ring. We believe Simon was the Canadian connection."

She wanted to sit down. But first she had to make sure Alice and Becca were safe.

She couldn't take in what they were telling her. She turned and hobbled down the street toward the white walls and jasmine vines that guarded the Scandinavian guesthouse. Becca. Just make sure she and Alice were safe.

She turned in at the white fence and rushed up the sidewalk, then stepped inside into cool. The front desk was empty. No one was at the pool. She tried the door to her room and it swung open. Alice's bed was its usual disaster. Becca's was made, but there was no one there.

"Phoebe…" Jeannie and Trevor came up behind her in the room.

"They're not here," Phoebe said, a slow panic bubbling inside her.

"Then they're likely out looking with Zamir. He's been as concerned as the rest of us."

She waved off their suggestion. "You don't understand. Avni is somehow involved in Simon's killing. She had Ijay Das and his men abduct me and—and—" she thought of Avni's chilling use of the phrase, 'at the moment'. "Avni more or less threatened Becca and Alice."

Jeannie's eyes widened. "Really?"

Phoebe looked skyward. "She said they were okay, then qualified it with 'at the moment'. We need to call the police."

Trevor nodded and pulled out his cell. He dialed a number just as whistling came from the lobby.

Phoebe pushed past him out to the lobby. Zamir came sauntering in from the street, saw her, and his expression bloomed into a smile.

"Phoebe! You're back!"

She rushed up to him. "Where're Becca and Alice? Trevor said they were with you."

He frowned and she wanted to claw the information out of his brain.

"We were just going out and the police called that you'd been found. Avni said she'd take them down to the station so they went with her."

"How do you know it was the police she was talking to?" Phoebe demanded.

He frowned again. "She said it was, of course. Phoebe, what is going on?"

But she was already swinging around to Trevor on the call. Already losing touch with her feet and legs and on her way to the floor.

She was already too late.

18

B etween Zamir and Jeannie, they managed to get her into a chair. The lobby spun around her and the overhead fans buzzed too loudly in her ears. Her mouth tasted of dust and decay and old mud. Her skin itched and none of it mattered because she'd failed her sister and Alice. They were gone who knew where. There was the entire Indian subcontinent looming darkly just outside this door.

"Zamir, she looks like she's going to faint. Get her some water and some food. Goodness knows when she last had something to eat," Jeannie said. She settled by Phoebe and held her hand. "You're freezing."

Phoebe nodded. She didn't know if she'd ever be warm again. Jeannie draped something lovely and periwinkle blue around Phoebe's shoulders, and brought a momentary warmth, but then she thought of all she'd lost and the cold set in again.

Jeannie was fingering the pashmina, her brows knit together. "Phoebe, where did you get this?"

Phoebe ignored her. Trevor had pocketed his phone.

"Detective Mathias will be right over with some of his men."

At least that was something. There might still be a chance. But this was Becca and Alice. How would they come through something like what Phoebe had just endured? Alice might. She was tough.

But Becca?

She was smart, yes. She was brave, too, though she didn't know it. But her first reaction was often to avoid conflict. How would she react when conflict was shoved in her face?

Phoebe had to console herself with the knowledge that Becca would die before she'd let anything happen to Alice.

Trevor had knelt in front of her. He held up the pashmina's corner. "Where'd you get this, Phoebe?"

She shook her head. "I don't know. From a shed. I was cold and muddy and I thought a pashmina might hide the worst of how I look."

"Phoebe, honey," Jeannie said, squeezing her hand. "That's not pashmina. That's shahtoosh, the king of wools according to the Persians. It's one of the rarest, most expensive scarves on the earth."

She tried to understand what they were telling her, but it didn't make sense. Hadn't Alice said something about shahtoosh once? And there'd been a magazine article, too, but she couldn't remember what they'd said.

Zamir arrived with a tray bearing bottled water and a bowl of what smelled like chana masala and a platter of nan. Her stomach turned.

Jeannie opened and bottle and put it in Phoebe's limp hand. "Drink."

It took just about everything she had to obey, but the cold fluid relieved the desert in her mouth. She heaved in a deep breath and upended the bottle, revelling in the cool liquid.

Jeannie dipped a corner of nan in the yoghurt sauce and held it up for her. "Eat."

Phoebe shook her head.

"Dammit, Phoebe. You need your strength. Your sister and Alice need you."

She ate. Small bites at first and then ravenously so that she had just about finished the delicious bowl of chana when the lobby door darkened and Detective Mathias walked in.

"Ms. Clay. You looked considerably the worse for wear. What has befallen you?" he asked, standing over her.

She told the story as quickly as she could, between the last bites of food. Then she stood. "Avni's taken Becca and Alice, I'm sure of it. She threatened that something might happen to them."

"Avni Kalki? I find that difficult to believe. She has held a responsible role here for years."

"Well, believe it." Phoebe's strength was returning and so was her ability to use her brain. "Tell me. Is Avni any relation to the old man I met at dhobi khana? He told me his name was Kalki."

Mathias did his head waggle. "She is his daughter. Tamils do not have last names, so they use their father's name in that position. Avni Kalki."

"Oh, God." She slumped back in her chair. "If I'd only known. She has a brother, doesn't she? A young man. He's studying medicine in Harvard. Do you know what his name is? Are his initials A.K.?"

Mathias shook his head, but looked toward a uniformed officer who stood by the door. He said something in Malayalam.

"Asiq is his name," Detective Mathias interpreted. "This officer knows the family."

It made sense. Too much sense. "Simon was meeting someone with the initials A.K. the night he died and Ijay Das described a young man who sounded like he was from here but had an accent. Time at Harvard could do that—change how you speak." And there had been the conversation Ijay Das had described, asking after father and school. And a sister. She closed her eyes.

Detective Mathias frowned. "And how did you know about the initials, Ms. Clay? That was police information only."

She sighed. "I searched Simon's iPad before you did, okay? You were blaming Becca and I had to know what evidence there might be to the contrary. Zamir had the iPad after he vacated Simon's room, so I borrowed it from him. When I returned it to him, I told him he had to turn it in to you."

For a moment he looked as angry as he probably should be at all her interference, but then he shook his head. "You are a most enterprising woman, Ms. Clay. But the Kalkis are an upstanding family. They work hard to keep their traditional business going."

"I'm sure they do. But to go to university at Harvard is an expensive business. How many shirts must be washed to afford it?"

"They could afford many years at Harvard if they had many of these." Trevor motioned to the blue pashmina. "It's shahtoosh, Detective. Do you know what that is?"

The detective looked puzzled a moment. Then his expression turned doubtful. "I have seen the alerts, but shahtoosh—from the fur of endangered Tibetan antelope—here? Surely that is impossible."

Jeannie shook her head and left Phoebe's side. She stuck out her hand. "Sergeant Jeannie Gerard of the Royal Canadian Mounted Police. This is Sergeant Trevor Smith. We've both been working with Interpol trying to track down a ring that's been selling shahtoosh into Vancouver."

Brows raised, Detective Mathias shook her and Trevor's hands. "And your tracking has led you to Kochi?"

"Unfortunately, yes. It may be at the heart of Simon Roy's murder."

"This scarf?" Zamir said from his place standing behind Phoebe. He fingered the edge of the fine material.

"And my sister and niece's abduction." Phoebe climbed to her feet. Everything hurt, but she was not going to sit here while they calmly discussed shawls. "Becca and Alice are missing. Avni apparently said she was taking them to the police because you'd found me. You hadn't, and I take it from your expression you never called the hotel to say you had."

Detective Mathias was shaking his head. "I did not call. Nor did my men."

"Where could she have taken them?" Jeannie asked.

"I can think of two possible places." Phoebe headed for her room to retrieve her sneakers. There was no way she was being left behind and she knew her poor feet couldn't take much more than they already had.

When she returned to the lobby, they were waiting for her, but the uniformed officer was gone.

"I've put out an alert for your sister and niece as well as for Avni and Asiq. Now where do you think your family might be held?" Detective Mathias asked.

"There's a place near the harbor where Ijay held me at first. It's in the warehouse area. I think I could find it again. The second is dhobi khana."

"The laundry?" Trevor and Jeannie said together.

"I saw Simon talking to a young man there. It might have been Asiq. They moved me there after dark and locked me in a shed. It was when I was escaping that I found that." She pointed at the pashmina—shahtoosh—she'd abandoned on the chair. No way was she wearing anything from an endangered species.

"Are you sure you're well enough to do this, Phoebe?" Zamir asked.

She caught his hands. "It's my family. We do what we must."

"I will come, too. While you are on my tour, you are my family."

The backbone he showed was a far cry from the indecisive tour guide she'd dealt with right after Simon died. She was surprised when he led the way out the door to where the uniformed officer was waiting with the police vehicles.

"Phoebe," said Mathias, "you will come with me, as will the two RCMP officers. Zamir may ride with my officer."

She climbed into the front of his Tata sedan while Jeannie and Trevor squeezed into the back.

"Where to?" Mathias asked.

Phoebe explained how she had followed Ijay through the tourist area and into the warehouse district.

"That is a large area with many buildings."

She thought a moment. "We hadn't reached the spice area yet. The large trucks were unloading rice and the road was the first one paralleling the harbor."

Nodding, he pulled the car out and headed toward the water. Soon he was driving down the street she recognized with its vividly painted three and four storied buildings. The traffic was almost as clogged as it had been yesterday.

"Stop here," she said, recognizing the purple building that had been where the rice truck had unloaded yesterday. Mathias pulled to a stop and the marked vehicle pulled in behind them and was joined by two other marked police cars. Traffic halted, blocked by their vehicles.

"Yesterday there was a truck blocking the road," Phoebe said. "Ijay and his men ducked around it, or I thought they had." She told them what happened. "There's a door close to the water. They held me in a cell there."

Mathias went to get out, ignoring the traffic. "You will remain here, Ms. Clay. We will look into this."

"Like heck I will." She scrambled out of the sedan as Jeannie and Trevor climbed out and Zamir and three other officers joined them. The world gently tilt-a-whirled and Phoebe leaned on the vehicle for a moment hoping no one was watching. When the world steadied, she stepped past Mathias and crossed the traffic to the narrow lane that led down to the water.

It wasn't quite as narrow as she remembered, and the stucco was smoother, though stained with age. She led the others toward the water, but stopped at a too-familiar thick-timbered door set two steps down in the wall.

Her mouth felt dry and her knees felt weak. She leaned against the wall. "This is it. There's a room inside and beyond that, a cell. That's where they held me. They took everything I had except my watch, passport included."

But a passport could be replaced. Becca and Alice couldn't be.

At Mathias's motion, the uniformed officer stepped up to the door. He thumped it with his palm and yelled an order in Malayalam.

For a moment there was silence. Then the door suddenly swung open and six men plunged out, bowling over the uniformed officer. He stumbled back. Mathias grabbed for one of the men. Jeannie and Trevor snagged two more. Phoebe tripped a man and grabbed the gamboling boy by the scruff of the neck. In the narrow space, it was Zamir who tackled the final man before he could reach the last two officers. Zamir's muscle-beach muscles finally were of use as he landed on top of the last man and dragged him up. Ijay Das glared up at him. He spat on the ground when he spotted Phoebe.

Detective Mathias shoved his captured man into his officer's arms and grabbed Ijay Das by the collar. Zamir crossed his arms, a satisfied grin on his face.

"This time I have you, Das. I have a victim and witness to your abduction. Unless you tell me where the other women are."

Ijay waggled his head, suddenly looking more like a squashed caterpillar than the one who confused Alice in Wonderland. "I don't know anything about other women or a girl. That one." He raised his chin and Phoebe. "That is the only one we took."

"He's lying," Phoebe said.

"I never mentioned a girl, Das. Where are they?"

"I do not know. I do not know anything about them." But he head waggled again and Phoebe wanted to grab him, thump his head against the wall. Instead she drew in a deep breath. "But you were going to help Avni get rid of them for a fee. Am I right?"

Ijay's almost black gaze slipped to her. "I am a helpful person as you know. I gave you much information for so little. Surely you can understand that I need to make money to support my family. So many mouths to fill." The head waggle again, as if to show his innocence.

"If you're so helpful, then tell us where you were supposed to take my sister and niece. We already know you know about them."

Detective Mathias leaned his arm across Ijay's throat. He sputtered and scrabbled at Mathias's chest and threw a desperate look in Phoebe's direction. "All right. All right. There is a ship. It leaves for North Africa tonight. Two blonde women I am told will fetch a fair price. It was a fate I offered for you, but Avni was weak—she would not make that decision." He shrugged.

The fact that the fate was planned for Becca and Alice said that Avni's resolve had strengthened, or someone else's had.

The uniformed officers took the men and the boy into custody. Mathias ducked into the open doorway and Phoebe heard the too-familiar clank and squeal of the inner door opening.

"No one here." His voice echoed out at her. Then he followed it outside. "Nothing here at all except for this." He held up a sweat-stained cotton travel safe that Phoebe recognized along with a sweat-stained passport and bank card. The money, of course, was gone.

"Thank God," Phoebe said and reached for them, but Detective Mathias held them back.

"Evidence of a robbery as well as abduction, Ms. Clay. We must think of the evidence needed for court." He handed her belongings to another officer who placed them in a ziplock bag.

Phoebe nodded. Having her documents held by the police was the least of her worries.

Becca and Alice were still missing, and if they weren't at dhobi khana, how was she ever going to find them?

19

———————

With Ijay and his men in custody and handed off to more of Mathias's men, Phoebe and the others returned to the two police vehicles. The day had advanced and the heat with it. Stark shadows filled the lines of Mathias's face and seemed to seep inside of Phoebe's hope. If Becca and Alice weren't at dhobi khana, where could they be? In a vehicle being taken to a ship? At the shipyards already? Already bound and drugged in a ship's hold?

She felt sick to her stomach. She rolled the Tata's window down and heaved in deep gasps of salt-stained air.

"You did well back there, Phoebe Clay," Detective Mathias said with a glance in her direction.

He steered the sedan through narrow streets, avoiding traffic jams until finally they emerged onto a broader, tree-lined, paved road that she recognized from her long walk home. The sky was blue. White egrets stalked tall grass at the verge of the road. It was beautiful, but she could barely see it given the shadows that lurked inside. She'd thought she understood the loss the families of her dead students had felt, but the dark hole in her heart was beyond anything she'd imagined —and Becca and Alice weren't dead.

Weren't lost to her. Yet.

She hung on to that.

Leaning forward in her seat when the Tata slowed, ahead she saw the broad field and its waving crop of blazing white sheets as if the whole field waved surrender. If only it was so.

Mathias pulled over and three police vehicles pulled in behind. He turned to her in the Tata.

"We need to plan this out. Your sister and niece are hostages. We cannot move too fast."

"If we don't move fast, they could be gone! What if they're already gone to the ship? We need to know now so we can get there before the ship leaves!" She let her fears spill out of her and felt the panic overwhelm. Her hands shook as she shoved the car door open. "You can plan all you want. I'm going to get them."

"Phoebe! Wait!" Jeannie climbed out of the car to stop her. "What are you thinking of doing?"

She wasn't exactly sure and knew that her actions could put Becca and Alice in more danger. If they were here. She heaved a sigh.

"You're right." She nodded at Mathias. "I'm just terrified for them. When I was held, it was in a shed in the last row." She pointed through the trees at the not-so-distant one-story buildings. "I escaped out the back over the stone wall. I—I thought maybe I could get in that way and see if they are there."

Jeannie studied the scene as if she could read something in the flat land, trees, and the houses beyond the stone wall. "It could work. What'd'you think, Trevor?"

He nodded slowly. "It'd work better if there was a distraction. If they're here."

Jeannie turned to Mathias. "If you and your men officially approach from the front, then Phoebe, Trevor, and I will go in through the rear. If we can free Becca and Alice, you can clean up the rest."

Detective Mathias considered and nodded. "But one of my men must go with you."

Jeannie nodded, but Phoebe was already starting down a side street that would lead to the houses that verged the rear of dhobi khana. The sun was harsh on her head and she desperately wanted shade, but Becca and Alice needed her. She kept going.

Trevor caught up to her. "You said you found the shahtoosh in a shed. The same one you were held in?"

She glanced up at him. His face was in shade, but it sounded like he was more concerned about the shahtoosh than Becca and Alice.

"The one next to my prison. I went in there looking for something to cut the ropes that bound my hands."

He thought a moment. "Was that scarf the only one?"

She glanced up at him. Jeannie had come up on his other side. "God, no. It was one scarf out of a bundle that must have held thirty, maybe forty scarves and shawls. And the bundles were stacked three of four high and four square. How many scarves does that make?"

"Jeezus," Trevor murmured.

"How many animals died to make them, is the better question," Jeannie said with a shake of her head.

"I've been thinking," Phoebe said. "Ijay said that he saw Simon meeting with a young man who brought him a package of something soft. It was wrapped like a laundry package. What a perfect way to smuggle the scarves. No one would suspect and there'd be less chance of someone trying to steal them, too. Simon could then take the scarves with him all across India and back home to Vancouver. It was a perfect distribution ring."

"Until something went wrong," Jeannie said. "There weren't any shahtoosh discovered with the body."

"Not even his bloody poof," Trevor agreed with a shake of his head. He wiped sweat off his forehead and scanned the quaint houses with their stone garden fences ahead of them.

"His poof?"

'You touched it, didn't you? Back at Ernakulam station? I thought he was going to hit you when you did. I'd been trying to get close enough to do so for the entire tour, but I didn't dare draw his attention. And then you go and grab it. Soft, right?"

Phoebe thought back. She'd been so aggravated with Simon at that moment, that she hadn't really noticed, but now…

"It was very soft. I thought it must be old. I remember it tickled my palm. I thought it was just worn out fabric with loose threads."

"Shahtoosh guard hairs," Trevor said with a nod. "We think it was his sample."

"Takes a lot of nerve to walk around with a twenty-thousand-dollar piece of contraband hanging from your hip pocket," Jeannie added.

But then Simon was that kind of guy.

They reached a spot in the stone wall where the rear of the sheds was visible through the flapping white sheets. Sweat poured down Phoebe's back and she felt faint, but wasn't prepared to show her weakness. Instead, she let Jeannie help her over the fence. The two RCMP officers gracefully vaulted over and the uniformed officer scrambled after. Then they set out single file through the field with Jeannie leading.

The sheets fluttered around them in a rhythmic wave as if the whole field breathed. The field swung around Phoebe in a slow loop-the-loop until she closed her eyes. The looping stopped. She drew in a deep breath and focused on the sheds she glimpsed through the shifting barriers of gleaming white that hurt her eyes.

When they were three sheet-rows away from the sheds, Jeannie stopped. "Which shed were you held captive in?" She studied the row of small buildings, Trevor beside her.

Phoebe eyed the line of buildings. She couldn't be sure, except...

"That one, I think." She pointed. "See how the door's off kilter? That's from me kicking it off two of its hinges."

Trevor glanced down at her. "There's a lot more to you than meets the eye, Phoebe Clay."

She shrugged. "The shahtoosh were in the shed to the right. So what do we do? Check them all?"

"Sounds about right," Jeannie said, scanning their surroundings.

Phoebe couldn't see anyone, but when she touched a sheet, it felt almost dry. Someone would be coming for them soon. They needed to act now.

A commotion from the other side of dhobi khana said Detective Mathias had moved in.

Jeannie started forward just as a man came running around the side of the shed. Phoebe couldn't be sure, but she thought it might be the young man she'd seen Simon with their first day here. He carried a gas can and hurriedly opened it and splashed the gas over the fronts of the nearest sheds. He lit a match.

Phoebe shouted. If he released that match, everything here could go up in flames. Clearly he was trying to hide something, whether shahtoosh or Becca and Alice.

The young man glanced in their direction and tossed the match in the gas. Jeannie bolted for the young man, Trevor and the uniformed officer at her heels. Phoebe ran for the shed row.

A whoosh behind her said what had happened. A wave of heat rolled into her.

"Becca! Alice!" she shouted and reached the farthest shed. She yanked open the door and inhaled damp darkness and the smell of old soap. She let the door slam shut, already running for the next shed and the next and the next. All empty. Her eyes watered in billowing smoke the wind blew across the sheds and field. The shed row's simple wood construction was perfect fuel and those at the other end of the row were already engulfed in flames.

Through the smoke, Trevor was slamming open shed doors and checking inside. The uniformed officer had the young man in custody. From somewhere Jeannie had found a hose and had turned it on the growing flames. She was joined by other officers.

The flames leapt from shed to shed. By the look of it, they'd jumped not only down this row, but the breeze was sparking flames in the other rows. All of dhobi khana could go up in flames.

She had to find Becca and Alice before that happened. If they were here.

Unlike the others, the next shed was padlocked shut. Wasn't this the shed where she'd found the shahtoosh? She stopped, certain she was right. She banged on the door. "Becca! Alice!"

There was no answer.

Sparks floated down and burned her head and shoulders. More sparks showered down on the metal roof and slid down into the brown grass along the shed row edges. Wisps of smoke rose and more flames.

Leave this shed and try the others? There were fifteen in all and Trevor was now helping Jeannie fight the fire. It didn't seem to be helping. Flames already engulfed the neighboring shed where she'd been held last night. The shahtoosh in the locked shed would be lost, too.

In the distance came more sirens, but they could be too little, too late.

She scanned turned back to the padlocked one. None of the others were locked up so tight. She needed something to break down the door, but there was nothing nearby except the drying racks and the fluttering white sheets.

She ran back to the nearest rack and yanked off the sheets. She tugged on the pole but it was deeply planted in dirt and probably had been for years. There were cross pieces though.

She leapt up and caught hold, putting all her weight on the cross pole. Something gave slightly. She dropped down and leapt again, using her weight to pull it down. Nails squealed in wood and suddenly she was on her bum on the ground, a piece of dried wood in her hands. She just prayed it was strong enough.

The smoke was thicker, the shed she'd been held in lost, and the shahtoosh shed was sparking. Blackened patches burned in the grass and out in the field a line of flames showed where sheets had candled.

She ran back to the shed and thanked God for the loose construction that allowed the door to give an inch outwardly, even though locked.

She slammed the end of the pole into the space, the shoulder she'd hurt trying to escape screaming in protest. The pain egged her on. She pried at the door. Her muscles strained, but the locking hasp was bolted deeply into the wood of door and frame. She managed to work her pry bar closer to the lock, but couldn't get the lock to come loose. Still, her effort had left the door looser in its frame. She pried it open as far as she could and peered inside.

For a moment she was blinded by the darkness, and the smoke

swirling around her. Then a red flicker showed at the rear of the shed, revealing shifting smoke inside. The fire must have run unchecked along the ground at the rear of the shed. This one was going up, or would soon.

Through the smoke the firelight revealed two bodies collapsed on their sides.

Becca and Alice.

Phoebe pulled back from the door. "Here! They're here! The shed's on fire!"

Trevor dropped the hose he was working and ran to help. He grabbed the pole and wrenched at the door. Again. Again.

Wood squealed and then suddenly the doorframe cracked. The door fell open releasing a plume of smoke. Trevor went sprawling onto burning grass. He scrambled up.

Phoebe ducked into the shed and blindly grabbed the nearest body, dragging it to the door.

Alice. It was Alice. She crumpled to the ground as Trevor dragged Becca out beside her. Then he dashed inside again. Were there more people there?

He came out carrying an armful of plastic covered bundles and dropped them beside Phoebe in a rainbow of colors. He repeated the action twice more before collapsing beside her. He leaned over and checked Becca's and Alice's pulses.

"I think they've been drugged to keep them quiet. You stay with them."

As if she'd ever leave them again. She nodded.

He gave her a soot-covered grin before returning to helping Jeannie, but nothing was going to save the dhobi khana sheds. In the fields more sheets were burning, but the sirens had arrived and arcs of water were sending bursts of steam skyward.

Through the smoke and steam, Detective Mathias appeared, accompanied by two other people. Their figures materialized into those of Zamir and the old man she'd met the first day in Kochi: Kalki, the father of Avni and Aziq.

That first morning in Kochi, he'd been so proud of his daughter

with her business degree and his son studying at Harvard. But now…
How could that man be the one who now appeared stricken and
ancient, barely able to keep his feet as he stumbled beside the
detective.

Phoebe went to stand, but Becca moaned. She rolled over and
rubbed her eyes, then looked up at Phoebe. At first she didn't seem to
register Phoebe's presence. Then two little furrows formed between her
brows.

"Phoebe? Is it you?" She sat up, coughed, and nearly fell over until
Phoebe grabbed her shoulders.

"It's me. You're safe."

"Alice! Where's Alice? Where are we?" She coughed again and
looked dazedly at the billowing smoke.

"She's here. Beside you." Phoebe pointed Becca's face at her
daughter and Becca crawled over to her to cradle her body, Phoebe
beside her.

"Baby?" Becca caressed Alice's face. "Wake up, honey."

"She's been drugged. You both were, we think."

Becca looked up at her. "We went with Avni. She said she was
taking us to the police to meet you. Then men grabbed us and I don't
remember anything else…" She closed her eyes and shook her head.
"This whole trip has been a disaster right from the start. I'm beginning
to think it's not safe to be around you."

Phoebe fell back, uncertain what to say. In some ways Becca might
be right. Phoebe *did* seem to be the center of a lot of trouble. But this
was no time to defend herself against a distraught mother, just as it
hadn't been a good time to defend herself against the parents and
school board who blamed her for the death of three students. It wasn't
her fault and yet there were many layers of culpability. She looked
away to Detective Mathias and the others, but they were lost in the
billows of smoke and steam.

She stood. "I'm sorry you feel that way."

"Step away," came a voice from behind her.

Phoebe swung around as a figure materialized through the smoke
from the far end of the sheds. Avni, like an Indian goddess of

destruction, clad in a golden sari stained red by the smoke-covered sun. She held one end of her sari over her nose. In the other hand she held a gun.

"You!" she growled and pointed the weapon at Phoebe. "You've ruined my family. My brother. My father…"

Phoebe drew herself up. Avni's gun barrel looked like a canon.

"I didn't ruin them, they did it themselves."

Avni stepped closer and Phoebe placed herself between Avni and her family.

"I knew you were trouble from the moment you entered the hotel. You watched everything. Questioned everything. You meddled where you never should have been! No normal tourist would!"

"I just tried to help my sister. I just tried to find an alternative version to how Simon died."

"You should have left it alone!" Avni screamed.

"Avni!" A male voice cut through the roar of the fire. "Avni, stop what you are doing! What's done is done and now we pay the price!"

From out of the smoke, Kalki advanced beside Detective Mathias. Zamir rushed past them, his hands clearly empty, and fell to his knees beside Becca and Alice. He clasped Alice's hand.

"Father! It does not have to end like this! We can still be free. Still have our lives!"

Kalki shook his head. Tears streamed down his face. "Our legacy burns!"

He stood beside Mathias who had his own gun aimed at Avni.

"Drop the gun, daughter. No one else needs to be hurt." Kalki's figure shimmered like an apparition in the fire's heat.

Avni shifted her gun so it aimed at Mathias. "Let my father go. He's done nothing wrong. It was me who killed Simon."

"Don't lie! Obey me, daughter! Think of your child." Kalki advanced on her, his face ancient. "I've already confessed. They have Asiq in custody, as well, for disposal of the body. Now stop and you may still have your life."

Avni's weapon wavered from Detective Mathias to her father. Her hands shook. The sari swirled around her in the wind of the flames. Then she swung back to Phoebe.

"You! You will know my pain!" She fired.

Phoebe screamed as the bullet blasted past her toward Becca and Alice.

Kalki lunged at his daughter. Avni swung back to him as Mathias fired. The bullet struck Avni in the shoulder and swung her around just as she fired again.

Kalki staggered. His chest blossomed with blood.

Avni lurched up, then screamed as Kalki went to his knees. Blood covered the white cloth over his belly. He swayed and reached for Avni, but she backed away, backed away another step, blood pouring from her shoulder.

"Stop!" Mathias ordered.

Ignoring him, she fled into the nearest burning shed. There came a shriek that rose and rose. It turned to keening that slowly faded, eaten by the fire's roar.

Kalki collapsed face down on the grass, the smoke a swirling pall.

Phoebe spun back to Becca, who was still on her knees. Becca's face was white. Her mouth was open in a silent scream. Zamir sprawled on the earth beside her, his face a horrified mixture of pain and triumph as blood pumped from his shoulder.

"He saved us." Becca came to herself with a gulp of smoky air. "Avni turned toward us and he leapt, putting himself between the bullet and Alice."

Relief stole the last strength in Phoebe's legs. She crumpled beside Zamir and bowed her head. It was over.

20

She woke to the soft whoosh-whoosh-whoosh of a ceiling fan and the gentle breeze running over her face and arms. Soft voices filled the air and dim light came through her eyelids. The scent of jasmine and green apple shampoo told her where she was as her consciousness gradually returned and she went to stretch luxuriantly in her Scandinavian Guesthouse bed.

Not a good idea. Her left shoulder, the one she'd hurt escaping, shrilled painful protests through her body and her eyes bolted open.

"Holy heck, who beat me up when I wasn't looking?" she asked the air.

"Finally! I was beginning to think you'd never wake up!" Alice's tanned face appeared in Phoebe's field of view, her blonde hair a corona around her head. Slatted light through the guesthouse window caught her face at an attractive angle that showed how her little-girl softness was slowly evolving into womanly angles that carried a hint of worry. And strength. For barely thirteen, the kid had seen, and been through, a lot, yet there was no sign of the terrifying ordeal she'd survived. She leaned in and gave Phoebe a perfunctory hug.

"How are you feeling? You've been asleep for over twenty-four hours." Alice pulled back and gave a little disapproving shake of her head that was so like her mother Phoebe had to laugh.

She shoved herself up in bed—or tried to until every part of her exploded in pain. With a groan she settled back on the bed. "Like someone took a crowbar to me while I slept. I don't think there's anywhere that I don't ache."

Alice's brows rose. "I think you said the same thing after kayaking. That means you're going to live, right?"

Phoebe gave a brief nod. Yup. Even that hurt. But she rolled to the side of the bed and managed to get her feet on the floor, her body upright. Yikes, she felt weak.

Alice stood over her, her hands on her hips. "Good. I'm going to get Mom. She's out by the pool with the others. I drew short straw so I had to watch you."

Through the bed-tangle of her hair, Phoebe threw Alice a sideways glance. "Short straw, huh? Get out of here!" She grabbed her pillow and heaved it at the girl.

Alice dodged it, of course, and danced out the door while Phoebe nursed the pain in her shoulder that the tossing had caused. God, she was getting too old for this. Too old to be battering down doors, especially. She rubbed her neck and shoulders and managed to find her feet and shuffle into the bathroom with some clothes.

The hot water revived her somewhat, though she still felt like she'd been hit and run over by a semi-truck. Twice.

Out of the shower, her joints felt like they moved a little easier, but the balls of her feet were so tender that she could barely walk. Her shoulder and hip carried a kaleidoscope of black and blue and green, and various cuts, scrapes, and additional bruises ran up her legs and arms. Her hair was singed in spots, too. She hadn't even noticed that happening during the fire. Her chest hurt when she breathed, as well. They'd said when they checked her and Becca and Alice over at the hospital that they were all very lucky that they hadn't inhaled more smoke.

All in all, she'd be remembering this trip to India for a good long time. Feeling it, too. She pulled on shorts and gingerly slid her arms into a bra, but her painful shoulders forced her to do up the clasp around her waist and then twist the bra into place. Another sign of an old woman when she couldn't even do up her own bra.

She pulled a favorite cotton t-shirt over her head, the blue one with white whorls like shells across the front, and looked at herself in the mirror. Same blue eyes. Same cropped blonde hair minus a few bits. Unfortunately, a familiar haunted look peered out at her, too. Old grief and guilt. She still couldn't believe that Avni had chosen to take her own life in the fire rather than admit what she'd done.

Sighing, she turned away, ran a comb through her hair, and left the bathroom. Moaning about the wounds she carried wasn't going to get her anywhere.

Becca was waiting for her just inside the room entrance.

She stood by the room door as if she wasn't even sure she wanted to enter. Her honey-blonde hair was pulled back severely from a face that showed a gauntness through the cheeks and shadows under the eyes that Phoebe hadn't noticed previously. She had on white capris, a t-shirt, and her hiking sandals that would be perfect for Kochi streets, but even though her clothing said 'tropical refresh,' her expression clearly did not.

Her lips turned down and her blue gaze was determined as she stood with her arms crossed. Instead of crossing the room to hug Phoebe, Becca simply nodded. "I'm glad to see you're up and around. More or less healthy, too, from the looks of it."

Her gaze caught on Phoebe's scrapes and bruises. "A little the worse for wear, I guess."

"A little." Phoebe went to find her hiking sandals, but then remembered that it had been her sandals that she'd lost in the mud while abducted. Instead she was forced to choose her soot-stained running shoes. She sat down on the edge of her bed to tie them. "Are you okay? And Alice?"

Becca shifted in the doorway but didn't answer.

Phoebe glanced up at her and stopped. Becca's expression waffled between pained and determined. Phoebe stood. "What's the matter? What's happened?"

Becca wouldn't meet her gaze. "We're leaving. Alice and I. We've got reservations for the train to Goa today and then flights booked to Bangkok and home tomorrow." She lifted her chin toward the wall. Previously unnoticed by Phoebe, two packed bags stood there: Alice's and Becca's. Phoebe's still stood unpacked by her bed.

Phoebe thought a moment, not sure what to say. "And you didn't bother to talk this over with me—or include me in the reservations."

With a heavy sigh, Becca stepped farther into the room. "This isn't working, Phoebe. I've thought about it a lot. I tried to tell you before Avni shot at us. Lord knows I've tried to be part of your life and adventures, but I never thought it would be like this. My daughter and I almost died, Phoebe. We were abducted. We were drugged! They were going to sell my baby to—to—to someone and steal her life from her. I —I can't let your need for adventure put us in such danger again."

She stomped one foot to emphasize her decision.

"But I didn't put Alice in danger, or at least not knowingly. I never would. I love that girl like she's my daughter. I love you the same."

Becca crossed to her and looked her up and down. "That's what's so tragic. You don't see how your little 'adventures,'" she hooked her fingers, "are too dangerous. I mean, look at yourself! It's—it's like ever since the school shooting you've been in self-destruct mode. You run into danger. I—I'm afraid for you, Phoebe. You're going to get yourself killed."

"I'm not self-destructive. I'm not going to get myself killed. If I go into danger, it's to help someone!" But this time and on the kayak trip it had been more dangerous than she'd realized. She *had* been truly afraid. Terribly so.

"And as long as you go on thinking like that, I'm afraid Alice and I will not be going anywhere with you. Nor will Alice be allowed to see you. I don't want you setting a bad example. She thinks the world of you, but she needs to realize that what you do isn't safe. *You're* not safe. You're not a police officer or a fireman who's trained for danger. You're a school teacher! A retired one!"

Feeling gut-punched, Phoebe sank down on the bed again. "But Becca! I didn't drag Alice into danger. Sure, she found the body, but I had nothing to do with that. I made sure she stayed safe with you, not with me when I went asking questions." Helplessly, she looked up at her sister.

Becca, the good one. The safe one. Their parent's baby who had always been protected and coddled. Phoebe, on the other hand, had always been told she read too much and told to go out and have real adventures instead of those in her books. She'd survived—*was* a survivor—though the word had come to have other meanings over the years.

"Well that didn't work, did it?" Becca said. "I know I chose this trip, but the reason we're here at all was because I was trying to keep you safe. But we were shot at, Phoebe. We were abducted and shot at. That woman shot her own father and she would have shot me. Or Alice. She would have if it wasn't for Zamir getting in the way. That's all that anyone can say. But for Zamir and the grace of God, it could be Alice dying in a hospital like that old man."

Phoebe's gut twisted. "I didn't intend for it to turn out like that. You're not being fair."

"Fair?" Becca shook her head and turned away, but her eyes were brimming. "I was fair when I took you in after the school shooting. I was fair and didn't blame you after the kayaking incident. I was fair when you wanted to go to Myanmar and so I made a deal with myself to keep you safe. We came here. The problem is, you don't want to be safe, do you? You keep running after danger. And I know it might not seem fair because you were doing it to help me when I got into trouble, but you didn't have to follow that man. You could have left it for the police. No, you have to push and push and push until people push back at you. Right now, I'm the one doing the pushing back and I'm telling you, I've made a decision. That's all there is to say. You need to take some responsibility for what you're doing."

"Responsibility?" Phoebe couldn't help herself. A sour chuckle burst up her throat. "And here I thought I was the poster girl for responsibility. I took the heat for the school board's lack of action when the students were shot. I did everything I could and got Alice back when we were kayaking. And here I was simply trying to make sure that someone caught the real killer so that Alice didn't end up with her mother in an Indian prison. But I guess that's not responsible enough." Damn it, there was no way these words were helping, but she was so damn tired of everyone dumping on her. She stood. "You know what? You want to leave? Let me help you."

Ignoring the pain in her feet and shoulder and the part of her brain that screamed not to do this, she shoved past Becca and grabbed the two packed bags.

"Phoebe, no!" Becca cried.

In Phoebe's condition, she couldn't lift the bags, so she dragged them to the door. In the lobby she dragged them outside to the curb.

"So get yourselves a taxi and maybe you can get an earlier train." She dumped the bags and left Becca helplessly standing there. When she stepped inside the hotel, Alice was there.

"Aunt Bee? What's going on?" She looked so young and Phoebe had to close her eyes against Alice's concern. Alice was everything. Family. Just as Becca was. And she was losing them.

It was probably a good thing. Inevitably, it brought trouble. The blame game.

"You're leaving with your mother because it's not safe here." With me.

Alice's eyes brimmed with tears. They rolled down her cheeks. "I know," she whispered. "I'm so sorry."

Phoebe swallowed back the horrible life-sucking grief and shook her head. It felt like she couldn't breathe. All air sucked from her lungs and the lobby—heck, from Kochi. Should she apologize to Becca? Agree to only do activities that Becca approved of? The thought of it left her dying inside.

And angry that her sister could even suggest it.

She looked at Alice and shrugged. "Me, too, sweetie. But these things happen in families. They break apart. Now come here and give your crazy old aunt a hug."

Alice fell into her arms and Phoebe thought she might die. The warm arms around her, the growing strength of the young woman she loved and might never see again if Becca's words were any indication.

She caught Alice's shoulders and held her away, but had to scrub at the tears that escaped to trickle down her cheeks.

"You know I'm always here for you, right? You can call me any time or place."

"I know." Alice swallowed and nodded. "I—I left you something in the room."

Through the guesthouse's front door, Phoebe saw a blue-and-white taxi pull up. Becca had clearly hailed one, for she and the driver loaded their bags. It was over. Done.

Phoebe nodded. "You keep your mother safe. She's not strong like you."

"Or you, Aunti Bee." Alice was openly crying. She rushed into Phoebe's arms once more for a hug and then left her for the taxi and her mother.

The taxi door thunked shut and the engine revved as the car pulled out from the curb and down the road. Phoebe listened to its tires on the pavement until she couldn't hear them anymore.

"That did not look pleasant." The quiet voice of Detective Mathias came from behind and Phoebe whirled around, palming tears off her cheeks. Beyond him, by the pool, sat Trevor and Jeannie and Zamir with his arm in a sling. They were deep in discussion.

She took a deep breath of the jasmine-scented air and hoped that the lobby shadows hid some of her emotions. She squared her shoulders.

"No. It wasn't. Saying goodbye never is." Saying goodbye forever even less so, when it was someone you loved. She looked up at Mathias.

Even in Kochi's tropical heat he wore a crisp gray suit, white shirt, and tie and managed to look like he wasn't even sweating. His gaze was different today, though. No longer assessing as if she was a suspect or at least a nuisance for the police. Instead he looked at her with concern and that was too reminiscent of how people had looked at her after the school shooting. As if she was something breakable and she could shatter at any time.

"So why are you here?" she said and was pleased when her voice sounded crisp and professional.

"I wanted to let everyone know what had happened with the case. After all, you were all there at the end. I thought you should know the results."

She raised her brows at him and met his gaze. "I seem to recall Kalki saying something about a confession before he was shot. How is he?"

She glanced at the lobby registration desk. Today a young man filled Avni's spot.

"Not good." He shook his head. "In someone younger there would be a fair chance of survival, but Kalki is not young and he seems to have lost his will to live. He loved his children very much." Detective Mathias caught her elbow and led her to a pair of lobby chairs. She almost shook him off—didn't want to be touched by him or anyone else at the moment. Not until she grew a harder shell, maybe.

But he sat and she sat facing him. "So?"

"Neither Avni nor Asiq were Simon's killer. Asiq was his business partner—recruited with the promise that it would bring him the money he needed to pursue his dreams. It apparently paid for Asiq's living expenses when he was studying abroad—his father never had enough to cover the costs, so Asiq took it upon himself and never told his father."

Phoebe thought about what the Detective said and about the old man she'd met at dhobi khana and how Kalki had reacted when he'd seen Simon and Asiq together.

"But Kalki knew about Asiq's relationship with Simon, didn't he?"

Mathias nodded. "He knew far more than the young man suspected. Simon told him. According to Kalki, he'd spoken to Simon about no longer seeing Asiq. You see, the relationship between Asiq and Simon was initially sexual, with Simon providing Asiq with money in return for the pleasure of his company. Kalki wanted it to stop. Simon's reaction was much like his response to your sister. He laughed at Kalki and boasted that their relationship was far more than sexual. But Kalki didn't see Simon for quite some time. Apparently, he thought Simon had stopped coming and Asiq was now safe. But when he saw Simon that first morning when you were in Kochi, Kalki knew that wasn't the case. His son would never be free of Simon. That night he followed his son, witnessed the fight between Simon and your sister and then Asiq and Simon's meeting and the exchange of goods."

Mathias went quiet a moment, his gaze searching the ceiling as if the rest of the story was there. "Kalki was furious. He waited until Asiq had left and then confronted Simon. The argument turned loud enough and heated enough that Asiq heard and returned—in time to see his father strike Simon and Simon go down—and hit his head. According to the pathologist, he died instantly. Together father and son moved the body and that was what Ijay and company saw. From there, it was Avni and Asiq trying to protect their father. Kalki had nothing to do with your abduction, nor with dragging your sister and niece into the whole thing."

Phoebe glanced toward the guestroom entrance, but Alice and Becca were gone—likely for good.

"If it helps, I told your sister."

Phoebe shook her head. "It doesn't. It's over. All of it." She stood, feeling battle weary and numb. "Thank you for telling me. At least Kalki did the right thing and admitted that he killed Simon. It leaves Becca in the clear to leave the country."

He looked up at her. "It does. And you as well, when you decide to leave."

"Then thank you for your time." She nodded and left him, feeling slightly unsteady as she covered the distance from the wicker chairs to her room. Across the lobby the sun shone over the swimming pool where Alice had lounged. Now the others sat in the dappled bougainvillea shadows laughing and chatting. They could all leave now. Jeannie and Trevor could close their case. Zamir could go home and finish sorting through Simon's estate. She had her passport and bank cards and could go home to try and patch things up with Becca or go wherever she wanted. She should join them to make plans.

Instead she retreated into her room to sink down on her bed. On

Alice's bed lay a flat, square, brown paper bag. She retrieved it and returned to her bed.

The bag held something folded, something soft. She pulled a rose-colored pashmina and a note from Alice that read "*Think of me when you wear this. You looked beautiful in it. Love always, Alice.*"

Phoebe's hands fell to her lap and she started to cry. Alice shouldn't have. The price of the pashmina would have used up all her spending money.

Kalki, now—he had done the right thing—one man amidst so many who had admitted his responsibility for what he'd done. Just as she had admitted her role in the death of Rick and the others. But no one else had.

What was it they said? That the truth would set you free?

She scrubbed at her eyes.

A whole lot of hooey.

Exhausted, she crushed the shawl in her fists. She needed to make plans. She had her passport, so she could go anywhere she wanted away from this place. Maybe start over. Heck, she might not have much money on her, but she had a pension and her teacher's credentials. Maybe she could teach English and start over somewhere else. Somewhere she was only responsible for herself.

Now there was a plan.

She looked down at Alice's extravagant gift and took pleasure in the softness, but the louvered windows placed shadows across her hands.

Read on for the first chapter of **Within Angkor Shadows,** the third
Phoebe Clay mystery, coming Spring 2022.

TO MY READERS

1. Thank you for reading *Under Malabar Nets* I hope you enjoyed it. If you did (and even if you didn't), it would be immensely helpful if you would leave a review. Reviews help other readers find this book.
2. Sign up for my Newsletter, and receive a free novel, a novella, and an award-nominated short story. To get your FREE eBOOKS, go to my website at www.karenlabrahamson.com.
3. While you're there, check out my website for information on my books, my adventures, and extra content.
4. For more links and offers, or to chat with me, check out Facebook at www.facebook.com/karenlabrahamson.

WITHIN ANGKOR SHADOWS
COMING SPRING 2022

Chapter 1

Along the Mekong River the overloaded barges chugged black smoke into the crystal blue sky, their gunnels mere feet above the river's sullen surface. Last night's rain had cleared the yellow haze and so far the morning was still relatively cool—not the sweltering heat that made sweat spring out on skin the moment you stepped from an air-conditioned room.

The barges sent water washing up over the muddy banks, rocking the small boats with the faded green, blue and red paint drawn up on shore. Though this was Cambodia, the fishermen were Vietnamese, and they lived on the small craft. During the day, they sold their catch in the market south of Phnom Phen's palace. This early, however, as the sun burned a gold band onto the water, the more industrious fishermen tossed circular nets out above the water with a mesmerizing soft whir and splash.

Phoebe Clay stood on the ferry dock watching the slow rise and fall of the fishermen's boats and the magical bloom of the nets like blossoms opening over the gilded water. Alice would be astounded. Her camera would be clicking like mad.

The thought brought a sad smile to her face. But Alice was no doubt in school back home in Langley, her days and evenings filled with extracurricular activities her mother, Becca planned. Safe activities, Phoebe was sure.

Around her the rumble of the barges and overfilled cargo ships were overtaken by the call of the ferry crew to the waiting passengers. Time to go aboard. Time to leave Phnom Phen and the slowly fading capital of the country, and head farther away from civilization to Angkor Wat, the temple complex that was one of the wonders of the world.

She shouldered 'Stoney,' her backpack, and, for the hundredth time since arriving in Cambodia three days before, turned to say something to Becca and Alice. They had returned home from India a few weeks ago and left Phoebe to fend for herself until, Becca said, Phoebe came to her senses and stopped putting herself in danger.

The unfair statement still made her angry.

And sad.

It wasn't like she went looking for danger to get into.

Sighing, she brushed her fingers through her short blonde hair. On the river waited the ferry that wasn't much more than an extra large cabin cruiser with an extra-large indoor passenger cabin and virtually no deck space. That was disappointing given she'd envisioned sitting in a deck chair in the shade and watching the countryside go by. But on this ferry, the only open area looked like it was the open prow that would be ungodly hot with not a stitch of shade…

She was already starting to sweat and it was only seven-thirty in the morning. God help her at noon. She'd thought Kochi, India was hot and humid, but at least it had the breeze off the Arabian Sea to cool it down. So far Cambodia in September was a sultry place of seemingly stagnant river and still air—and rain. Lots of rain and it wasn't even monsoon season yet. These were just the 'little rains' she'd been told as she waded the streets of Bangkok while she waited for her visa to Cambodia to come through.

It had poured two of the three days she'd been in Phnom Phen so that she hadn't done any of the sightseeing she'd planned. Instead she'd hunkered down in her room, only stepping out in search of new accommodation after the rain began to run down the inside wall of her room in her low-cost lodging. Thankfully she'd found a better place to stay and had sat in her room watching the wall of monsoon water fill the streets and overwhelm roof gutters. Maybe it was Becca and Alice's absence—Alice was up for anything—but Phoebe had braved the downpour only enough to buy a plastic poncho and food before retreating to her room. Beyond that, a break in the rain had allowed her to visit the Royal Palace and find the flower market, both of which Alice and Becca would have enjoyed.

Looking back at the city strung along the river, she shook her head at what she might have missed. If she was honest with herself, she was a little nervous about this trip alone. She'd never done solo travel in such a foreign country. England and France, yes. Even in India, the people spoke English, while here, beyond native Khmer, French was the second language. On the other hand, the Vietnam war and tourism had increased the number of English speakers big time.

She joined the line of tourists and locals, behind a father holding his daughter's hand. The man wore a plain, white shirt and chino trousers gone soft with age, while the girl wore a blue sarong like so many women seemed to wear, and a chaste, white blouse with lace at the collar. The girl could have been as young as twelve or as old sixteen. Maybe older. Phoebe couldn't be sure given how young most Cambodians appeared and this girl was so delicately boned the word fairy came to mind—certainly something magical. The girl had black hair twisted up behind her head and a blue plastic flower clipped above her left ear. Fly-away strands framed her smooth forehead and almond eyes that seemed almost too large for her delicate skull. The girl smiled up at Phoebe until her father noticed, then her long lashes veiled her gaze. He nodded at Phoebe and tugged the girl closer to him as if he considered Phoebe a threat.

Frowning, she made the long step over the river to the gunnels of the white cabined river ferry and then had to decide whether to follow father and daughter into the cabin that filled most of the ferry's length and breadth. Inside, there would be air conditioning, but inside she'd be confined to peering out what looked like perilously grimy windows. The alternative was to edge around the cabin to the prow of the ship. A few young people had already done so and had staked out spots to suntan while watching the scenery go by.

A good place to get a sunburn, Becca would say. Alice would roll her eyes.

Phoebe grinned at the image and edged away from the door. If she was in Cambodia for an adventure, she might as well go whole hog and she seriously was *not* going to miss her family. She'd promised herself that when she booked this trip. Wobbling along the narrow cabin edge before stepping down into the railed prow, she then found free deck space at the railing and settled onto the warm metal with Stoney at her side. The prow space wasn't large. The wedge-shaped area could hold perhaps ten people all seated on the floor. There were eight people seated here now. Most of the youngsters had taken up positions in front of the cabin, so they could use it as a backrest, but that didn't allow the best view. Phoebe's position almost under the flag on the prow seemed like it would provide a better vantage. From her daypack she claimed her hat, sunscreen, sarong and a large bottle of water. She'd save the oranges and rolls of cookies and crackers for later, in case food at the planned stop for lunch was inedible.

"Looks like you're all prepared," said a male voice with a faint British accent.

She glanced back at the cabin. Against the peeling white paint of the pilot's cabin, between two groups of long-legged, tanned, twenty-something tourists, sat an older man in worn sandals, cream-colored trousers and long-sleeved shirt rolled up over his forearms. He wore a broad-brimmed hat that shadowed his eyes, but his wide mouth was smiling from within a few days' worth of gray-blond beard.

"Trying to be," she said and slapped her Canuck's hockey team ball cap on her head. Two could play at hiding their eyes.

"Been to Angkor before?" he asked.

She shook her head, wondering where this was leading. It wasn't as if she didn't have *tourist* emblazoned all over her. She'd heard enough horror stories about the things that could happen if you took up with strangers. Becca had made sure of it. She still sent Phoebe links to newspaper articles, even though she hadn't responded to any of Phoebe's emails.

The stranger leaned forward and stuck out his hand. "Trevor Morgan. Trev to my friends. I live in Siem Reap. I manage a non-profit there." On shore the last of the tourists came aboard and the ropes tethering the ferry were cast off. Out in the channel a fisherman hauled in his net and shifted his small wooden boat out of the ferry's path.

She considered his hand. Long fingers. Clean nails and skin. His movement had released the faint scent of laundry soap and she caught a glimpse of two piercing blue eyes under his hat brim. Could someone with eyes like that, who made sure his clothes were clean be that bad? Besides, he was sitting on his fanny on the prow of the boat, just like any tourist.

She accepted his hand even as a small part of her said, "If you wanted to bilk a tourist, what better place to meet them."

Of course, if he was out to bilk someone, he was going to be terribly disappointed in Phoebe Clay. She was traveling on a very strict budget.

"Phoebe Clay," she said. "And yes, to answer your question, I'm one of the tourist hordes headed to Angkor." His grip was surprisingly cool and dry compared to her sweaty palm. The rumble of the ferry engines vibrated up through her seat as the vessel left the dock behind. She turned to look upriver as they started to move and a blessed breeze ruffled her hair and lifted the sweat from her skin.

"From the States?" Trev asked.

"Nope." She glanced back at him and tapped the flag patch Alice had carefully sewn to Stoney before they'd all left Canada. "Vancouver. You?"

"London. But that was a dim and distant time ago. I've been in-country for the past fifteen years."

"No wonder you're not sweating! You're almost a native!"

He chuckled and slid his bum forward beside her at the prow. "I fear that will never happen. The Khmer people have been through a trauma that someone who hasn't survived with them, will never know. I think the entire country is dealing with PTSD."

Just what she needed to hear, given she'd been dealing with the condition since the school shooting that had led to her forced retirement. She glanced sideways at Trevor. "You a counsellor or something?"

He shrugged and stuck his legs through the ferry rails to her left so his feet dangled down the side of the boat and turned toward her. "Sometimes it comes with the job. You see things, you know? Luckily the internet gives you access to all kinds of expertise. I've got experts in Australia and London who come to visit now and again. They triage people and give me and my staff the direction about how to best help."

"Interesting. So what do you do, then?"

"Like I said. I manage a non-profit. There's a lot of us NGO types here helping the country rebuild."

On shore, the city fell behind, but there were still plenty of buildings and the spires of new temples under construction. Gold spires stuck up out of the trees. Here and there white temples caught the sun. Alice would be like a kid on this ride. She couldn't imagine Becca not enjoying it either.

Phoebe tilted her head back and basked in the wind streaming over her face. Her white blouse fluttered around her and so did her pantlegs.

"A lot of temples and buildings were destroyed during Pol Pot's regime. A lot of people were killed. A lot," Trevor said.

Even though she'd read about it before coming to Cambodia, his bald statement sort of put a damper on the bliss she was seeking from the fact she was here adventuring on her own. In fact she still was reading about the reign of terror of the Khmer Rouge, where nothing like modern medicine was allowed, anyone with any education was killed, and the entire population was basically enslaved.

"It's tragic on so many levels," Trev continued. "Historic Cambodia was the source of much of the rich cultural traditions found throughout Southeast Asia. The fusion with French culture during colonial days led to a vibrant second cultural tradition. The Khmer Rouge wiped all that out. Today I see a lot of people who don't know and don't care about their history or traditions—only about the money they can make."

"That's so sad," she said

"The Khmer Rouge thought the Chinese didn't go far enough with their cultural revolution." He shook his head. "Anything vaguely educated, cultured or capitalistic had to go."

"Back home Canadians are struggling to deal with the cultural genocide of our First Nations people. In schools we're even teaching First Nations history so our Aboriginal students learn to be proud of who they are. We're seeing higher graduation rates for Aboriginal kids." She could imagine how the lack of tradition would leave youth anchorless and with little guidance to help them live their lives.

"Let me guess. You're a teacher," Trev said. Beyond him, the broad river had widened further and there were more small fishing boats along the shores, and overloaded barges and steamers passing up and down river. An egret lifted from the edge of water in a flash of white.

"Guilty as charged. At least I was… for twenty-eight years. Some things stay with you for a long time."

Beneath the brim of his hat, Trevor's brows rose. His blue eyes were studying her. "But you left?"

For a moment her throat tightened and she swallowed back the loss. The school shooting had apparently been the beginning of the end of so much she'd thought would be forever. Her career. Her relationship with her sister and niece.

"I—retired." Hopefully that would put an end to his prying. This level of sharing was simply too much. Maybe Trev whatever-his-last-name-was felt comfortable divulging all his secrets, but she did not.

A slight sound turned her around to see the young girl she'd seen earlier swiftly traverse the narrow walkway from the cabin door to the space over the prow. She stepped down into the crowded space to pick her way over outstretched legs to where Phoebe sat. She glanced at Trev, folded her legs under her and sat behind and between them as if she had something to say and something to prove. The sunlight caught on the flowered clip in her hair.

"H—hello," she said in a soft voice barely audible over the ferry's engines and the wind. Those long lashes still demurely veiled her eyes as if she had secrets to preserve. "You are American? From America?"

Phoebe shook her head. "Afraid not. I'm from Canada." When the girl looked confused, Phoebe pointed at the flag on Stoney. "Not America, but we are right next door to them."

Of course the girl wouldn't understand. Since Phoebe had arrived in Asia it seemed few people understood where Canada was—if they'd even heard of the country.

Trev said something Phoebe didn't understand and then looked at her. "I translated for you."

"What is your name?" Phoebe asked. On the shore, tall stands of bamboo swayed over stilted houses while water buffalo wallowed at the river edge or chewed their cud on shore.

"Sokha," she girl said and tapped her breast. "My name is Sokha, Aunty." She said it with a flourish as if proud of her English. She didn't even have any accent.

Phoebe pointed at herself. "Phoebe. My name is Phoebe and this is Trev."

"Trev?"

"Exactly," he nodded and smiled.

"Are you traveling with your father?" Phoebe asked.

Sokha looked at her blankly until Trev translated. Then she solemnly shook her head and they conversed in what must be Khmer.

"She says he's her uncle, but I'm not sure. She doesn't seem to want to talk about him or where she's going."

A little flutter of concern ran through Phoebe, but she tamped it down. Becca always said she went looking for trouble. Here was proof it wasn't so. The girl's business was no business of hers.

As if on cue, a male voice called Sokha's name. Her uncle stood in the cabin doorway, one foot on the narrow pathway to the prow.

The girl turned to Trev and spoke some more as she shook her head. She looked unhappy, but then climbed gracefully to her feet, smoothed her sarong, and nodded goodbye before picking her way over the tourists to join her uncle. He nodded once more in Phoebe's direction, but caught Sokha's upper arm and seemed to haul her down into the cabin. Or maybe he was just steadying her and Phoebe was misreading given she'd already decided she didn't much like the man after the way he had acted on the dock. They disappeared inside and the door closed behind them.

Phoebe sat there a moment, a knot of concern in her stomach, but she couldn't say why. She turned back to Trev. "You think everything's okay?"

He frowned, apparently surprised at her concern. He shook his head. "Probably. People here can be pretty relaxed about their kids—or else they aren't. Parents love their kids a lot, but they can be pretty demanding of obedience. I wonder what drew her out to talk to us?"

"You'd think she'd be attracted to all the youngsters. They're clearly more fun." And a girl between the age of thirteen and sixteen is pretty sure to be attracted to kids just a smidgen older.

As if to prove her point, from behind them came a burst of laughter from one of the groups of young people.

She and Trev Morgan talked casually as the river narrowed and the scenery became more rural. The sun lifted and the air filled with the murky scent of muddy river water. A haze made the distances soft, but the landscape that flowed away from the river was mostly flat. Farms and fields with ramshackle stilted houses built on the riverbank.

"I imagine it floods here," she said. "That's why the stilted houses."

"That's one of the reasons, but even houses not prone to flooding are often built on stilts. A lot of household life takes place in the shadows under the houses. It's cooler there. But once a year, during the monsoons, the deluge out of the Tonle Sap will flood a lot of the landscape—more so since logging took out most of the jungle. Not as much flooding here as around the Tonle Sap, but let us just say that stilts are prudent."

The air heated and the breeze couldn't stop the sweat running down Phoebe's back. The river split into two broad channels and they left the main river. At noon they pulled into a floating restaurant that stood off-shore from a small village and passengers were free to disembark into the restaurant for a thirty minute break. There were more covered boats like the Vietnamese boats she'd seen in Phnom Phen—long and shallow-drafted—but these were larger with curved, half-moon walls and ceiling forming living quarters. Women cooked in open areas on the sterns of the boats. Children leapt from the sides into the murky water and splashed about. One boy leaned out a boat's window and held out a huge snake. Phoebe recoiled.

"Is that a pet?"

"Maybe. Or they plan to eat it. In Cambodia everything is fair game. There's a town north of here that specializes in deep fried tarantulas. They're not bad actually."

She looked at him in horror until he burst out laughing—a good hardy laugh. "You really haven't done a lot of traveling in less developed countries, have you?"

"Tarantulas?"

"Yup. Nice big crispy ones on a stick."

In self defense she pulled out a package of crackers and offered Trev one. "This is about as crispy as I want."

After they left the restaurant, the river had broadened out into a wide lake that seemed to stretch on forever. Here and there, small, treed islands stuck up from the water, some with small farmsteads on them. Here the water was the same blue as the sky with shimmering reflections of puffy clouds so for a moment she felt disoriented except for the rumble of the deck under her.

Becca would love this. She'd always had a weakness for the water.

"Tonle Sap Lake. Those islands you see are actually hilltops. The monsoons have flooded the lake. Twice a year, the river changes direction due to the volume of water. In between, thousands of acres of rice fields are under water. The river hasn't even changed direction yet, but the rains have come early."

A small, gas-powered boat passed them hauling a second boat full of tree branches. A man steered the first boat past them. With him was a young girl who met Phoebe's gaze and held it as they passed by. She was perhaps the same age as Sokha—maybe fifteen—with the same long dark hair coiled up behind her head and the same sad expression. That was the thing about Cambodia. She might not have been out and about a lot in Phnom Penh due to the rain, but the shopkeepers and even the manager of the second guesthouse had all seemed to have an air of sadness around them. As if the whole country was grieving.

She understood about grief.

Sighing, she looked out over the water and let herself just 'be,' caught between the vast sky and the shimmering expanse of water as she steadied her breathing. The wind ruffled her hair and she took her hat off to let the sun drink her sweat. She closed her eyes against the glare and inhaled the ferry's diesel and the scent of the lake. Overhead, the Cambodian flag on the prow flapped and slapped in the wind.

These were the experiences she wanted. Things that took her out of her comfort zone. Things that were totally foreign. Surely it would be easier to set aside her history and the shooting in a place this unfamiliar. She could be someone else. Become someone unfamiliar to herself.

Maybe that had been the issue in Kochi. Sure she'd been in a foreign country far different from Canada, but she'd been with Becca and Alice. She'd brought 'her' country with her by travelling with them. On her own, she wouldn't have to take care of them.

"Water hyacinth," Trev said beside her.

She opened her eyes and glanced at him. He was leaning his arms on the railing, peering out at the lake much as she had been. He noticed her noticing him.

"Beautiful, isn't it."

"It looks pristine. Untouched. Not even much garbage." She lifted her chin at a pop can floating on the water.

"Unfortunately, you're wrong. There are a lot of problems including garbage. It's just that the currents run the garbage together under the trees so you don't see it here. And there's rampant overfishing, not to mention the environmental disaster that's water hyacinth."

He motioned to an undulating patch of green they were nearing. Spikes of lush purple flowers bloomed above the tangle of green leaves.

"It's everywhere. It clogs waterways. It kills endemic plants and lowers the oxygen content in the water. Eventually, if it's allowed to spread there won't be any fish for fishing. An entire way of life will be destroyed and people will starve. Damn stuff is everywhere in Southeast Asia. Should never have been introduced."

"Let me guess: because it looked pretty?"

He shook his head. "Of course. There are people trying to save the fish stocks in the lake, but they are fighting an uphill battle. I don't envy them. Dealing with the government doesn't make anything easy and there are always people in opposition to progress."

He stared out at the water as if considering the effort of those others—or maybe his own attempts to deal with that same government. Should she ask him about it? She looked back at the lake. No, asking about his problems might pull her back into her problem-solving mode and hadn't Becca said that was at the heart of her issues – always rushing in to save people…

It was some world where you weren't supposed to help people.

She turned back to Trev. "Sounds like you've run into the government, too."

"It's nothing really. Just red tape and general interference when a foreign non-profit is involved. And you've always got officials and others demanding to be paid off. The usual business."

"So that's what you do? Pay off corrupt officials?"

He gave her a sheepish smile and looked back to the lake. "If it gets the job done, yeah. We're building something here. Changing communities. We're doing good work and I'm not allowing some bugger with a bit of authority, or someone who sees us as a rival, to stop us." He spoke passionately with his hands. His work was important to him—whatever it was. Once she'd felt that way about teaching…

"What are you smiling at," he asked.

"You. You care about what you do. A lot. I'm not exactly sure what a foreign NGO does in Cambodia, but given what you've said I think maybe the Cambodian people are lucky to have you on their side."

"Well, thanks, I guess. Kind of you to say, but what we're trying to do is build for the future. Give them the opportunities and jobs and skills so that they won't need outsiders like me anymore. That's what I want to see, the Cambodian people celebrating their culture and their pride."

Regardless of her vow to remain uninvolved, her curiosity got the better of her. "That sounds like a tall order. How do you do that?"

An hour later, after Trevor regaled her with talk of working with specific villages to build businesses, constructing schools, and international fund raising, they came to a floating town. The ferry had ploughed through channels cut through acres of hyacinth-covered water to reach the village of boats seemingly trapped between the undulating hyacinth invader and a man-made, gravel and stone jetty. The ferry eased into shore and plank gangways were laid from the deck onto gravel. Then the cabin passengers stumbled out onto the land. Phoebe scrambled to her feet with the others from the prow, and hefted Stoney onto her back to follow behind.

Without the boat's movement the sun was a heavy hammer on her head. The humidity made it worse so her body was immediately covered with a sheen of sweat. Her shirt clung to her and her capris had racing stripe lines of sweat down the front of her legs. After wobbling across to land, she picked her way up the loose gravel and rock of the steep-sided jetty. At the top of the jetty, a few passenger vans and a line of motorcycles and motorcycle taxis waited in a parking area to take the passengers into town.

Along with most of the local people on the ferry, Trev headed over to the motorcycles. Then he turned back and returned to Phoebe who had just found what seemed to be a shuttle van into town. She hoped. The driver had nodded when she'd said Seim Reap and had taken her money, so she had to figure that was a good sign.

"Here's my card," Trev said. He handed her a green card with the name *Cambodia Prosperous* scrolled in a darker green across the top. His title was managing director. "I realize I don't even know how long you're here for, but maybe we could meet for a drink while you're in town. It can be lonely here on your own."

Someone important. She was a little surprised.

"Thanks. I'll see how things go. No firm plans here, you know. I'm just going with the flow." She grinned, accepted the card and stuck it in her day pack. She wasn't really here to have drinks with strange men.

On the other hand, wasn't that part of the whole idea of adventure? Meet new people? Talk about new things? Things that matter? With people who didn't know her history?

Trev patted her shoulder. "Enjoy your stay in Siem Reap—and enjoy Angkor!" With a wave he went back to the motorcycles that were quickly being taken by Cambodians. He climbed aboard the back of one and the bike roared past her as she climbed into the van.

She settled in a seat in the back and wished she hadn't. The air was close and the smeary window beside her wouldn't open. She fanned her face and spotted Sokha and her uncle. They were standing with another man in a crisp navy suit at the open rear door of a dark blue Audi sedan, which was a surprise given the worn state of the uncle's clothing. Sokha looked like she was studying the toes of her shoes, until suit man caught her chin and tilted her face up to him. They stood like that a moment as if Sokha was being inspected, and then he released her. And smiled. The two men spoke and then the suit man caught Sokha's arm and urged her toward the rear seat of the car. Sokha hesitated and said something, but the man shoved her in.

Then uncle spoke to suit man before the man in the navy suit climbed inside the sedan beside Sokha. Uncle walked away to one of the motorcycles and climbed on the back. The car and the motorcycle both pulled away from the parking area.

Phoebe craned around in her seat to watch them go. Something about the whole experience with Sokha left her uneasy. The uncle certainly wasn't in any way affectionate to Sokha. And what uncle basically hands their niece over to someone who, judging by Sokha's reaction, was a stranger, or certainly someone she was appeared to be afraid of?

A heavy clot of anxiety formed in her stomach and she could almost see Becca shake her head and throw her hands up.

Watch for ***Within Angkor Shadows*** coming April 2022.

ABOUT THE AUTHOR

K.L. Abrahamson writes fantasy and romance as Karen L. Abrahamson and mysteries as K.L. Abrahamson. Her best known books are the unique Cartographer series in which secret agents of the American Geological Society use their powers to take on the purveyors of dark magic. Her romantic suspense and mysteries take readers on adventures to dangerous locations around the world.

Her short fiction has appeared in numerous magazines and anthologies, including Realms of Fantasy and Ellery Queen Mystery Magazine; her short fantasy story "With One Shoe" was nominated for an Arthur Ellis Canadian Crime Fiction Award.

Karen's background includes time as a police officer, corrections officer, and probation/parole officer.

To find out more about her and her writing, visit www.karenlabrahamson.com

MYSTERY, FANTASY AND ROMANCE

If you enjoyed this book, you might enjoy other titles from K.L. Abrahamson that can be found in your local bookstore or wherever e-books are sold.

www.karenlabrahamson.com

THROUGH DARK WATER: Eagles, Orcas and a killer stalk the kayaking Mecca of Pirate's Cove, British Columbia. On a holiday with her niece, school teacher Phoebe Clay has to solve the case to protect herself and everything she loves. Find it at http://www.karenlabrahamson.com/books/through-dark-water/

*AFTERBURN: Vallon Drake, agent of the American Geological
Survey, the secret arm of Homeland Security that protects
America from illicit changes to its landscapes, discovers her
partner smothering in a wall. Now someone is rewriting the
Seattle maps and killing AGS agents. Their actions threaten the
safety of the entire Northwest and only rogue agent Vallon can
stop it.Find it at http://www.karenlabrahamson.com/books/
afterburn/*

SHADOW PLAY: Star reporter Kaitlin Blackwood arrives in Cambodia and lands right in the case of her missing father. When men try to abduct her, the wrong man rescues her: B.J. McCallum, ex-man of her dreams, who comes with his own heap of trouble. The two must put aside their differences long enough to solve the case—and maybe save themselves in the process. Find it at http://www.karenlabrahamson.com/books/shadow-play/

www.ingramcontent.com/pod-product-compliance
Lightning Source LLC
Chambersburg PA
CBHW020754190726
48285CB00006B/2019